THE
SILENT
WOMEN

Notes from an Asylum

AVRIL JOY

Published by Linen Press, London 2023
8 Maltings Lodge
Corney Reach Way
London W4 2TT
www.linen-press.com
© Avril Joy 2023

Cover art: Arcangel
Cover Design: Avril Joy and Zebedee
Typeset by Zebedee
Printed and bound by Lightning Source
ISBN: 978-1-7391777-6-8

For Elsie, Freja and Lilah

About the Author

Before becoming a full-time writer, Avril Joy worked for twenty-five years in Low Newton women's prison in County Durham. Her short fiction has appeared in literary magazines and anthologies including Victoria Hislop's *The Story: Love, Loss & the Lives of Women*. Her work has been listed in the Bridport, the Manchester Prize for Fiction, the Fish Short Memoir and the Raymond Carver Prize. In 2012 her story, *Millie and Bird*, won the inaugural Costa Short Story Award. Her novel, *Sometimes a River Song*, won the 2017 People's Book Prize for outstanding achievement. Her poetry has appeared both in print and online. In 2019, her poem *Skomm* won the York Literary Festival poetry competition. Avril lives with her partner near Bishop Auckland in County Durham.

www.avriljoy.com

https://avriljoywritingdays.substack.com/about

Books by Avril Joy

The Sweet Track, Flambard Press, 2007
From Writing With Love, Createspace, 2014
Millie and Bird, Iron Press, 2015
Sometimes A River Song, Linen Press, 2016
Going in With Flowers, Linen Press, 2019
this One Wild Place, Linen Press, 2021

Praise for Avril Joy's writing

Sometimes a River Song

An amazing, accomplished, beautifully written book. Masterful storytelling. Gorgeous, captivating, innovative lyrical prose…(we) want to recognise its inspirational content to women all over the world that despite an unfair society one can lift oneself out of misery through the strength and love of the women who fight together for a better life. A magical book that speaks to every sense and to your heart.
– The People's Book Prize judges

Avril Joy has produced a work of haunting beauty which celebrates the courage and resilience of the human spirit.
– Jenny Gorrod, Dundee Review of the Arts

An amazing, beautiful book with echoes of Eimear McBride. Avril Joy knows how to draw you into the story, right into the soul of the narrator. Aiyana's voice is the voice of the river. I could have gone on listening to that song for ever.
– Kathleen Jones, author of *A Passionate Sisterhood*

A tour de force. The narrator's voice sings… I can almost hear the insects and the dip of the oars… original and beautiful… I read it in one great gallop.
– Sharon Griffiths, The Northern Echo, author of *The Accidental Time Traveller*

A great feat of literary imagination...this beautifully written novel will enchant readers, young and old, across the world.
 – Wendy Robertson, author of *Writing at the Maison Bleue*

Completely stunned by it! The power of Aiyana's voice, the exquisite rendering of the river setting and life around it, the characters – it is incredibly engaging, immersive and moving. And although there are shocking and brutal events, there is beauty and hope in abundance, not to mention love.
 – Isabel Costello, On the Literary Sofa

Triumphant ...This book, with its hopes for Aiyana being dashed and thwarted so many times along the way, could so easily have fallen at the last, but the conclusion, brought about by Aiyana herself, whose spirit is unbroken, is triumphant. I felt, by the end, that I had been reading an epic tale, not a novel – rhythmic, mystical, poetic.
 – Alison Coles, Book Oxygen

Going In With Flowers

Poetry is a natural place to express the most intense feelings. But for it to work it has to be more than just expression; it has to be transformational...Avril's poems have that quality. Skomm is an absolutely shattering poem and it's not going to leave me.
 – Clare Shaw

Women in prison are neither seen nor heard, their stories seldom told and even more rarely understood. Avril Joy spent twenty five years teaching in prison and as well as teaching, she listened and tried to understand. She wanted to give the women she'd known a voice so they could be heard. In this selection of scene-setting prose and powerful poetry, she has succeeded brilliantly.

Avril's work is unsparing but humane, a plea for understanding for those women on the margins of our society who all too often end up in prison, doubly victimised. Buy this book, keep it by your bedside and read it over and over again .

Listening to Avril Joy yesterday was a treat. She is simply captivating. She also made me cry. Not an easy task with my heart of stone...I've been thinking about Lisa since yesterday. Her words about her have left such an imprint on me.

The highlight of Durham Book festival 2019 was Writing from Inside. Inspiring readings and stories of prison life from all three writers... I was close to tears at times at the beautiful poetry and emotionally charged stories from the writers involved – a special event.

A little madness in the Spring
Is wholesome even for the King,
But God be with the Clown,
Who ponders this tremendous scene-
This whole experiment in green,
As if it were his own!

Emily Dickinson

He who reveals the secrets of a prisonhouse must have
been in it. Even so, gentle
reader, is it with lunatic asylums; therefore, to tell thee
that I KNOW whereof I affirm in this little book and
am prepared to PROVE every statement made therein,
is to tell thee that I have dwelt in asylums for lunatics.
Whether as matron, keeper or patient, I leave to thy
discrimination.

The Bastilles of England, Louisa Lowe, 1883

The Asylum

To the north, a wild and uncultivated fen, where paths vanish under water and hollows fill with winter rain, where reeds lay down in the wind and bittersweet hides. And deep in the black soil, the fossil beds, ammonites as big as a man's fist. To the south, chalk downland, a covering of lady's bedstraw and a spring-fed stream flowing into the Cam, gin clear and mineral rich, where brown trout nose the watercress. To the west, the pumping station, where the new steam pumps move water, day and night. To the east, Keeper's Wood.

The purchase, three hundred acres known as *Long Meadow*, is made by the agent, John Tiplady, in November 1855. The Asylum is to be situated a good distance from city and village boundaries so as not to trouble their inhabitants. Yet, as the walls, chimneys and water tower of the new County Pauper Lunatic Asylum rise, they come to dominate the view. There is not a soul in the County who does not know the name Long Meadow, who does not wonder what might transpire behind its walls, or what power lie in the hands of its newly appointed officers. Truth be told, there are none who do not fear incarceration with no prospect of release, who have not dreamed of the darkness that lies in wait on their doorstep. Except perhaps those who work there, good and bad. Those who make a living from madness.

September 1875

The air is ripe with the scent of rotten apples and damp earth. Seed heads rattle in the grass and the wet, yellow leaves of willow stick to the boots of eel catcher, Michael Corey, as he makes his way to the river. Above him the sky is autumnal blue. The smoke from Long Meadow's chimneys and the low throb of the pumps hang in the air. He is hoping for a good catch to sell in the town market. For wicker hives and griggs fat with silver eels. And enough left over for chopped eel, fried in best butter, for tea when his mother comes home from attending the mad women of Dormitory Twelve, women who believe they speak with Jesus, who claim to be the Queen herself. Women who believe that eels have taken root in their stomachs and suck their lifeblood.

The newspapers had championed it 'to better the condition of lunatic paupers,' or so the Chronicle said. But now he wonders at it. This parade of the afflicted seen in the fields and along the river, always accompanied by their attendants. A circus of lunatics. Are there not better places for such a project? The filthy disease-ridden cities for one? It should never have been built on their land, so the locals say, and he agrees, though he is mindful that the land is no longer theirs. It has been parcelled up and sold off. Now there are new ways to make a living, as in the Asylum, ways that pay as much as thirty-five shillings per annum for a mere attendant.

Michael Corey steps onto the riverbank, wades in among the rushes and reaches down in anticipation for the first hive. But his hand alights on something softer than wicker.

There is cloth beneath his fingers and there is flesh. A limb. An arm, he thinks, full grown, half-hidden in the reeds. And there is more.

With all thought of eel and hive forgotten, he wades further in and begins to heave and drag a body up through the mud and onto the bank. The shock and the effort leave him breathless. He looks down on the corpse he has pulled from the river. It lies green and swollen in the grass. He puts his hand to his chest. His heart is alive and beating fast, thank God. He takes off his hat and offers up a prayer.

May 1875 –
5 months earlier

Patient Confinement

71. No Patient shall pass beyond the grounds of the Asylum until discharged by due authority, unless the temporary absence of such Patient be permitted under the power contained in the said or some other Act; or unless the Resident Medical Officer and Superintendent shall give express directions for that purpose.

Rules for the Government of the Pauper Lunatic Asylum situate at Long Meadow – prepared and submitted by the Committee of Visitors thereof, by virtue of the 53rd section of the 16th and 17th VIC. CHAP 97

Long Meadow

A Room Adjoining Dormitory Twelve

Simone Gastrell

She dreams of the child. She dreams of spinning glass, of an ascension of larks. A sky blistered with wings. She dreams of the black water's edge, a tangle of river weed as she is sucked under, her skirts dragging her down. She wakes breathless. Her head aches and the familiar, sweet, scent of rotting hyacinth curls about her. She opens her eyes, looks up, and wonders where she lies.

Then she remembers.

In the dark, airless silence she hears the beating of her heart.

A cold sweat on her skin, she sits up, lowers her feet to the stone floor, moves across to the window and draws up the canvas blind. A sky like a bruise, a pale moon with a ghostly trail of stars hang above her and the distant thud, thud of the pumps echo the beat of her heart. She turns from the window. Moonlight spills into the room, falling on the wooden chair and table, on the mottled cover of a Book of Common Prayer, on the buttons at the cuff of a linsey dress draped on the chair back. It settles like snow on a corner of the iron bedstead and in the narrow gap beneath the

17

locked door. It lights the blanched face of the counterpane, the whitewashed walls, the waxen bed linen. Nothing here familiar, no colour, no comfort, no ornamentation, no ceiling rose, plaster cornice, curtain, carpet. All absent. All leeched of colour. But then on the corner of the pillowcase a freckle of dried blood, set in the heat of a wash. The blood of another woman? Who might she be? Did she inhabit this room? Is she now gone from Long Meadow? A glimmer of hope, a ruffled feather on a raven's wing, catches her. Perhaps such a woman walks freely in the world. If so, then how? How might a woman captive, entombed, be set free?

Simone turns back to the window and reaching out to the world she has lost, presses her forehead and her palms on the windowpane. She is the wax flower under glass, taxidermy beneath the dome, butterfly, bird stilled, captured, unheard. If only she had foreseen what was to come, she would have shaken off her grief, escaped the house, run, thrown herself on the mercy of strangers, gone into hiding like a deer in the forest. But her reason had been veiled in laudanum and her will, bound, contingent, subjugated at their whim.

She peers out into the night. Beyond her lie outbuildings and a stretch of grass scattered with the small stone crosses of a graveyard. She can make out a chapel roof and further still the black, yew hedges and high walls of her confinement. In the far distance are trees, their feathery tops clotted with nests. A wood, perhaps a forest? She knows nothing of where she is. She knows nothing of how her incarceration might end, though she fears that only a man will have the power to free her. The husband who put her here, the doctor and apothecary who lent their signatures, an officer of the Asylum. Perhaps a man such as William Blakely, Medical

Officer, who boasted of the cleanliness and godliness of the place, who told her how the walls were painted regularly, how as a private patient she would be entitled to a room of her own, to this room, adjoining Dormitory Twelve. William Blakely, the man who had greeted her on the forecourt and escorted her in.

It is dusk when she steps down from the carriage onto the gravel drive. At first sight, the Asylum appears like a fine country house, not unlike the one from which she departed but an hour ago, with gables and parapets and an ornamental porch. But as she raises her head and looks skyward, a chill runs through her. Its very size is forbidding, the stretch of its wings east and west, the looming body of its tower. It is as if a giant bird hovers above her blotting out the sky and the last of the day's light. She approaches the steps, her heart fast, her mouth dry. She stumbles. He reaches out and offers her his hand. It is warm and strong, and she takes comfort in it.

In the Receiving Room, every surface is cold and slippery, porcelain and metal, tile and sink. There is a weighing machine and a bath. On the walls are cabinets filled with bottles, boxes, cartons. In the corner squats a chair of rough-hewn wood with leather straps on its arms. She is weighed and must bathe under the supervision of a female attendant dressed in a grey gown with white, starched collar and cuffs, crimped hat, apron, and a belt hung with keys. Simone is issued with two green linsey dresses, a cap, four pairs of knee length drawers, stockings, boots, an underskirt and two nightshirts. The attendant says she must wear these for now, but may wear her own clothes, once laundered, seeing as she is admitted as a private patient and not a pauper.

She is a private patient. Of course. Her husband Everett has money enough and will not want the world to think him anything other than concerned for his wife's welfare. Poor man, they will say, what a tragedy, have you heard? A wife in the County Asylum. Drowned the child, so they say. He pays for her to have every privilege and comfort you know.

And he who pays the piper calls the tune.

Is this to be her life now and no reprieve but at Everett's bidding? Her fingers fumble at the buttons on the cuff of the dress. A familiar, sharp pain has started up on the right side of her head, making its way down through her neck to her shoulder. Its pulse is insistent. If only she could close her eyes, lie down in the cool and dark, somewhere away from the sour smell and flickering of the gas lamps.

The attendant escorts her upstairs to a narrow room where she is seated behind a desk. Blakely enters and sits down facing her. He smiles but all the while he is watching. She cannot avoid his attention. She looks for something to fix on in the room, away from his gaze, but it is empty, soulless. She cannot escape. How he observes her, looking again and again into her eyes, as if seeking out an explanation, as if searching her very soul. He presses questions upon her, makes notes on all manner of things: her height, complexion, the colour of her hair and the condition of her tongue, her appetite, peculiarities and marks. He wants to know every intimate detail, everything from the regularity of her menses to the consistency of her bowels.

She is photographed wearing the linsey dress.

He asks if she has thoughts of taking her life. He asks what she remembers of... he hesitates, 'the accident,' he says, using the word as if it is in question.

'I have no recollection,' says Simone.

'Have you ever had thoughts of harming a child before that day? It would not be so unusual,' he adds.

'No,' she answers. She puts her hand to her temple as if to press away the pain.

What of her child, the stillborn? What of her marriage? Her husband? Her jealousies? The accident? He refers to the paper in front of him. Though she views it upside down, she can read the title, *Admissions Form*, and she recognises Eames's writing, her husband's physician, and the words *suspicion*, and *intentional*.

She swallows hard. Her head throbs. She does not know how to answer. His face shimmers with stars and there are flashing lights at the side of her vision. Her arm grows numb and she fears soon she will be unable to speak, at least sufficiently to give a sensible account of herself. The pain tightens in a band about her head.

'I have a headache,' she says. 'Please. I beg you. May I sleep now?'

He offers her a poultice of opium and vinegar for her head. The attendant escorts her downstairs, through a series of long corridors and a silent dormitory of sleeping women, to what is to be her room. Once in bed and with the poultice administered, Simone falls into a deep, dream-troubled sleep. Until the moonlight wakes her.

She moves away from the window leaving the blind drawn so that she might watch the sky and climbs back into bed. Her headache is fading. Dull now. Moonlight wanes, replaced by the rose light of dawn. Then voices. People calling out their goodbyes, leaving, going out into the break of a spring day. She pictures them free, under a wide cloudless sky, breathing in the cool morning air.

A morning to be up and out, the kind of morning she and Constance would set out early with a picnic of breakfast rolls, freshly baked by Cook, salted meat, cheese, preserves and ginger beer. A day to linger in the water meadows, with the cuckoo flowers and the small blue butterflies, Constance playing with her Dutch dolls, Simone with a book open on her lap. The scent of grass and apples. The memory catches her like a rogue wave on a sea blown up by the wind and rising to a storm. She is cast on its rocks.

The light turns from rose to grey, the hint of sun already retreating. The building shifts and creaks as if its bricks and mortar, its walls, corridors, dormitories and stairways breathe. She listens for the chorus of women who have come before her, for the heartbeat of trapped and stifled lives. Beyond her room, muffled voices float like gulls far out at sea, keys rattle and she hears the trundling of passing wheels on the linoleum floor.

Then silence.

Then a scream.

A scream that pierces the air, high and long, followed by shouting, running, boots on the floor, a commotion and a piteous wailing. Simone jumps out of bed and begins to dress, not knowing why, only knowing if something terrible is happening that she must be dressed and ready.

Gradually the voices calm and die away.

She lies back on the counterpane, waiting, with no notion of what may come, fearing that there has been some great tragedy, that she is forgotten and may remain locked away until the day passes and it grows dark again. But before long a bell sounds, a key turns in the lock and her door is pushed open. She sits up. A plump, red-haired, freckled attendant in uniform and cap stands in the doorway.

'Mrs Corey, ma'am. My job it is to keep watch here now. Show you what's what. That was the morning bell. Time to get up. Pick up the pot, dear, and follow me.'

Simone does as she is told. The clock on the wall in the corridor shows three minutes past six o'clock.

Women are already gathered in the washroom. Mrs Corey shows Simone where to empty the chamber pot, where to get her stand-up wash, though she must wait for the dormitory women to finish first.

In the washroom mirror, her face as pale as ash. Mrs Corey hands her a washcloth and a thin, grey towel. There is only carbolic, no rosemary water, no scented powder.

As the last of the women drift away, Mrs Corey looks in their direction, 'You'll not mind me saying,' she says, 'but next time you'd be best to come in your chemise, like the others. Better for a wash, I always think. What's more it would be a good idea to make yourself known to them. They're your neighbours now, Dormitory Twelve. They'll be in and out. Mostly we keep the doors unlocked. We are not a prison house.'

Simone nods. 'I heard a noise earlier, a scream,' she says, as she picks up the empty pot and follows Mrs Corey along the corridor back to her room. 'Is someone hurt?'

Mrs Corey tuts, 'Nothing for you to concern yourself with. Just Alice Semple, at it again. God help us. It sets them all off. Now if you don't mind me saying, though I am just a poor attendant, it's my observation that it be best for you to be employed. Time passes more quickly in useful occupation and there is plenty to be had here. And if you don't want to be watched night and day, then you will need to persuade the powers that be that you intend no harm to yourself. If you get my meaning. Now, I must search your room.'

While the attendant goes about her work, Simone brushes and knots her hair.

Mrs Corey lifts the mattress first, then opens the small wooden cabinet next to the bed where Simone has stored her linens and shawl, and what few possessions she has brought with her, packed by her housemaid Maria: her tortoise shell combs, her white kid gloves, a copy of *The Child's Guide to Knowledge*, a childhood gift from her sister, Clara, and a pansy flower pressed in a lace handkerchief.

When Mrs Corey is finished her searching she says, 'Breakfast is taken in the Dining Hall, Mrs Gastrell. Seven o'clock sharp. This way. Follow me.'

Simone does as she is bid. She keeps her head down, eyes on the muddy hem of Mrs Corey's skirts. They pass the entrance to the washroom, then through a moulded archway into Dormitory Twelve, a large and lofty room, measured out in bays of iron framed beds. Identical beds, on either side, each with the same white counterpane as Simone's, all neatly made. Or so it seems on first glance, which is all she dares, preferring to look ahead only.

The floors are wooden, the walls panelled. There is a whiff of carbolic and vinegar, no lavender, no Maria with the smell of lemon about her as she polishes. The floor is wet from mopping. The room is lit by the towering windows, one after another, that stretch the length of the walls, letting in a flood of light. How can it be that a place so illuminated is yet a cave of darkness?

They stop.

Simone looks up from the scuffed heels of Mrs Corey's black shoes to see two women by a bed at the end of the room, one on her hands and knees scrubbing the floor, another washing down a wall. The wall and the floor are stained with blood. Mrs Corey tut-tuts thems under her breath and hurries out into the corridor. She stops when she reaches a square vestibule with a glass lantern in its roof.

From this quiet, empty vestibule, a place where you might rest and listen, where you might hear the furthest footstep, hear even the echo of a heartbeat, Mrs Corey pushes through the double doors into a cacophonous Dining Hall.

Simone follows her into the din, into the smell of meat and boiled cabbage, into a flock of women bristling like sparrows fighting over crumbs. Her entrance does not go unnoticed. The women look up from their plates. A startled silence is followed by a fluttering of whispers, then silence again as if the flock has flown. Except they are there still, every one of them, all eyes now on her. Head to foot black looks, as if they wish her ill, as if they wish her as dead as Constance, as if they lay the blame squarely at her feet. For she is not foolish enough to think they will not know something of her situation, news travels fast in the County and in a place such as Long Meadow. Simone holds her head high and thinks of William Blakely's hand reaching out to steady her.

Mrs Corey indicates a table, empty apart from a lone girl. She is to sit there. The girl is young, not past seventeen Simone estimates, fair of skin and hair like Constance, though it is patchy and thin and there are bald places on her head. A plate of rye bread sits before her, untouched. She mumbles and hums under her breath. She is too thin or else her dress so ill fitting that it drowns her. She has the appearance of a beggar on the street, of a poor lost child in need of a mother's care. The skin on her wrists is marked with cuts and grazes, the blood dried and brown. Simone is about to ask her name when the girl's eyes grow wide, her head goes down and a new silence falls over the Dining Hall.

'Matron,' the girl whispers and the tin cup in her hand begins to shake.

Phoebe Baines

The Dining Hall

the bees are back, they come when i am asleep
tapping at the window glass, whispering
still it is not done
they say i must find the knife or some such means
by which to drain his blood
they wish to see him on a slab
white as the belly of the whale,
white as candle wax
they want him butchered and hung like pork meat
my purpose to rid the world of him
shadow like the devil looming on the wall at dusk
flickering in the gaslight, beer on breath
smell of vinegar and frost
smell of cod and cockle
my hair lost stolen
stuffed into my shoes, stuffed between the bedsheets
in the day room and the dormitory, out in the airing
courts, my linen drawers
and nightshirt full
hair in my mouth and my cap
hair pulled out, where it should not be, on flowers and
grass
on my head spots as bald as my stepfather's pate

27

there are semolina cakes for breakfast
heads bent to plates mouths bursting with crumbs
my teeth break as on the cobbles
kites and crows in the clerestory suck light from cathedral
walls
nails curved and narrow as claws black hair on skin
black as coal in the coal cellar I shouldn't wonder
watch for the boots watch the floor for their approach
hear the gossips whisper *she's for it no mistake*
bees cannot keep me safe
i have a pencil hidden in my skirt, the smell of parchment
consoles me
i beg a book for drawing in and a sharpened pencil
still my hair falls out
they will not change my brown linsey dress to green
even though it is spring
they are whitewashing again
they say i
am alone too much, they say they will lock the door of
dormitory twelve if i do not stop my wanderings at first
light
if i do not stop dancing with the magpies and the gold
crests
i will be moved to the dormitories of the watched
better still he says he will put me in the padded cell
i do not eat
black bread makes me sick
hair in the butter more of it lost
whitewash, they whitewash the walls to cover the blood
i would feed the gold crests and the magpies before the
morning bell
but Alice Semple cut her throat with a table knife

they came running boots on the floor
back to beds water mop blood whitewash
water mop blood whitewash
Alice in the infirmary seventeen stitches in her throat
i hum under my breath the sweetest songs tell sad
thoughts
they watch me eat
watching is what they do, for apron strings and sheets,
cords, handkerchiefs, tied to gas brackets and window
handles twine and calico
knives are not the only tools
the new woman comes and sits by me
on her plate two slices of black rye bread and butter
she does not eat
the women whisper all eyes on her
the gossips spittle in the air about her
bubbles of vinegar drops of spite
curses for the killing of a child
who to trust, a woman who cries out in her sleep
larks, larks of glass or some such
i hear her through the shadows, my bed being the last in
the dormitory
hers the next room along
she smiles at me
perhaps she has been in the airing courts when she
shouldn't
dancing with the birds
perhaps we are sisters, they sit outside her door
she is pretty dark eyes bows for lips her hair is not falling
out
like mine which the bees take to their hives to make beds
ants for their nest hair spoils the honey

larks are birds I think, though I haven't seen one
except once in a book
the bread is thick with butter and hair
i cannot eat
now this
matron
matron is in the dining hall
look up look down pretend to eat
matron brings her muffling cloud, silence
matron like a stalking cat tight-corset waist thick hair
eyes like frozen puddles
bitch
from nowhere, one minute the mind at rest dragonfly on
a green leaf
bee nestling in the flower cup white foxgloves by the
watercress stream,
the next matron
then him
he is standing beside her a pair, matron simpering
acid in my throat i swallow it down cannot eat
my tin cup shakes
the new woman looks at me
she is yet to know matron
she is yet to know them

Medical Officer

31. He shall be under the control of the Superintendent, whom he shall assist in the performance of all his duties.

32. He shall prepare the Medicines and take care that they are properly administered.

33. He shall in the absence of the Superintendent, perform his duties, and be responsible for the condition of the establishment whilst under his charge.

Rules for the Government of the Pauper Lunatic Asylum situate at Long Meadow – prepared and submitted by the Committee of Visitors thereof, by virtue of the 53rd section of the 16th and 17th VIC. CHAP 97

William Blakely

Medical Officers Quarters, above the Dining Hall

He extracts the blade from its handle and sharpens it on the leather strop. As the blade grazes his skin a skein of blood blooms across his fingertip. It reminds him to go carefully, he does not want to do his rounds with dried blood and cuts on his face. It reminds him of his dream. She was standing in the meadow among the grasses and ladies' bedstraw and there was blood on her skirts.

He works the brush into the soap and lathers his chin. He has no time for the new fashions, for the unkempt beard and unruly moustache. His own moustache is neat and small. With one hand he stretches the skin at his chin while with the other he draws the blade over the stubble. He watches its progress in the mirror on the washstand. He knows there are those who consider him handsome, prominent cheekbones, fine jaw and uncommonly bright, some have said arresting, green eyes. But he is not always sure of his looks. What he is certain of, is that when he looks in the mirror it is his father's face he sees looking back at him, a face he'd prefer to forget. But the mind has its own workings and despite the best efforts of fine men, still far from fathomable.

He'd been alarmed to dream of her last night. He rarely, if ever, dreams of a patient but he had dreamed of Simone Gastrell on the very first night of meeting. Perhaps it had been her late arrival when the swifts chased about the tower and the light leeched from the day. Perhaps that she had stumbled and needed his hand to steady her, that she was gentle and quiet, showing no signs of mania or dementia, no puerperal insanity but a melancholia brought on by grief and a suicidal disposition which she had vehemently denied. There was the question of the dead child of course. As well as the habitual loss of consciousness, a condition she appears to have suffered since childhood and described by her physician, Eames, as *fainting fits*. But apart from this, Simone Gastrell was a fine and handsome woman who had seemed entirely out of place in his Admissions Room.

He puts the razor down, washes his face and towels it dry, inspecting it for minor cuts. He's pleased there are none. He applies a pomatum of sandalwood and combs it through his hair. He fetches his grey broadcloth suit from the wardrobe, and with it a white shirt, a collar and a green necktie. While he dresses, he prepares mentally for his meeting with Cornelius Stafford, Superintendent of Long Meadow, a meeting that takes place every weekday at 8 a.m. when they review matters concerning staff and patients, both the men and women, who thank God, inhabit separate wings of the building, rarely coming together. They go through the diary and ensure the general smooth running of the establishment. It is his job to brief Stafford on issues of control, self-harm and attempted suicides, as well as details of those admitted and those released. It is an opportunity to show competence and knowledge and he puts great store in performing well. He has, after all, ambitions to one day be a Superintendent of his own asylum.

As he fastens his collar, Blakely runs through the notices, reminding himself that Alice Semple had attempted to cut her throat. Again. Matron had sent a *Note of Harm* to his quarters. He would have to visit Semple in the Infirmary. No doubt Stafford would want the gloves on her. Though he himself was not sure that such drastic solutions as locking heavy gloves without fingers onto a patient's wrist were beneficial and did not cause more harm than good. He sighed. On the Men's Wing a minor fight had broken out between Smith and Grainger in Dormitory Five over accusations of petty theft. They had been placed on Report and would appear before him later for adjudication. There were no patients due for release.

He'd learned fast what Stafford needed or wanted to know and what he, as the Deputy, was expected to deal with. They were well acquainted. In private, on first name terms. One evening most weeks, they shared a bottle of burgundy in Stafford's cottage in the grounds. Above all, the Superintendent valued his freedom to work on correspondence and research, particularly in respect of his latest fascination – the treatment of insanity by electricity – which Blakely considered to be bordering on obsession. By and large, Blakely observed that Stafford was uninterested in the patients other than as subjects for his investigations.

There had been only one admission yesterday, Simone Gastrell. Blakely had finished writing up her notes at 10 p.m. the previous evening. He was nothing if not dedicated, nothing if not professional.

He runs through them now in his head…*Simone Gastrell, aged twenty-six, no children, a stillbirth at full term. No epilepsy, though suffering from fainting fits and loss of consciousness since childhood. No hereditary disease. Bodily condition on admission, good. First recorded attack – duration being two days. The patient can read and write. Is educated to a good standard. Causes of insanity, predisposing: jealousy, claims husband is engaged in adultery with his cousin. Exciting: death of child by drowning. Causes as cited by local physician Dr Eames: jealousy, undue interest in reading, neglect of household and wifely duties, intention to harm a child, subsequent hysteria. Whether suicidal? According to Eames, the patient threatened to throw herself off Fullerton bridge. Mrs Gastrell has no memory nor gives credence to such a threat. Whether dangerous to others? Says she would never harm a child, though considers herself in part to blame for the child's death. Speaks of a liaison between the drowned child's sister Henriette Gaule and Mr. Gastrell, the patient's husband. Denies any jealousies.*

In conclusion, I could find in her no intention to harm. Patient is suicidal, without the presence of insanity, due to obvious moral and emotional cause. Twenty-four-hour watch to be reviewed.

Blakely adjusts his necktie, pulls at his cuffs and checks his appearance in the long mirror on the back of the wardrobe door. As he does so, he remembers that Marianne Vaisey and whoever joins her, for they must come in pairs, are to visit that morning. Knowing her, thinks Blakely, she will already be on the premises. He sighs. In his view, the members of the House Committee are all too good at poking their noses in where they're not wanted. Though he is forced to admit there is something about Miss Vaisey that piques his interest.

The House Committee

6. Not less than two members of the House Committee shall together, once at least in every two months, inspect every part of the Asylum, and see and examine as far as circumstances will permit, every Lunatic therein.

The Visitors' Book

8. The members of the House Committee shall make entries in a book kept for that purpose, called the Visitors' Book, of the result of their visits and minutes of their proceedings as they see fit...

The Infirmary

56. One Ward on the men's side and one Ward on the women's side shall be appointed as Infirmaries for the different sexes.

Rules for the Government of the Pauper Lunatic Asylum situate at Long Meadow – prepared and submitted by the Committee of Visitors thereof, by virtue of the 53rd section of the 16th and 17th VIC. CHAP 97

The Visitors' Book

May 10th, 1875

Alice Semple has today been issued with three pencils and a book of plain paper by the House Committee in lieu of her desperate act and in consideration of the fact that the knife she has taken to her throat has rendered her temporarily speechless.

M. Vaisey

Alice Semple

The Infirmary

From the window, Alice Semple takes comfort in the fat, grey clouds that have replaced the early sun and now gather over the Airing Courts. She watches the women taking the air. Before long it will rain and they will be drowned like rats at sea. But not her. Water flows off her back.

She is born in a storm. Her mother squatting in the bog myrtle, her grandmother the midwife. She is goose-footed having a sixth toe on her left foot which some say marks her as a witch. Her family are Simplers, wise woman who make their living from the land seeking out its herbs and roots, angelica, feverfew, hemlock and foxglove, though it is not enough to know what they may cure. The Simpler must know where the cure may be found and in what seasons and weathers. She must cast her eye on the shift into winter and the colour of the rowan berries. She must heed the omens, the spilled salt, the smell of roses in a dream.

Before she met him, Alice Semple swears there were no omens, or else her nose had grown cold for it. Clare. John Clare, poet and traveller, too fond of ale, too fond of women, who professed to love a happy ending, who loved her, so he said, for a brief season, was it weeks or mere days, when the hedges were full of bloom?

She meets him in The Bluebell. Barely twenty, she has taken refuge in the warm interiors of public houses and in the comfort of a glass. She has a taste for it. She is tired of sleeping always alone under the stars. He is twice her age. They fall into drink together, wander the wild heath, green meadows, crooking brooks and the dark woods. They camp out with the gypsies. They rub up against each other like a pair of farts in an old man's breeches, so he says.

He is always scribbling and never without a pencil, his pockets crammed with crumpled paper. Never enough paper to satisfy. It is where she learns the habit of writing. She is literate, taught by her grandmother.

He is lustful but so is she and why not? Their time brief. He is a man of heart, would rather watch the butterfly settle on the leaf than stick it with a pin to cork. But he is wary of being seen, of trespassing, afraid of this new world, afraid he will be forgotten, that his poetry will not last. The drink only makes such anxieties worse and the money of course. They have no money, they eat with the gypsies, badger meat, hedgehog soaked in vinegar, a dose of flatulence if ever there was. The fields are their church, the dykes their pillow, together they imagine they might journey beyond the horizon to the world's end. It ends in acrimony. Two drunks fighting over what? For one thing he has a wife and a family to keep.

She cannot remember now how it started, their falling out, she doesn't care to. He left her, finding work as a hedger, better than selling apples, he said. She never forgets him. There was a time, when she first came to Long Meadow, fourteen years ago, when the drink had undone her and she believed herself to be his first love, Mary Joyce, of whom he so often spoke. A madness born out of want. Not so now. No, faculties returned, she stands apart in her captivity and observes, she knows the way of the place, its people, their tracks, its hidden rooms, the wheels that run in the corridor at night. She has learned that to protest, to lay claim to one's sanity is, in their eyes, nothing but proof of lunacy.

Clare is dead now. He died as she will. Incarcerated. Only she strives for it to be at her own hand and mourns her ill-fated attempted that morning that has left her without the power of speech but in a whisper.

Alice Semple moves away from the window and takes up her newly acquired notebook and her pencil. Outside, as the rain falls, the pumps grow ever louder. A bell rings and an attendant calls, 'All ladies in, all ladies in.'

Matron

39. She shall be under the control of the Committee of Visitors and the Resident Medical Officer and Superintendent and take care that all orders and directions as to the management of the Female Patients, and the directions of the Resident Medical Officer and Superintendent as to the medical and moral treatment, be enforced and carried into execution. She shall superintend the domestic management of all parts of the Asylum where females are employed – shall be responsible for the condition of the Female Wards – shall have control over all the Female Servants and, in common with the Superintendent, over the Nurses of the establishment, with power to suspend the Female Servants if she deems it necessary.

40. She shall visit the Female Wards and see every patient at least every day, shall from time to time visit the Wards during the Patients' meal times and at uncertain times before the attendants rise in the morning and at night after the Patients are in bed.

Rules for the Government of the Pauper Lunatic Asylum situate at Long Meadow – prepared and submitted by the Committee of Visitors thereof, by virtue of the 53rd section of the 16th and 17th VIC. CHAP 97

Simone

'Matron,' announces Mrs Corey in a voice like a curtsey.

Simone has met women like Matron before, though mostly they are older and not as slender or as pleasing to look at. They are polite and dutiful in their manner yet in everything they do, they manifest an air of superiority. Such women may instill fear with a mere smile. She had such a governess once, Mrs Powell, after her Mama and Papa died, when she and Clara went to live with their aunt Elizabeth. Mrs Powell's aim was to have the sisters at a word, like dogs at heel, begging for scraps. And she might have succeeded had there been just one of them, especially if sad and grieving, but together Simone and Clara were ungovernable, headstrong, recalcitrant.

Matron stands waiting in the open doorway and as Simone rises to greet her, she thinks of Clara, if only she were here now. She determines that she must get word to her sister as a matter of urgency.

Matron steps into the room, about her waist a belt laden with keys. Her eyes are everywhere, searching as if seeking something she has lost. She does not look at Simone as she speaks, 'Good morning, Mrs Gastrell. I trust you slept well and have breakfasted. I wonder that you are not out in the Courts taking the air. You will find our doors mostly unlocked, so that you may come and go to work, to dine and to take the air. Fresh air is recommended for all our patients, and walking, most soothing.' Then glancing at the window, 'Though it has come on to rain now I fear.' She runs her hands over the counterpane on the bed, then moves to the pillow. 'What is this? Is this blood?'

'I believe so, though not mine,' Simone says.

Mrs Corey bustles forward, smoothing her apron, hand on her cap.

'Have it changed immediately,' says Matron to Mrs Corey. Then mutters to herself, 'Enough blood already for one morning.' She looks at Simone for the first time. 'I trust you will be comfortable here with us, Mrs Gastrell. I have assured my brother, Dr Eames, I think you know him, your husband's physician?' She pauses, smiles, and turns to the door. 'I have assured him I will do everything in my power to keep you so.'

'Please, before you go, Matron,' says Simone, seizing her chance, 'I must contact my sister so that she may know my whereabouts. I need writing paper and a pen and the means of postage.'

Matron turns slowly. 'Your sister,' she says, with what Simone detects to be a hint of suspicion in her voice, 'I was not aware you had a sister, Mrs Gastrell.' She pauses, 'But of course, paper and pen, if agreed, it is possible for a small charge. You have the means I assume?'

'I do,' Simone replies, though she is unsure of it. She has no money with her and no knowledge of how such funds are arranged. All she knows is she must have paper.

'I will look into it,' says Matron and leaves.

Mrs Corey looks up to the heavens, tuts and disappears, taking the pillowslip with her. She returns with a clean pillowslip and resumes watch outside Simone's room where she sits on a stool and, taking a needle, a skein of wool and a sock from her pocket, commences darning. The door is to be left ajar.

Simone lies on the bed, slowly easing her neck onto the newly covered pillow. It is always this way, her neck stiff and painful after one of her headaches. If only she was with Clara now. Clara would have rubbed Simone's neck with a camphor liniment and eased the pain. It was always Clara who had cared for her. And though they lived at a distance from one another, they shared their troubles too, chiefly hers with Everett. Simone thinks of what she will write to her sister. She must tell her everything, all her misfortunes, hiding nothing. She must tell her of Constance's death. And of her life confined here in this room.

She looks about her. The room comprises a window, a bed, a small cabinet and two chairs, which admittedly is more than the women in the dormitory have. One chair is wooden and fits into the small table she supposes is a desk, though as yet it has none of the trappings of a desk and no books except a tattered copy of the Book of Common Prayer. The other sits beside the bed and is upholstered in rough grey wool. It is comfortless as such chairs so often are. All colour and texture are absent, all furnishings bare, there are no brocades and velvets, no soft silks to run through fingers, no tapestries, no carpets. Nothing to soften the edges of this new world. Nothing is familiar, and there is no voice, face, attitude, no scent, no touch that she knows. All that she was and lived is gone, replaced by brick and iron, carbolic and blood, walls to keep her in, ceilings that echo the keening.

How shall she live here? How shall she survive?

Simone is dreaming of Clara. They are by the sea, sat together under a dazzling sun, picnicking in the dunes and Clara has a baby in her arms. She shields the baby from the sun with a muslin cloth. Clouds gather in the sky above them. The sea grows dark and the waves threaten. The baby begins to choke. Her mouth is stuffed full of sand. Simone cries out to warn Clara, but no sound comes out – only the ringing of a bell.

A hand is shaking Simone's arm.

She opens her eyes. A freckled face and red hair, Mrs Corey is standing by her bed. It is time for dinner, she says, and Simone is to find her own way to the Dining Hall.

She makes her way out into the corridor and through the dormitory. She follows a pair of stragglers, who look back at her and stare but say nothing. When she reaches the vestibule, she pauses in front of the double doors and looks up at the roof lantern. The rain has stopped but the glass is scattered with raindrops like a spill of stars.

The stragglers go through the doors. Simone stands beneath the lantern. There are voices behind her. She turns, a breeze wafts over her face, and she catches the scent of wet earth. An attendant calls, 'All ladies in, all ladies in.' A small group of women come through an open door on the other side of the vestibule. Simone glimpses the sky, trees dark from rainfall, a high hedge and a gravel path. Last through is the attendant who closes the door but does not lift a key from the bunch at her belt to lock it. The women push past Simone, a bony elbow digs in her arm.

She follows them into the Dining Hall and looks for the girl with the thin hair who reminds her of the child Constance but there is no sign of her. Simone sits alone facing the doors, her back to the throng. She is joined by several other women, mostly silent, fixing on their boiled meat and potatoes. She is grateful for their lack of interest in her. She eats her potatoes and drinks a cup of beer. It is noisy, and noisier still when women begin getting up, scraping their plates into bowls of swill, and throwing their cutlery into the water bucket.

Dinner is all but over when the girl appears. The doors open and she stumbles into the hall, as if pushed. She stands frozen, dishevelled, cap awry, skirts black with coal dust. One of the *silent women*, older, perhaps old enough to be a grandmother, though it is hard to tell in Long Meadow, gets up from her seat and takes the girl by the arm. She steers her gently to a seat at Simone's table.

Simone turns to the woman and asks the girl's name.

'Phoebe,' whispers the woman, 'Phoebe Baines.'

Alice Semple's Notebook

Dormitory 12 – An Inventory.

I am! yet what I am none cares or knows
– John Clare

I write to name us, so that the world may know who is hidden here.

Emma Brewer – believes her husband is coming to kill her, tries to choke herself with her fingers, once jumped out of a window.

Mary Ann Holdsworth – collects pieces of fruit and scraps of bread and calls them her babies. They go green and mouldy, but she does not like to part with them.

Amelia Grey – stands on her head and sings bawdy songs, bangs on the walls and doors at night, fearing her father is come to take her to his bed.

Esther Knox – has fits and softening of the brain, she cries a lot, more than you would think possible for one woman. She claims to speak with the Queen.

Anne Bickerdale – believes she is Mary Magdalene but there's no sign of Jesus here. She works in the kitchens, the source of much news and gossip.

Phoebe Baines – eats hair and talks to bees, poor child spends half her life in the coal-cellar and everyone knows why.

Katharine O'Sullivan – says she saw the devil come out and dance at dawn in the woods round about. Claims her husband was shot for poaching in Keepers Wood though his body was never found.

Ivy Cole suckled thirteen children before falling into black moods and debility, she does not speak.

Eveline Web cuts herself where you cannot see. I know, I have loaned her the means, for it brings her relief. She believes her stomach to be filled with eels.

Gladys Carter offers her virgin flower to all and sundry, does handstands up against the Chapel wall. Likes to dance.

Dorcas Fisher wears a mask. Her face beneath is crumpled and scarred. She was but five years and tied to the chair by her mother when her flannelette nightshirt caught fire. She is often force fed.

Stafford is a galvanic pig and Blakely his piglet. They know nothing of poetry. God save the Committee of Visitors, Miss Vaisey, and the Chaplain. Matron is a witch and a hedge whore. I was once married to the poet, John Clare, in a daisy field with two trees in the distance and a lark above us...

Simone

Simone sleeps through the afternoon. It is not so unusual the day after a headache.

The supper bell wakes her.

Mrs Corey arrives and tells her she must hurry it is quarter past five and she will be late. 'You've been asleep a good while. You've missed 'em all. His Lordship, that's what some call him, Mr. Stafford, the Superintendent, he makes his rounds once a day, at least he's supposed to. Then Mr. Blakely, his Deputy. He looked in. You can rely on him for his rounds, never known him miss. Asked me how you'd been getting on, what you'd eaten, and if I thought you were a danger, to yourself. And I said I didn't think so and he nodded. But as you can see, I'm still sat here watching you. Now hurry up.'

'I won't take supper this evening. I've no appetite. If I could just wash,' Simone says. Already she finds she cannot face another mutton-grey meal, nor the way time is ordered, bell by bell, meal by meal, the day measured in joyless routine.

The attendant hesitates. Simone senses her reluctance, but after some thought she says, 'Well, I suppose so. You are new here, after all. You can wash while the others are eating. I could bring you your pint of tea if you like. I can send Anne Bickerdale up from the kitchen with a slice of bread?'

And although Simone doesn't want bread or tea, she nods

and says, 'Thank you, Mrs Corey.' For it seems as if the woman has a kind heart and never has Simone needed kindness more.

Resident Medical Officer and Superintendent

16. He shall be the principal Officer of the Asylum, to whom its general management is entrusted and shall give up the whole of his time to its duties without other occupation or engagement. He shall have the direction of the medical, surgical and moral treatment of the patients, and of all general arrangements within the Asylum.

17. He shall have control over all the male Attendants and Servants, shall regulate their duties, and have authority to suspend them whenever he may deem it expedient...

20. He shall classify the Patients and see each once a day: and in case of his not making such visit, he shall state the cause of omission in his journal.

22. He shall never absent himself for more than one night without the previous written consent of one of the Committee of Visitors, such absence to be recorded in his Journal.

Rules for the Government of the Pauper Lunatic Asylum situate at Long Meadow – prepared and submitted by the Committee of Visitors thereof, by virtue of the 53rd section of the 16th and 17th VIC. CHAP 97

The Superintendent's Cottage

'Damn, the bloody woman,' says Stafford. 'Damn Semple.
I'll have the gloves put on her. She's a thorn in my side.
Always has been. As for our Miss Vaisey, have you seen
what she's given her? Pencils, and a notebook full of blank
pages. Have you seen what Semple writes in it? An inventory
of her own making no less. Patients' names and so-called
afflictions. Sheer bloody nonsense. The Committee should
leave well alone. But of course, they think themselves experts,
when they are simply folk with money and county titles.
Power beyond their wits and women to boot.' Stafford sighs,
shakes his head and puts his glass to his lips.

Stafford and Blakely sit opposite each other in carved
spoon backs either side of the leaded fireplace. No fire is lit.
Blakely pulls his coat close around him. Despite thick velvet
drapes, the parlour bears the damp and chill of a spring
evening. The cottage is situated some distance from the main
building and lies in a hollow where the mists gather, so that
returning to his apartment, Blakely often finds himself
stumbling through a fen fog.

Stafford puts his glass down and fills it from the decanter
of claret next to him on the side table. He offers the decanter
to Blakely, but Blakely shakes his head. He's had enough to
drink for one evening. He'll do his best to avoid answering
Stafford's questions about Alice Semple. Experience tells him
it won't be a problem. Stafford is happiest to hear his own
voice and Blakely does not want to admit he has not yet

seen Semple's jottings though he's read the entry in the Visitor's Book. He merely nods.

'Does Vaisey not stop to think that a pencil might constitute a dangerous weapon? Have your eye out in a moment and, knowing Semple, quite likely to poke her own out once she's finished with her rantings. We can't have it you know, Blakely, paper flying about all over the place. God knows if they have unfettered access, all kinds of trouble, love notes, filth I shouldn't wonder, accusations, letters to the newspaper, all uncensored, smuggled out. It's not as if they're poets, like Clare is it?' He laughs. 'Well, not on my watch. And Matron agrees. I can't have it, Blakely. I want all rogue paper gathered up and destroyed. No paper without my express permission, and in the event I allow it, each sheet to be numbered that includes sketchbooks, drawing materials. Do you understand? It's in the rules of Governance, damn it – sixty-four.'

Blakely nods and smiles inwardly. The whole place knows how Stafford ignores or cites the rules according to his whims. There will be no arguing against the claret and no arguing against the joint will of Stafford and Matron. Not when he considers the way the air around them crackles with their teasings and come hithers. It is their power, Blakely thinks, that attracts them. That and the comeliness of Matron which cannot be denied, and which Stafford never misses a chance to remark on, especially in drink. The time he'd been down to London and 'as it happened,' according to his account had found himself in Holywell Street and unable to resist a series of lascivious engravings. He'd shown them to Blakely on his return. 'Doesn't the whore remind you of someone?' Stafford had asked. 'Doesn't she have the look of Matron about her?'

'As to the Gastrell woman,' says Stafford, pouring himself another glass, 'decent chap, Gastrell, pays well and God knows we need the money, of good reputation too, and Eames, the physician, he's Matron's brother, did you know? I'm not sure I concur with your diagnosis. Though I've yet to interview her. But, no, I incline to puerperal melancholia, mania even, after all there are indications of possible derangement and murder. This stillbirth… are we certain it was not infanticide? Was there an autopsy? We might at least assume that she failed to act in the case of the child, that she encouraged her to the water, that she watched the drowning, held her down without aid. Does she speak of the child, express grief?'

'No, not as far as I'm aware, not that I, or Mrs Corey who is watching her, have observed, but surely her grief would…'

'There you are, no guilt you see, a clear sign they're not like us, Blakely, not anything like, no conscience you see. I warrant she did it out of jealousy or revenge. The child was not hers I understand?'

'No, a cousin of her husband's. She claims an adulterous relationship between her husband and the child's older sister who is nineteen, I gather.'

'Jealousy and revenge are powerful motives. The Kent case, remember it, killed her half brother?'

'Wasn't the motive questioned? Beside Mrs Gastrell claims no jealousies.'

Stafford does not reply. But looks over the top of his glasses in disbelief at Blakely.

Blakely leans back in his chair, then tentatively, 'Well, I'm not sure the Commissioners would agree, you know. They might even lean to a belief of wrongful confinement.'

'Heavens above, man. God's Blood. The woman's in need of protection. Do you doubt Eames? She's a danger to herself and others.'

'But as far as the Commissioners are concerned, she may present as quite sane. The press has been full of their laxity in these matters. They will want to make redress. If they inspect, they may deem her detainment unlawful. If she is not a danger…'

'A new-born and a child, what more do you need man? As for her composure, the lunatic is always the queen of deception. It's her very appearance of sanity that marks her out. God forbid, it's not as if we've got the woman chained up, no whips or camphor, no quicksilver. Oh, I grant you ours can be an uncertain business but nevertheless it must be left to our judgement and diagnostic skill. You'll need to interview her again. No. On second thoughts leave it to me. She will make an interesting case study if I'm not mistaken. She may in fact be an excellent subject for the use of galvanic current once we begin the treatments. Though God knows when that will be what with the Committee and the Chaplain and their nonsensical objections.'

Blakely refrains from commenting on Stafford's frustration. In truth, he shares the Committee and the Chaplain's reservations, though for different reasons, and therefore prefers to avoid the subject. 'Matron tells me she has asked for paper. To write to her sister.'

'Hold off, for as long as possible. Let us pray the likes of Miss Vaisey and her House Committee don't get word of it. And if there are letters, then they must be censored. The women's letters must be censored, Blakely. And don't bother with forwarding them to the Committee. You know as well as I do, they need protecting from themselves. Women such as these tend towards the self-revelatory and indecorous in their writing. It is to be discouraged at all costs. Now. Did I tell you I'm corresponding with Bryce from the Alabama Institute in the United States? He judges it to be beneficial in most cases, 'valuable in a majority', those are his words. For our purposes, Mayer and Meltzer have the instrument of choice, a constant battery of considerable power with an induction apparatus in the very same box. Perfect for the medical practitioner. I'm preparing a paper for the sub-committee. I can rely on your support?'

Blakely nods, gets to his feet and brushes down his coat. He pulls at his cuffs which are soiled. The shirt will go straight to the laundry when he takes it off. 'It's late, and time I was away, Sir,' he says.

'Before you go, remember to fill in the Journal for today. I've no time for it. All these damn rules and regulations, can't keep up with them. I swear they spend their days dreaming up new ones just to frustrate us. They have no thought for the demands of the real work itself.'

Blakely makes his way back to his quarters, above the Dining Hall. The night is moonless and chill. The insistent rhythm of the pumps weights the air. The grass is damp and his heart heavy. He deeply regrets Stafford's interest in Simone Gastrell. There are those, and he is among them, who think Stafford an unprincipled, even dangerous man. He thinks of going to Simone's room. He tells himself it will be by way of reassurance, so that he can know his diagnosis was correct. But it is late, and surely not within the bounds of propriety for a man in his position.

Simone

Simone sits at the wooden desk, dressed only in a chemise, with a shawl about her shoulders. Outside, the sky turns to ink and a thin mist hangs above the ground. There is a chill in the air, as so often, here in spring. She shivers and pulls her shawl tight around her. She thinks of Constance and of the river that morning. Surely, she had wanted to save her. Just as she had wanted her own child to live. She closes her eyes, but the underwater soup and tangle of river weed leave her blind. She is afraid of uprooting memories of the sea and the shipwreck which so altered her and Clara's young lives. If only she could remember. How had the day of Constance's drowning begun? Had she been alone with her that morning and what of Everett and Henrietta, where were they? And where are they now?

She tries not to dwell on what is happening on the other side of Long Meadow's walls, for these are matters beyond her influence, on which she can have no bearing. It is best not to torture oneself with imaginings. But she cannot help but think of them now, her husband and Henrietta sipping port together after dinner, on the terrace, the lilac bursting from its bud. The lilac she would pick, as she did every year, with Maria, filling the drawing room and hall vases, drowning the house in its perfume.

Here there is no such scent. The air is thick with the tar of carbolic, and beneath it the iron smell of blood, and a stale miasma of bodily fluids. On the surface Long Meadow is clean and well-ordered. Built, she daresay, with the best of intentions, but it has taken her no more than a day to see beneath the whitewash to the peeling walls, to a place that God forgot. To the women he abandoned.

The lights flicker and begin to fade.

Simone gets up from the chair and kneels by the side of the bed. She prays for Alice Semple, whoever she might be, for what possesses a woman to cut her own throat she cannot fathom. She prays for the poor girl, Phoebe, who plays in the coal, for the *silent women*, for the woman who sang her heart out and pirouetted through the washroom that very evening before bed, making them smile. She thanks her. She asks God not to forget them. She asks for what she craves above all else, forgiveness.

She is praying for the strength to resist when she hears voices outside. The door opens slowly. Simone gets up from her prayers. William Blakely appears in the shadows. He steps into the room. He smells of wine and the damp night air. He sits on her bed.

'Please, sit here, beside me,' he says, patting the bed. 'I have some matters I'd like to discuss with you.'

She sits beside him. He reaches out and touches her arm. Beneath the wool of her shawl, she feels the heat of his hand on her skin.

When he is gone, she stands at the window looking out beyond the mist to the edge of the forest. She feels the imprint of his hand on her arm still. Sandalwood perfumes the room. His voice gentle, insistent, lives in her ear, pleading with her to remember, telling her it is of the utmost importance.

Outside in the corridor she hears a shuffling of feet, boots on the floor, an urgent stifled, whisper, and the trundling of wheels.

The Treatment of Patients

63. All the Attendants shall be instructed to treat their Patients kindly and indulgently, and never strike or speak harshly to them; and they shall be responsible for the safety, cleanliness and general condition of the Patients, and for the ventilation, proper warmth and good order of their respective wards.

Rules for the Government of the Pauper Lunatic Asylum situate at Long Meadow – prepared and submitted by the Committee of Visitors thereof, by virtue of the 53rd section of the 16th and 17th VIC. CHAP 97

Phoebe Baines

Dormitory 12

the bees are silent no tapping at the glass
night falls
still it is not done
at night he comes with the wheels
wet dog wet dark coal black and blue
back pressed into brick
dust in mouth hair in mouth
they say sleep, but my ears wide awake
pricked hare in the field of corn
nightjar owl quartering
i am owl in the forest a ghost with wings.
hear him at her door
see his shadow in dusky light
the wheels come when he leaves
i cannot keep my boots clean
black spots on the leather
on my apron matron scolds
but not her pet, all fluffed and golden, goldie in feathers
feeds it titbits every morning
morsels of flesh through the bars of its cage
cage in the day room golden canary in a cage
they forbid me to feed the morning birds keep the
entrance locked

before long i shall unlock it
i will set us all free
no cellar
one step two step one at a time like counting cobbles
hopscotch in the yard before I was sold
a stone in a pocket might make a wound
head wound sticky blood a push might make a fall
headlong over down not moving
heap of coal at your feet trolley falling
shovels sharp blades pencils with points
shovel on a head pencil in the eye of sour breath
fumbling skirt up
i close eyes, mouth, watch the spider in its web
spiders have eight legs bees have six
cobweb, spider, grunt cobweb, spider grunt
i am spider hanging above on the low ceiling
looking down on a girl's cap
the bees know the taste
smell of cupboard back in the shop no customers
two hands britches down
laugh when the bees sting his arse
laugh slap lock laugh slap lock
unlock errands bees follow buzz
laugh all the way to the close
stung his arse cried like a baby
me dancing on the cobbles cherry blossom like snow in
the wind
is Ivor Houndsworth's job to shovel coal pull the trolley
light the fires trap the cold
attendants' work
but HE, HE says GO leave it to me
ears stalks wheels he comes when he will

and nothing to stop him spoiling my boots
i hide the pencil under my pillow
Alice Semple says she will give me a whole sheet of paper
says she will write it all down
still they whisper it is not done
they say i must roast and spike him like a fat pig on a
spit
burned and blacked in the fire
skinned buck red flesh, blue vein dried blood, chopped eel
wheels
even the bees cannot keep me safe
he comes and no one to stop him but a pencil and a
shovel

Chief Attendant

52. He shall be responsible, under the Resident Medical Officer and Superintendent, for the condition of the Male Patients and Wards, and shall have control over all the other Attendants, shall superintend them in the performance of their duties in accordance with the Rules, Orders, and Regulations prescribed by the Committee of Visitors, and with the directions of the Medical Officers shall report to the Medical Officers all illnesses and casualties as soon as they occur, and he shall see that the Male Patients are employed according to directions, and that all orders with regard to their treatment are properly attended to.

Rules for the Government of the Pauper Lunatic Asylum situate at Long Meadow – prepared and submitted by the Committee of Visitors thereof, by virtue of the 53rd section of the 16th and 17th VIC. CHAP 97

William Blakely

Medical Officer's Quarters above the Dining Hall

Six thirty a.m. and Blakely sits at his desk, his eyes on the clock. He is waiting for the Chief, Amos Farrell. Where the hell is he?

His thoughts drift back to Simone Gastrell, to the evening, a week ago, when he sat with her in the shadowy dusk. He has not dared to return, and yet the memory is as fresh and troubling as ever it was. She'd been praying, he was sure of it. If he closes his eyes, he can still see her pale chemise, smell the faint scent of carbolic on her skin, glimpse the outline of her breasts beneath the cotton when she lifted the shawl to pull it closer around her shoulders. He can feel the air around them, how it pulsed with a forbidden energy. He thinks of little else, especially when he lies in his bed at night.

He looks again at the clock. Six forty. He wonders if he should pleasure himself now, quickly, to relieve the tension, though he regrets such a necessity. Decides no, now is not the time to be caught with his trousers half down. Not the time to induce palpitations and a flushed countenance nor to enervate the body.

Six forty-five a.m. Farrell is fifteen minutes late.

Blakely picks up April's copy of the *Journal of Mental Science*, which lies open in front of him on the desk. He is attempting to read an article entitled, *Note in Regard to the Prevalence of Insanity and Other Nervous Diseases in China,* George Shearer M.D. Liverpool, but is failing abjectly. He reads the same sentence three times over: *the condition of the insane in a country like China, where there are no asylums, is truly pitiable.* He scans down the page to Shearer's appraisal of the Chinese character: *smooth, placid and unexcitable.* He could wish for more of such characteristics among Long Meadow's patients, especially its women. He sighs. He closes the journal and throws it back onto the desk. Where the hell is the man? Here, there and every bloody where, including where he shouldn't be, no doubt.

The problem with Farrell, as Blakely sees it, is that he's been at Long Meadow longer than any of them. Too long. Stafford relies on him and defers to him in matters of restraint and keeping order. They are on first name terms. Amos Farrell is more than happy to do Cornelius Stafford's dirty work. Truth be told, to do all their dirty work. Blakely has to admit they need men like Farrell. Where would they be without him when trouble starts, as it inevitably does? He can't deny Farrell is accommodating. He works with a ready smile and has the strength of three men. But he is not a man to be pinned down, nor crossed and he has about him an air of mystery and worldliness, lacking in most of Long Meadow's attendants who do not dare venture beyond the County. In his long tenure, he has been the source of considerable curiosity and rumour. Some say he was a defrocked priest chased out of his parish after a scandal with a parishioner. Others that he was master of a sailing smack out of Yarmouth, journeying as far as Iceland in the West, the Baltic to the East. Others insist he was a Death or Glory boy, having joined the 17th Royal Lancers at sixteen and served in Crimea at the Battle of Alma. Blakely thinks such claims to be exaggerated but whatever the truth of Farrell's origins, he saw how he garnered a degree of sympathy due to a sick wife who, though she lived with her husband in quarters in the Asylum grounds, was rarely, if ever, seen. He was said to be devoted to her care.

Blakely gets up from his desk and paces the room, finally settling in front of the window. The grass is webbed with dew and the morning lit with the coppery rays of the rising sun. A sun that looks in on her. Is she at her window? Jesus, he needs to get a grip. He must blunt this obsession with Simone Gastrell. He needs Farrell. Damn the man. Then just as he despairs, thinking he will have to go off in search of him, there is a loud knock at the door.

'Come in,' shouts Blakely.

Farrell pushes open the door and steps into the room, 'Sir. You wanted me?'

Blakely is always surprised that the Chief is somehow not taller. Farrell is stocky, thick set and wide shouldered, with ruddy cheeks and hair that is thinning at the front. He has a labourer's physique. Most likely, thinks Blakely, it's true what Matron says, that his father was a bare-knuckle fighter and well known in the County.

'Yes. I did, Farrell. Baines, Phoebe,' says Blakely, 'Stafford wants her taken upstairs and fed. She's too thin again by half and we can't afford a wasting death, not with the Committee on our heels.'

Farrell nods his assent.

'This morning in the Dining Hall, as breakfast concludes, would seem as good a time as any. Preferably while the women are dispersing. As quietly as possible, with as little fuss as can be managed. Hopefully Matron's gentle persuasion will succeed. Bring Houndsworth with you if you think it necessary.'

'Yes, boss,' says Farrell in a manner which suggests it will be followed by a salute and the knocking together of feet. He leaves, pulling the door behind him. Perhaps it is true after all, thinks Blakely, perhaps he had been a Death or Glory boy.

The Airing Courts

57. During the day the Patients of both sexes shall be employed as much as practicable, out of doors: the men, in gardening and husbandry, or other suitable employment; the women in occupations suited to their ability: and as a principal of treatment, endeavours shall be continually used to induce patients to take exercise in the open air, and to promote cheerfulness and happiness amongst them.

60. The Airing Courts shall be accessible to the patients for at least three hours in the forenoon and three hours in the afternoon of every day, when the weather is favourable.

Rules for the Government of the Pauper Lunatic Asylum situate at Long Meadow – prepared and submitted by the Committee of Visitors thereof, by virtue of the 53rd section of the 16th and 17th VIC. CHAP 97- state

Simone

Simone is up and dressed before dawn. She puts on her cape and bonnet and steps out into the corridor, then silent as a cat, steals through the dormitory of sleeping women to the vestibule and the door to the Airing Courts. If she is lucky, it will be open and she will get her first glimpse of the day beyond Long Meadow's walls. She thinks of this as her stolen hour. She tries the handle. She is in luck.

As she slips through the door and out onto the gravel path, the sun is rising over the trees in the east, above Keeper's Wood. She knows the wood by name now, having learned it from the women who whisper of poachers shot on the ancient track that runs through it, of bodies thrown in the brackish pond at the wood's heart, among the alder and ash. She has heard tell that the body of Katharine O'Sullivan's husband is one of them. They say there is no finer bluebell wood in all the County. Simone wishes she were among bluebells now. Breathing in their scent.

She gathers her cape close about her and takes a deep breath, pulling the air down into her lungs. In the Courts, the air is different. Here, there is air enough for the world. Here despite its high walls, she is afforded a glimpse of the world beyond. She tastes the morning sharp and clean on her tongue like a lemon from a glasshouse.

Inside Long Meadow, the air is fetid and stale, doomed to cycle back and forth through its corridors and dormitories, catching the scent of despair and sickness. Here, the air is clean and Simone is returned to her true self, to morning meadows dappled with dew, to the pale, yellow stone of Bath and her aunt's house, to Paris where she stayed with Clara, where the air was filled with the ripe scent of horse dung and jasmine from the flower sellers.

She follows the winding path, down from the parterre, past the flower borders which are greening fast, past the benches where the women sit, down to the boundary wall with its iron-barred gate leading to the kitchen gardens and beyond to the gently sloping water meadows and the river. If she stands here, looking through the gate, then she can imagine herself to be somewhere else entirely, far away from here.

She pauses and drinks in the silence. The morning changes its colours as the sun rises. Wind weaves the long grass and clouds shift across the blue. Over the meadow, the pale wings of a harrier hover like a ghost in the sky. The child's face appears before her, then her daughter's a baby dead in her arms. And, not for the first time since her incarceration in Long Meadow, the notion that she is an unfit mother takes hold. It stands to reason she is unfit else why would God take her baby from her. She had fooled herself for a while with Constance, believing the child in need of mothering. Her mothering. But it had ended in tragedy, just as before.

Simone turns to look back at the Asylum's black, imposing façade. The place in which she must atone. Days of repetition and routine, slow and numbing. What is there in Long Meadow to distinguish one hour from the next? There are bells, there is black bread, and little else. The minutes and hours fall slowly and vanish into nothingness. And yet she must stay alert, she must keep her wits about her, for she is unsure as to where the dangers lie and in whom she can trust.

He has not been back since the evening when he found her at her prayers. She had presumed then that he might be her champion, her saviour even. His tenderness and concern had led her to hope. He had asked her to remember. She had tried harder than he could know, but her memories of the drowning remain clouded and distant. She searches for them like a blind woman, uncertain and fumbling in a place she knows something of but can no longer see. The little she does recall, she is afraid to tell. She cannot tell. There is the spinning light of her dream, always the spinning light and then the darkness and out of it the child's face, pale as a swan's wing, a cry, a hand reaching out. A struggle. If he comes to her again, she will disappoint him, no doubt, but she has thought to share with him something of what happened to her parents and to herself and Clara. This she can remember. This is written down.

She is still waiting for paper and pen with which to write to her sister, though she was promised it days ago. Mrs Corey, who no longer watches her but is often to be found nearby, declared that Matron herself would deliver it. But Matron has not come and Simone waits still. Long Meadow is a waiting game. This much she has already learned. A waiting and withholding game which serves to undermine and deaden the spirit. This is the fate of the powerless, the anaesthetising of hope and expectation, of spontaneity and surprise, of everything that might run contrary to the good order and discipline of the institution. Routines and constraints, these are the opium of the Long Meadow. Already she has grown used to its daily rituals: black bread for breakfast, boiled meat and potatoes for lunch, boiled meat and potatoes for dinner, an occasional pie, and once, an Irish stew, meat more gristle than flesh. Already she feels her clothes loosening.

She has grown accustomed to passing the workshops where women spend their days shredding paper and mending clothes, as she makes her way to the Day Room. It is here the women gather when the weather is inclement. She cannot deny the room is pleasant enough, being light and airy, with high and low-backed chairs, birch settees and tables with checked cloths. There are potted plants, though mostly they are yellowing and sickly, a serving hatch from which an attendant may pass hot water for tea, though she has not witnessed it, and an upright piano in need of tuning. There is a small library of books and games against one wall. In the corner by the stove, hanging from the ceiling in a gilded cage is Matron's canary, Goldie, a yellow Norfolk, a much-prized bird that according to Mrs Corey cost two pounds and ten shillings. In the bay is a window seat from where patients may look out onto the Airing Courts.

It is time to go. Simone makes her way back through the garden, stopping to admire the red feathered tulips aflame in the parterre. As she approaches the door, she cast her eyes on the building and marvels at the alchemy of the sun as it turns Long Meadow's windows to fire. Even here there is gold and beauty.

She slips in through the vestibule door, takes off her cape and bonnet and hurries into the Dining Hall. She is late for breakfast. The women are already gathered, the air consonant with their laughter. Gladys Carter and Amelia Grey, the jesters among them, known for bearing their backsides to one and all, especially the men on the way out to the kitchen gardens or to the Committee of Visitors including Marianne Vaisey who blushes like a peony in bloom, are entertaining them with a bawdy ballad and a jig. It is not uncommon. Any and every opportunity for laughter is seized upon. It is their unspoken rebellion. Simone has witnessed how uneasy it makes those in charge. How they seek to dampen it. But how joyful are those who instigate it. How, when rills of laughter roll through the corridors of Long Meadow, it is like a sun breaking through cloud.

Simone looks for the table of *silent women* and as she does so, she catches sight of William Blakely. He is standing in a group with Matron and Dr. Stafford, the Superintendent, who has interviewed her twice now, intent on the loss of her baby, exploring the finest details, who was present, who witnessed, how the child had appeared, the colour of its lips, the nature of its limbs, and all regardless of her distress.

There are two others in the group, the man they call the Chief who she has seen often wandering the women's corridors and another she does not know. They stand in a huddle next to the table with the water jugs and tin cups, arms crossed. Finding an empty table, Simone sits down, within earshot of the group.

'I see the grotesques are out to entertain us this morning. Time to shut them up,' says Stafford.

'They'll soon tire of it,' says the Chief. 'Let them be, the women will be in a better humour for it.'

'Breakfast is nearly over. I'll speak with her now,' says Matron.

'Best be ready, Houndsworth,' says the Chief to the man beside him. 'She's a fighter that one, have your trinkets and no mistake.'

Matron approaches the table where Phoebe Baines sits. She bends her head and whispers in Phoebe's ear. Phoebe jumps up, screams and lashes out, clawing at Matron's face. They are on her in a flash, the Chief and the man he calls Houndsworth, pinning her to the floor with their arms and knees. They are ruddy-faced with the effort of it and breathing fast. Matron falls back, putting her hands to her face, wiping away the thin trail of blood that drips from her cheeks. The men drag Phoebe to her feet and away, out into the corridor. Her screams fade to muffled cries and then to silence. A hush falls over the Dining Hall. The women clutch each other's hands, put their heads down and retreat into their plates of bread. Simone's palms begin to sweat, her arm grows numb and nausea overwhelms her. Her vision grows dark and narrow. She is drawn into a tunnel. Everything crackling and black. The smell of rotting hyacinth. She is falling, and the floor is coming up to meet her.

Phoebe

Upstairs

Out of bed, get her out of bed, on the chair,
is Stafford and his mutton chops
hard wood cold floor
tip it back, that's right back, tip her head back
my head back cap off hair falling my hair is falling out
they pull knots of it make nests of it
Tie the ankles, wrists, pull them tight. Pull the ties. For
God's sake tighter, like this. See. Yes. Now press on her
knees. I said press, man. The sheet now, across her neck,
use your hands man, across her throat.
sweat on my face my dress
sweat sting smell sweat sting smell
ripe with lust ripe with anger
stafford's sour breath
i cannot move my head i must atone tie me down
pin me to the crucifix
Open her mouth, get your fingers in. Keep them there.
The gag.
Get the gag in place. There, she'll not bite now.

cannot speak cannot move my mouth full of hair and
bees.

Press her tongue down. I said down, man. Pass the tube.
Pinch her nose.

in my mouth fat black-nailed fingers
tube pressing, forcing
pain
i cannot breathe i cannot breathe
pain heave the tube up
trail of vomit on my dress his suit.

Damn it man the tube's up. For pity's sake wipe this off
me. Open her damn mouth. Ready? And again. Her nose,
pinch it, pinch while I push the tube in. Good. Wait...its
done. Pass the funnel. Hurry.

voices ride in air
red faced sweating swearing under breath
pulling heaving coughing
i see all from my seat on the ceiling
learned long ago my escape to watch from afar
a bee watching from its hive
they fill the funnel with milk and eggs brandy cream
i swallow
no more yellow sick
receive all without choice mine to regurgitate
then she says
enough surely enough
matron with a tear in her eye
can it be
she stands apart.

She has no stomach for it, he says. Stomach, ha! He

laughs. They laugh.

all is laughter now but for matron
i come down
watch her turn her back and leave

Simone

When Simone woke and found him sat at her bedside in the chair, the world had seemed at once vivid and promising. The darkness had lifted, leaving no trace. No lingering headache, no stiff neck. He put his hand on her arm and said he was glad to see her wake but that he must go soon. She asked how the girl Phoebe was. He told her it had been for her own good, that she was in need of feeding else she might die.

Before he could go, she begged him to wait. Then sitting up and bending to the cabinet beside her bed, she lifted out her copy of, *The Child's Guide to Knowledge*, and from between its pages, took a folded cutting from *The Liverpool Echo*, now yellow with age.

She was five years old when her world, the world that encompassed her parents and her sister Clara, shifted from the cosy, contented life of the nursery to the cold, unknown, the domain of an orphan whose parents lay at the bottom of a fathomless sea. At least that's how she imagined it, when she remembered them, lying on the seabed, nosed by blind fish, prey to the vicious teeth of the monsters who haunted the deep, monsters only a child could conjure. Since that day, she'd been afraid of water, of sea, lake, river, always the one standing back from the edge, urging caution, not willing to dip even a toe in the shallows.

They had been on their way to see their father's sister, aunt Cecily, in Glasgow when the Orion went down. A clear, placid morning by all accounts, the water limpid like a lake, when the ship hit the rock. She remembers nothing but darkness and terror transmitted by the crying out and the clutch of Clara's hand around hers. Then the cold, the icy cold as they entered the water. Her mother's voice, she thinks. Trying to soothe. Then it is just her and Clara, the black water, a fleeting memory of a fire, her toes stretched out towards it, a blanket and Clara next to her, they are drinking cups of broth. How much of this she truly remembers, she is not sure, or how much Clara's account has become hers. She dreams of it sometimes, but her dreams are impenetrable, black and airless, as if her head is being held underwater and she cannot breathe.

'My past, before Everett, before my childhood had barely begun, is here, reported in the newspaper, and I remember it all,' she said, handing him the cutting. She waited then until he finished reading, then said, 'After our rescue, from Portpatrick, we were sent to Glasgow and from there to Bath to live with our mother's sister, Aunt Elizabeth, and her second husband, James Priest. My aunt was prone to staying in bed with the curtains drawn and the housemaid in attendance. James Priest was not a man to be crossed and before long we were bundled off to Mrs Williams Seminary for Young Ladies to be instructed in needlework and grammar. I might have stayed there, even past sixteen, had Clara not eloped to Paris with Edward Gibson, a good man as it happens, and it is Paris where she remains, which is why I beg you for paper to write to her, so she can know where I am and what has befallen me.'

He stared at the newspaper cutting. She wished he would look up at her so she could gauge his thoughts. She was eager for his response, but his head remained down. She had no choice but to continue. 'By then, by the time Clara eloped, although I did not know it, my step-uncle had promised me to Everett. I was married to him the day after my fifteenth birthday. It was a matter of business. A transaction, if you will. There was nothing of love between us from the start.'

Blakely's eyes remained firmly fixed on his lap. He opened the newspaper cutting, then folded it. Then opened it again. He was unsure of what to say. He had encouraged her to remember, no doubt. Yet he had not expected this.

'They imagine me jealous of Henrietta,' she said. 'They do not know what it is to live with a man who forces himself upon you, who puts his hands to your throat so that you think you might die, while he splutters and chokes his pleasure. No. I am relieved whenever Everett's attentions turn to a body other than mine, as they so often have.'

Blakely got up, put the newspaper cutting down on the chair and leaned towards her. He brushed his lips against her cheek in the ghost of a kiss, and whispered, 'I'm sorry but I must go. I will bring you paper to write to your sister. Sleep now. Rest.'

She heard his footsteps leaving, halting, then fading away.

She wasn't sure she knew what love was although she prayed, hoped, it was about kindness, a tenderness of touch, a look, a thoughtfulness, a fast-beating heart, something like the feeling she had when she held her baby. Something like the feeling she had when she told her story and he sat beside her smelling of sandalwood.

Alice Semple's Notebook

John Clare. Three farthings for a sheet of paper. Shop paper of all colours. Old copy books and never without scattered notes and sixpenny romances. Could recite the psalms and the poems of Job, every one. Was fond of the wildflowers, of daisies, and of nightingales. Who loved the pasture with its rushes and thistles. The wild marshy fen. The henshaw in a melancholy sky. A fossil stone in his pocket. Because he is gone and I am old does not mean I do not crave him still, crave such love. Either that or to be gone from this place and all my sorrows winging above me.

They hide us away like knives in a locked drawer, sequester us in their cellars and their padded cells. We are trapped in iron like the creatures of Keeper's Wood. A week now since the commotion and Phoebe Baines is abed still, upstairs, strapped in like an animal, caged to be fed and plumped like a Christmas goose, made to eat beef until its lodges in the windpipe and takes her breath. If the spoon does not work, head on the pillow, tube in the nose, port wine, brandy, eggs. Food fit for a queen. Ha. Tis the moral treatment, gag, funnel, tube. It will kill slow but sure.

If she is mad, if I be mad, then so be you. Be quiet they say, be silent, stay out of the light. You know too much, travel too far. I would rather out in the fields, digging the earth, I would rather tether a goat, ride a horse, plant for the good.

Instead they wish me to take up a needle and sew, shred paper, mend breeches, head down. Slavery. Obedience. God Bless Marianne Vaisey whose cheeks flush pink as a poppy and eyes grow dark as the flower's sooty heart whenever Blakely appears. As for him. He blossoms and bathes in it. A half-hour gentleman him. Goes out of his way. The same with all women, the new woman, Gastrell, a case in point. Matron herself, though her pretty face is marked now in blood. The Chief was too slow to save her. They say he held back. They say he smirked. There is no love lost between those two.

Many have forgotten, many were not here at that time, for it was before Stafford and his crew, but I have not forgotten how she accused the Chief. Molestation, she said. It was after dark, one winter night, said he jumped out at her as she passed the Chapel on her way home. Fought him off. She had a black eye all right and a bruised wrist. I gave her comfrey for it. They did not believe her. They said she invented it, for the attention. It is something they say about us and our deeds, that we are attention seekers. He said she was old and ugly, a dried-up prune, why would he bother with the likes of her.

Though it is forbidden, for no rogue sheets are allowed, I have torn a page from this notebook. On it I have written what I know about the Chief, and poor Phoebe Baines, though it might just as well be Blakely or Stafford himself. Tis one of them. I have folded the paper and addressed it to Miss Vaisey. I intend to hand it to her myself. If they insist I must stay alive, then the cat will prowl among the pigeons. As do they.

The Visitors' Book

I have today spoken with the Patient, Alice Semple, who has provided me with a written note concerning the conduct of certain Asylum officers. I have informed Medical Officer, William Blakely of its contents and have passed the note to the Superintendent, Cornelius Stafford, for his attention. I have been assured the matters raised will be investigated thoroughly.

M. Vaisey

Upstairs

An Empty Treatment Room

'I want it snuffed out. Do you hear me? Nipped in the bud and you're the man to do it, Blakely. The ravings of a mad women, that's what this is.' Stafford waves a piece of paper under Blakely's nose. Have you seen it?'

Blakely nods.

Stafford stretches out his arm and indicates the door to a treatment room. Blakely opens the door with caution, checking the room is empty before he ventures inside. Stafford follows, pulling the door closed, and Blakely catches a faint whiff of vomit about him. No doubt it is from the force feeding, which in his opinion goes on too long but which Stafford appears to relish. For his part, Blakely finds it unnecessary and distasteful.

The treatment room is long and narrow with a high window of frosted glass, and pale green walls. Blakely perches on the edge of an iron framed bed covered with a rubber sheet.

'By God, man, she's ungovernable,' says Stafford, pacing up and down in the meagre space so that a metal trolley beside the bed, complete with instruments, scissors, syringes, atomisers, scopes, speculums, as well as bottles, bowls, liquids and powders, rattles and clinks.

Blakely wishes he would stand still.

'The woman is dangerous. It's what comes of women denying their true nature, allowing themselves to believe they might be equal to men. A bit of learning and she fancies herself a poet's wife, mark my words she never set eyes on the fellow. Stuff and nonsense, fabrications on a scrap of paper she shouldn't have had in the first place. I predicted this. Words stoke rebellion. Words committed to paper take on a power of their own. It'll be up to you now to thwart this Blakely.' Stafford comes to a halt. He pauses, breathing heavily. He leans back against the wall. His shoulders drop. He waits for his breath to return. Then in a gentler, more persuasive tone, he says, 'Everyone knows you have a way with the ladies, Blakely, especially our Miss Vaisey. You will be the one to convince her the claims are unwarranted. I want this rumour quashed before it takes hold. You can vouch for him. The man wouldn't harm a fly, devoted to his sick wife, a fine soldier who does not deserve to have his reputation sullied in this way. We'll be next, mark my words. You see what she writes. He flourishes the paper again – *it might just as well be Blakely or Stafford himself. Tis one of them.* I ask you. Vaisey will believe you, Blakely, enamoured as she is.' He folds the paper and puts it in his pocket. He sighs, noisily. 'I blame myself. Too soft by half. I should have had the gloves put on her. I should have insisted and it's too late now. If we do it now, it will look too much like revenge. We need to step very carefully through this, no scandal, we need it to stop here. We don't want it brought in front of the whole damn House Committee. We need to keep our slate clean. But mark my words, as soon as this dies down, that notebook will disappear, and the gloves will come out. A long spell in solitary confinement might be just the thing to stop her infecting the place with her lurid fantasies. There's no time to waste. I've seen the way Vaisey looks at you, and you her, might I add, that Gastrell woman too. You have a certain fondness for the species and they for you. Use your charm. See it as a courtship of sorts, that's what's required. Dare I say, if it were to go as far as compromise it might not be such a bad thing, if you get my drift. In all honesty what hardship would it be. She's a peach waiting to be plucked. Ripe for the taking. And a wealthy father to boot.'

'Well,' said Blakely, 'I hardly think…'

'Don't think, man, do. Do as I ask for all our sakes.'

'But have you considered…'

'Considered what?'

'That there may be some truth in it. I've heard the odd rumour, that he is not always where he should be.' Hadn't Blakely seen him with his own eyes, that night in the corridor? Pulling the coal trolley towards the open cellar door, the glimpse of a skirt in front. But the lights were extinguished and he couldn't be sure it was Farrell. A cry muffled by the trolley wheels. Had it been the girl? Best to remain silent. He had no wish to put himself in conflict with Stafford. And if it had been the Chief, what business of his? After all, men were only human.

'Hogwash. Rumours. The place thrives on them. A coven of witches will stir the pot and no mistake. They're attention seekers, every last one of them. It's in their nature, you should know that. They can't help themselves.'

'I gather Semple's asked that the Chaplain visit.'

'God help us.' Stafford raises his eyes heavenward. He makes for the door and then turns sharply back. 'Oh, and by the way, Blakely, I've informed Matron no ball, no dancing this month or next, and Alice Semple is prohibited from any walks beyond the premises. I believe a Magic Lantern show is organised for Sunday. See that Matron gets the support she needs and only those who can be relied on to remain calm and compliant are to attend. Now, go and find Miss Vaisey before she leaves the premises. Before we have the lot of them down on us, demanding an investigation. And while you're at it, you better see the Chaplain and get him on side.'

He would be better served working with men, thinks Blakely, as he steps out across the grass towards the Chapel in search of the Chaplain. He has had no luck as yet in tracking Marianne Vaisey down.

Men were more straightforward, and the matter of sex, well, it would have no bearing on the situation. He would be entirely safe. Damn Stafford. Damn them all, he mutters beneath his breath.

Do they think he hasn't suffered? That he does not know what it is to contemplate a night without stars or a coming dawn? He could so easily have fallen by the wayside, into a ditch like Clare, had he given in to the grief.

He blames his father for her death, his mother's heart broken by a succession of his dalliances, his drinking and his profligacy. Blakely despises him, swears he will never be like him. Yet whenever he looks in the mirror, it is his father he sees looking back at him. And it is not simply a matter of countenance.

Are they alike? He wants to believe not, that he can be a good and faithful husband one day. Surely that must be true. And yet he knows he has a weakness for beauty and charm, a fascination with the fairer sex, the quest for something, the smallest thing to remind him of her beauty and gentility. To remind him of his own powers of attraction which he so enjoys. He cannot deny he searches out the affection and adoration of women, particularly those he considers handsome. And there is no shortage, even in a place such as this, each with her different and distinct charms. Truth be told, he rarely finds a woman who cannot delight him in some way, and whose conquest does not please him, though he draws the line at Semple and her likes.

He must be careful. He must mind himself.

On reflection, he finds he regrets having that morning, via the good offices of attendant Mrs Corey, provided Simone Gastrell with the necessities for writing and posting a letter to her sister. He makes a mental note to speak with Matron. He must ensure the letter comes into his possession before it is dispatched.

Patients' Letters

64. All letters from Patients, unless addressed to the Committee of Visitors, may be inspected on the male side by the Superintendent, on the female side by the Matron; and what may appear objectionable shall be submitted to the Committee of Visitors.

Rules for the Government of the Pauper Lunatic Asylum situate at Long Meadow – prepared and submitted by the Committee of Visitors thereof, by virtue of the 53rd section of the 16th and 17th VIC. CHAP 97

The Letter

May 17th
Long Meadow Asylum
Cambs

Dearest Clara
I hardly know where I might begin, so much having happened since my last letter to you.
But begin I must by telling you that a number of misfortunes have befallen me of late, worst among them, the drowning of Everett's niece, our dear child Constance, whilst I was in attendance. I will not venture to go into detail. There is much I struggle to remember about that fateful day. My fainting fits have become more frequent and suffice to say, I find myself presently, at the behest of Everett and Dr Eames his physician, a patient here in Long Meadow Lunatic Asylum, living among its sad and pitiful women, locked away from the world, in the dark, with no knowledge of when I might be released. It is only the kindness of the doctor, William Blakely, who attends me, that has provided me the means by which to write to you. Dearest Clara, I beg you to come at once to visit me and to secure my release. For though I may be sad and pitiable, I am not a madwoman. Not a lunatic. Of this I am sure, though I believe too long in a place such as this may be liable to infect the sanest of minds. Please, I beg you, hurry, my sweet sister. I have never needed you more than I do now. I am afraid of what might

become of me in this place. I pray for your coming. I await your urgent reply.

Your loving sister
Simone.

The Chaplain

35. He shall devote the whole of his time to the duties of his office and shall report quarterly to the Committee of Visitors.

36. He shall perform Divine service twice on Sundays, Christmas Day, and Good Friday, and preach at least one sermon on each of those days. He shall also perform service once a week, and shall have access to every Patient at all times except in any peculiar case where the Resident Medical Officer and Superintendent might think it injurious and shall give his special attention to any Patients whom the Resident Medical Officer and Superintendent shall consider peculiarly likely to be benefited thereby.

Rules for the Government of the Pauper Lunatic Asylum situate at Long Meadow – prepared and submitted by the Committee of Visitors thereof, by virtue of the 53rd section of the 16th and 17th VIC. CHAP 97

The Chapel

Blakely rarely goes to the Chapel, avoiding Sunday service when he can. There is something about the act of stepping inside its stone porch and onto the tiled floor of the nave that reminds him of her funeral procession, eyes downcast, fixed on small, polished boots, the air around him thick with the perfume of white lilies and the weight of his sadness. Yet once he overcomes his reluctance, he finds the Chapel's cool, unfussy interior can be a balm. A settling. A pause in a long day of duty and myriad responsibilities.

On his very first visit, he had been struck by the Chapel's size. The Chaplain, Daniel Hawkins, younger than he had expected, informed him it was designed to seat over two hundred worshippers. Set apart from the main Asylum block, with its buttressed facade, single bell tower and buttercups edging its walls, it was much like any ordinary country church. Daniel Hawkins however was no ordinary country Reverend, of that William Blakely was sure.

'Ah, Reverend,' says Blakely, raising his voice as he calls down through the nave to the altar where Daniel Hawkins appears to be rearranging the altar vessels and the white linen cloth.

Hawkins turns, he holds a candle in his left hand, a chalice veil hangs from his right. 'Ah, Blakely,' he says, 'just doing a spot of tidying.' He puts the veil and candle back on the altar. 'What brings you here? How can I help?' When Blakely hesitates, Hawkins continues, 'are you in need of prayer, or is it a patient you wish me to visit, perhaps?'

'Not exactly,' says Blakely.

Hawkins walks towards him nodding at the first pew, 'Shall we sit?' He brushes his hand over the wooden seat. 'I hope there's no dust. The pews are in need of a good polish but Alice Semple who has taken the job upon herself is… er…well, as you know, is indisposed. It's a sad business. But we pray together, and I am hopeful of a good recovery.'

'Indeed. As it happens it's Semple I've come about,' says Blakely, settling onto the pew. 'It seems she is suffering a form of mania, voices and so forth, and she has convinced herself that the Chief, Farrell, has been up to no good with one of the women.'

'One of the women? A patient?' asks the Chaplain, leaning forward and cocking his head to one side.

'Yes,' says Blakely. 'Unfortunately, she's written a note to that effect to the Committee of Visitors. I understand she has also put in an application for a visit from you.'

'Has she,' says Hawkins, 'well of course I shall visit immediately, today, as soon as possible.'

'Well that's just it, there's no need. The Superintendent has asked me to let you know the matter is in hand and a visit might in fact be injurious.'

'No need? Injurious?' he pauses. 'Ah well, thank you. Is that all?'

'Yes. that's it. I'd better be getting back, plenty to do as always, if you'll excuse me,' says Blakely, relieved not to have been grilled by Hawkins for more details.

'Of course, off you go, ' says Hawkins.

The Chaplain stays seated, looking at the chancel and the altar. He draws air deep into his lungs, breathing in the

Chapel's scent, a must of plaster, the yellowing paper of donated prayer books and bibles. New and second hand, all is subject to the dampness of low-lying places, a dampness that seeps even into stone and wood. Daniel Hawkins is ever watchful of a peeling back, of blight and black mould in his fen chapel. But today, although rain threatens, a pale sunlight falls through its tinted windows, catching the spinning motes of dust about the pillars, illuminating the mural texts and images of the evangelists on its walls. The Chaplain is reassured and grateful that everything is as it should be in God's house.

As for the Asylum, as for what lies beyond God's house, everything is not as it should be. Not by a long shot and he cannot say it surprises him. Injurious or not, he determines he will visit Alice Semple that very day.

Simone

It is her habit now to sit with the *silent women*, then, when breakfast is over, Simone follows them out into the Airing Courts. To be among them is to be as if alone, just as she is in her stolen morning hour, their voices like the soft murmurs of nesting birds whose beaks are stuffed with moss. There is safety and gentleness in their company. There is quiet. She has watched them fuss over Phoebe since she is back from being fed, smoothing her hands to quieten her distress, feeding her titbits, and brushing the dust from her skirts. Like shades, they hover above the anguish and turmoil of the Asylum. They have become her anchor.

This morning, the *silent women* are reluctant to leave the vestibule for the Airing Courts. Rain threatens. They mill about by the entrance but Simone does not hesitate. She is out, down through the parterre to the lower terrace, past the lilac in bloom, she follows paths littered with fallen blossom to the border with the kitchen gardens and a bench in the shelter of the high yew hedge. She sits alone under the pewter sky, breathing in the damp air. She has brought a book with her, in the hope of distraction, though she finds since entering the Asylum that she can no longer properly concentrate on the written word. She opens it on her lap and is about to begin reading when the first spit of rain lands on its page.

She closes the book and lifts her head to the sky as if to greet the rain. How she would welcome its cleansing power, its silvering of green, its droplets fastened on the spirals of newly unfolding ferns, on grass and bloom, on her gown, drawing out the smell of pasture and damp wool. She closes her eyes and is transported to a sudden downpour in the Tuileries, in spring in Paris, when she and Clara had hoisted umbrellas and hurried to the safety of the Louvre. She is reminded of how she wished, that day, she could stay with her sister and never return home. How she wishes even more that she were there now and she closes her eyes and prays that her letter will arrive without delay.

Her prayer is interrupted by the sound of footsteps and the rustle of fabric. A voice, low and rasping, brings her back to the present and to Long Meadow.

'You won't mind, if I sit here a while, will you?'

Simone opens her eyes and sees Alice Semple standing before her. She is wearing a black wool shawl. There is a scarf tied about her neck and she carries a notebook beneath her arm.

'Please do, I shan't mind,' says Simone edging to one corner of the bench.

Alice sits down and places the notebook on the bench between them. 'I'm Alice, you've heard of me no doubt, Alice Semple, you'll excuse my voice, and you are Mrs Gastrell, I believe?'

'I am,' says Simone.

'The murderess then. A child was it?'

'No!' says Simone. 'It was not... I am not. I am no murderess. I would not take the life of a child.' She is indignant and yet she is fearful. Consumed by doubts. If only she could recall the morning of the accident in something more than dreams and snatches of memory. She looks for substance where there is none. Had her own fear of water played its part that morning? Had she failed a drowning child? Had she coaxed her into the water and drowned her, like Everett said.

'Blackout was it, like them you have in here?' croaks Alice.

'I cannot be sure.'

'Well, never mind, I've brought you something.' Alice rummages in her pocket and lifts out what looks like a brown claw dusted with soil, and hands it to Simone. 'Valerian, nothing like it for afflictions of the head. Infuse it in boiling water to make a tea. I guarantee it will help.'

'Thank you', says Simone, taking the tangle of roots, its wilting stem and few forlorn leaves and putting it in her pocket. 'It is very kind of you, I'm sure.'

'Growing just down there by the stone wall, they are,' say Alice, her voice reduced now to a mere whisper. 'Valerian likes stone and such. Picked it before the rain. Though I think it might hold off now or perhaps not. Would you like to hear a poem? I usually read them to Phoebe, but she is a bed today, poor child. It's not mine, it's John Clare's.' She doesn't wait for a reply. She picks up her notebook and turns to the back where she has penned several poems in a scratchy copperplate. As Alice reads in her dry, ragged voice, Simone leans back into the bench and looking up through the gardens, sees William Blakely on the path above. He is not alone. He is with a young woman and they are strolling together beneath an umbrella. Simone catches her breath. She feels her pulse quicken.

The couple sit down together, on a bench by the lilac. They are just in sight and although she cannot make out their words, it seems to her that they are sitting closer than is seemly for the unattached. He bends forward, then leans in, offering her his undivided attention. She giggles like a schoolgirl. Simone can hear the giggling even above Alice's recital.

'There,' says Alice when she finishes, then looking up. 'Oh, I see your attention is elsewhere.'

'No, indeed I liked the poem very much. Thank you. But I was wondering who that young woman with Dr Blakely might be?'

'Ah, that is our Miss Vaisey, a member of the House Committee. They make the rules. Keep their eye on things, on the likes of our Superintendent for one, the Chief for another. I got this notebook given by Miss Vaisey. Now here is something that might interest you. My inventory. But my sad, old voice is giving out. Read it for yourself, if you care to.' Alice hands Simone the open notebook just as the rain begins to fall. A bell sounds and the cry of, 'All ladies in, all ladies in,' drifts through the gardens. 'Oh dear, that's no good, my paper will get wet,' says Alice, snatching the notebook back but not before Simone has alighted on the name Phoebe Baines.

Simone is about to ask Alice what is meant by *spends half her life in the coal cellar and everyone knows why* when she looks up to find William Blakely and Miss Vaisey have risen from the seat and are heading in her direction. She cannot watch, nor does she wish to encounter them. Foolish though she knows it to be, it pains her to see them together and so enamoured. It is as if he betrays her, which is preposterous for she has no reason to believe she is anything other than just one of his patients. He owes her no loyalty and yet she had begun to think, dared to wonder, if there might be something more between them. What nonsense she dreams up.

'We must go now,' says Simone. 'Before we get wet. ' She stands, hoping he will not see her.

'Aye,' says Alice, standing, her voice so low now that Simone is forced to lean towards her to catch her words. 'I am expected in the Chapel. Before evensong. The Chaplain has asked to see me. Tis private there. Take no heed of him,' she says nodding in the direction of Blakely who comes ever closer and seems intent still on his companion. 'He's a popular lad, like my John, and a foolish one, but not dangerous, not like some here. Pleased to have made your acquaintance Mrs Gastrell. I believe you are a good woman, as are most of us here. Come to evensong at four thirty. It is balm for the soul and there's little else of that in here.'

Four-thirty in the Chapel. The rain taps on the roof and the glass. The light is dusky and the walls flicker with candlelight. Simone stands among a scattering of women attending the service. Alice is beside her, silently mouthing the words of the hymns. They are an unharmonious choir, loud, yet plangent, with Amelia Grey's voice soaring above the others, surprisingly sweet. She has a voice like Clara's, thinks Simone, for she too sings and plays the piano. Has her letter been posted yet? Surely it will arrive soon and when she receives it, Clara will come immediately. She will not hesitate. Then her nightmare will be at an end. Paris beckons and with it a new life. She will never go back to Everett. She is determined now. She will never again have to bear his sour breath or the weight of his body pinning her to the bed. Her spirits lift and for this she gives thanks to God.

She has infused the valerian root with the boiling water brought from the kitchens by Anne Bickerdale, and drunk the earthy, bitter, tea. The lights out, her prayers said, she is preparing for bed, half-dressed, and loosening her hair, when there is a gentle knock at the door. Uncertain as to who it might be at this late hour, Simone hesitates.

A voice whispers beyond the door. It is his voice. 'Mrs Gastrell, may I trouble you a moment?'

Her breath catches in her throat. She smooths down her bodice and underskirt and pushes back her loosened hair. 'Come in.'

He pushes open the door, steps into the room and closes it behind him. She stands before the window, a shadow in the dusky light. Her face pale, her hair unpinned.

'I'm sorry to come so late. I hope I haven't disturbed your prayers,' he glances at her prayer book open on the pillow.

'No, I had finished,' she says, reaching over to pick up the prayer book.

As she does so, her hair falls about her face and he is struck by a desire to put his hands to it and pull it back, to feel it slide between his fingers.

'How can I help you?' she asks, clutching the prayer book to her chest, 'I'm afraid I have still remembered nothing more of the day in question though I have tried my best.' She sighs and sits down on the bed.

'May I?' he says, gesturing to do likewise.

She nods and puts the prayer book down on the counterpane.

He sits beside her. He cannot help but look at her, at her lustrous, uncoiled hair, at her breath rising and falling beneath her bodice. He is breathing faster than he should. He hopes she cannot hear it. He reminds himself of why he came and how he must strive to overcome his weakness for her.

'It is about the letter,' he says. 'I thought if you'd finished it, then I should be the one to take charge of it to ensure it is posted. Letters do sometimes go missing in here I'm afraid, or are censored and rendered incomprehensible…'

'Oh dear, I'm afraid I gave it to Matron this morning. I was hoping it might already be winging its way to my sister.'

His shoulders slump. It has been a long day and longer still now he must track her letter down. He tries to remember if Matron is still on duty. He wonders if it really matters other than it may incur Stafford's wrath. But there is the Semple note to think of, an excess of paper, too many words committed for public consumption. Who knows what Simone Gastrell has had to say in her letter to her sister?

'Well, never mind, I'm sure Matron has seen to it. Your letter will be safe with her. Your sister lives in Paris, I believe?'

'She does. Such a beautiful city. I had many happy times there,' says Simone. She lifts her eyes to the window as if travelling there in her mind.

There is a fragility in her beauty, he thinks. There is a sadness in her soul that he recognises, that makes her dangerous to him. Such a contrast to Miss Vaisey, who is all chatter and simper. But why won't she look at him?

She cannot look at him. She dares not meet his gaze. Her eyes are growing moist with tears. She cannot let him see, nor must she hope for solace from him. And yet he must sense her grief for he reaches out and places a hand on her arm. Her body inclines to his. He lifts her hand, puts it to his lips and places it back in her lap. He touches the bare flesh of her arm and begins to stroke it. His touch is gentle, back and forth. His fingers trace up to her shoulder. She shivers. His hand grazes her neck and comes down slowly to rest on her breast. She does not move. A liquid rush, her

105

breast swells, her nipple hardens, she is opening like a flower to his sun.

Then he is up, all at once, adjusting his coat. He has thought better of it. 'I'm sorry, I must go. Forgive me, Mrs Gastrell. It's been a long day.'

Once outside, Blakely leans against the corridor wall, takes several deep breaths, and shakes himself down. It won't do. It won't do at all. Now, if he's not too late he must go and find Matron and retrieve the letter.

A Magic Lantern Show

There is something about the darkness imposed by the extinguishing of the gas lamps and the pulling down of the blinds that allows dreams and fantasies to surface more readily, for an intimacy to thrive, such as is kept hidden in the daylight. The women whisper, putting their lips to each other's ears, hands are held, fingers entwined, a stray hand rests in a lap, on a thigh, a finger seeking out the forbidden place. The air is stirred with laughter and undercover lust. A rustling of skirts, a shushing and shifting while they wait for the photographer setting up, for the first lantern slide to appear on the white wall of the darkened Day Room.

Simone slips into an empty row at the back. Matron and Mrs Corey have persuaded her it will be a good thing to attend. She has barely slept since he came to her three nights ago and when she finally succumbs to sleep, it is but for an hour or two, in which he stalks her dreams like the longed-for ghost of a loved one. Matron has offered her laudanum. She has refused. She knows its dangers, how quickly the dose must be increased to have effect. And how easy to come by in Long Meadow, for there are patients with visitors and, it is rumoured, attendants more than willing to smuggle in whatever is needed. Moreover, she desires a peace of mind and freedom that no drug can deliver, that only her release from Long Meadow can provide. She thinks of him. One minute she is listening and longing for his return, her life blood draining away, siphoned off like water from the pumps.

Another she is on her knees, a penitent, praying for forgiveness. She thinks not of his betrayal but of his soft breath, the brush of his coat sleeve, his hand on her breast. She looks for him now, in the inky light of the Day Room but he is not here.

Alice Semple's Notebook

The Magic Lantern Show – An Inventory

Present, forty-six women – or thereabouts. Tis not easy to count heads in the dark.

Four attendants including Houndsworth.

One photographer, Mr. J Downham Esq. with all necessary equipment, lanterns, slides and such like.

A fine black box case.

The Chaplain, Daniel Hawkins, as helpmate, there to introduce and assist.

Six rows of wooden chairs facing the bookcase wall, the bookcase having been removed for better display of the slides.

Matron.

A bird in a cage.

I am not allowed. The red-nosed porker, Stafford forbids it. What do I care, for I am in a state of lunacy, so he says, in which case I can know no better. Besides, I take no heed of a lush with his nose in the trough, fat and addled, not fit to be in charge of a madhouse. What does he know of the earth and all the precious things in it? He is no watcher of birds and flowers. No lover of women but for his own wicked ends. He threatens to take away my notebook. Best be done with it, says William Blakely. That's his advice. I do not think they will dare, our Miss Vaisey will not allow it. But should they confiscate it, no matter, for I will make paper of my own as Clare did, from birch bark, and better still my own ink from green copper and nut galls and bluestone soaked in a pint of rainwater.

I sneak in and sit at the back next to Phoebe and our so-called murderess, Mrs Gastrell. She is one of us now, still wearing the linsey dress of uniform when she is entitled to wear her own, and not giving herself airs and graces as some private patients do.

I make myself small so as not to be noticed, like I did with Clare when the police were after us for the public house robbery, which we did not do, though we acted as lookouts, outsiders, as we always were. How can a poet be anything but? Houndsworth spots me. I see him look but he turns away and says nothing. Perhaps he is wary, wary of what I know of who brings the trolley and collects the coal.

The Chaplain blesses us. The lantern casts its light on the wall and the slides begin. The room is a chapel of stained glass. We await the prodigal son, suffer the crucifixion, and Bunyan's torment. We worship the golden calf but all the while we lie in the mossy, flower strewn edges, of the stories and the songs.

Rescue the perishing, care for the dying
Snatch them in pity from sin and the grave
Weep o 'er the erring one, lift up the fallen
Tell them of Jesus the mighty to save

Will he snatch us from sin? Will he save us, and if not, if we are sinners past the saving, what do we care? We are here for the entertainment of the dark. We are here for our own small amusements. For the comfort of women, such as takes place under the covers in the dormitory at night. The likes of which Stafford and Blakely can do nothing to prevent. And why not, when we are so starved of love? Of the touch of another? Of the pleasure that can sweep us away in its moment.

We are here too for the making of mischief. Always mischief, part of our living and breathing, of knowing we are alive. Tis no surprise, then, when halfway through the show, comes an agonised cry from Matron followed by a fluttering of golden feathers swooping overhead. The women shout, tis *Goldie, Goldie is out*. The lantern is switched off. The blinds are lifted. Goldie's cage hangs open and empty, for all to see.

The bird circles the room, wings flapping at walls, beak at glass. She searches blindly for her escape. *Go on Goldie*, we shout. *Go on*, we cheer. We are in the ascendancy, drubbing the floor with our boots, whooping, chanting the bird's name, our laughter bold, loud as a drunk's spilling late from a public house. We taste rebellion, breakaway, we come alive. In a flash the window is open, and she is out, flown into the dusky night, and Emma Brewer, who is no stranger to windows and their escape, stands grinning, her hand resting on the window sash.

There are consequences.

They call for the Chief.

The show is over.

J Downham Esq. packs his lantern away.

The Chaplain does his best to quieten us.

Emma Brewer is removed upstairs to the padded cell.

A search party is formed to go looking for Goldie – happily for the bird, to no avail.

Matron is off somewhere being comforted.

We sit in silence, no singing permitted, until we are led away a row at a time to our beds.

Simone

It begins with the commotion of Emma Brewer pinned to the floor. A rocking back and forth, a trembling, a hand reaching out for hers. It is the girl, Phoebe. Simone takes the small, frail hand in hers, hardly bigger than a child's and squeezes it in the hope of offering some comfort and reassurance. It grows quiet around them. The laughter and calling out subsides. As they carry Emma Brewer from the room, the hullabaloo transfers to the garden. Outside they are whistling and calling at the hedges and the trees, *Goldie, Goldie*. But it is dusk now and the bird has flown and who can blame her.

Simone keeps hold of Phoebe's hand for she is still trembling. The women are ushered out row by row. When it is their turn, she and Phoebe are held back by an attendant and told to let the photographer pass. He is laden with equipment. Strapped over his shoulder is a large, black box case embossed in gold. Simone reads the lettering, J. Downham Esq. The name is at once familiar. Does she know this man? Has she perhaps done business with him? She takes in the figure. He is taller than average, bearded, and his lean face is framed by a mop of unruly white hair. She knows at once who he is.

J Downham Esq. is the photographer called by Everett to photograph Constance, after her death. It is as if an aperture opens and widens in Simone's mind. A flood of memory, images and scents rush back, the day of Constance's death, the accident and its aftermath come racing at her from a distant haze to a near and sharp focus. It returns to her in an unspooling reel which she clings to.

A pulse starts up on the right side of her head, lights flash at the corner of her vision. She fears darkness, oblivion, but she must hold off. She leads Phoebe along the echoing corridors, back to Dormitory Twelve. She leaves her standing by her bed and promises to come for her in the morning.

Once in her room, Simone closes the door and lies down. She keeps her eyes open and fixes on the faint, brown-edged maps that have formed in the damp plaster of the ceiling above her. Fear catches in her throat. She is the creature struggling to escape its snare, her heart racing as she allows the memories to rise like waters in a lock, until they spill over. Until she remembers. She remembers everything.

June

Simone

A damselfly day. Hot and fine enough for swimming in the river, though Simone does her best to persuade Constance otherwise. Everett is with them and Henrietta lurking behind him in the shadow of the willows.

'Let the child go in. She'll come to no harm. She's a good swimmer.' Everett insists. 'For God's sake, try not to infect her with your own cowardice, Simone. She is not one bit afraid. Go on, off you go Constance.'

With that, Everett and Henrietta disappear. Constance tears off her clothes, slides down the bank and slips into the river. She is splashing at the edges, chasing imaginary fish, step by step making her way further in. The hairs on the back of Simone's neck prickle in the heat. Soon the child will be out of her depth. Simone's palms sweat. She consoles herself with the thought that Constance cannot stay in the water for ever, that before long she will be out and sat beside her, drying off on the bank. Everett is right. She is a coward when it comes to water.

Seeking to distract herself, she takes the lark-glass, from the picnic bag. She turns the stem with its spangled, mirrored head over and over in her hand, watching it catch the light, entranced by its fluttering signal. How simple it is to lure a songbird to captivity, to its death even. She shivers at the thought of being so caught, so caged. In that moment, a desperate and pitiful cry rises up from the water.

'Help, help me. Simone...'

She drops the glass, is on her feet in an instant. Constance is a good way from the bank, out in the middle of the river, her arms flailing and her blonde curls disappearing beneath the surface of the water.

She shouts for Everett. She shouts for Henrietta. 'Help. Help. Someone. For pity's sake help me,' she cries, but there is no answer. Everett and Henrietta are nowhere to be seen. She is alone on the riverbank and the child is crying out again, each time more desperately, 'Help me, Simone.'

Simone lifts her skirts, pushes her way through the gap in the reed bed and launches herself into the water. She dares not think of the shipwreck, of the loss of her mother and father, of life rafts and cold seas. Her feet sink in the river's muddy bottom. The water is thigh high now and the river weed is tangling about her legs. If only she could swim. But she cannot. She can only wade out, the water growing ever deep around her.

In a moment Constance surfaces again, crashing up through the water, sending a brace of moorhen and a mallard flying up into the air.

'I'm here, Constance, I'm coming,' shouts Simone. But by the time she reaches her, the child has disappeared and the river has stilled to a pool of concentric circles.

'Help, God help me!' howls Simone. There is nothing for it but to dive beneath the water. She must find the child. She must. Again and again, she dives, only coming up for air when she must but it is dark and opaque below the river's skin, and she is hampered by her skirts. She dives until her lungs are fit to burst and she has no breath left. Until she can dive no more. Until she is left alone, standing in the river, water lapping at her chin.

She struggles for the side, clutching at the roots and

branches of willow. Somehow, she does not remember how, she hauls herself out and falls onto the bank, wailing in her grief. Constance is gone, drowned, three days before her seventh birthday. A shadow settles over her. She looks up and sees Henrietta and Everett standing on the riverbank with their backs to the sun, watching.

He had been angling for it for some time, of course, ever since his cousin by marriage, the nineteen-year-old Henrietta Gaule, had come to live with them following the death of her mother, bringing her younger sister, Constance. The drowning gave him all the excuse needed.

In the days that followed, Simone learned that a man of means needs little if any excuse to have his wife locked away while he entertains his mistress.

They pulled the child's body from Swanford Lock. Simone begged to see her, but despite all her pleadings, they would not let her near. Hadn't she done damage enough? She was not safe to be around children, Everett said. An unfit mother. Hadn't God seen to it that her own child had not taken breath? She was a witch, a murderess.

Everett's physician, Dr Eames, was summoned. He took little persuasion in calling the apothecary and arranging to have her committed. It took two men she barely knew, and a matter of minutes, to sign away her life, citing her troublesome nature, her jealousy and hereditary tendency to weakness. She had, they said, an unnatural interest in reading and writing which had caused a softening of the brain and kept her from the proper duties of mother and wife. What else they saw fit to write she cannot remember. She should be grateful that she was not charged, that they were men of mercy. She was confined to her bedroom and the lock secured.

The apothecary prescribed laudanum, forty drops.

Her housemaid Maria brought it, measured it out into the tea, one by one, forty drops of tar. And with it, a plate of small, pale, sponge cakes.

'Eat something Ma'am please, just a trifle, it will stop the sickness that comes with such medicine, and you have a journey ahead of you tomorrow, though God be praised it is not a long one,' said Maria.

Simone drank the tea and picked at a sponge from the plate. As the laudanum took effect, the edges of her world began to blur. The bedroom and all its furnishings floated away like thistledown in the wind.

In the morning, Maria took her to see the child in her coffin. Constance was laid out in her white Sunday dress with eyes painted on her lids and rouge on her cheeks. When Simone saw her, she fell weeping to her knees. Maria helped her up, pleading with her to be quiet, else the master would come and she would be sent upstairs again.

The casket's edge was trimmed with a garland of willow and cypress with the small, wan faces of viola and pansy peeping out like jewels. Simone picked a pansy the colour of the morning sky and put it in her pocket.

Everett called for the photographer, J Downham Esq.

Constance was lifted out of the coffin. Simone and Everett were to pose with the child propped on a chair between them, stiff and cold. It was then Simone began to shake from head to foot. Everett ordered her to be still or else he said, it would be worse than any Asylum.

What could be worse, Simone wondered, as she lay on her bed, gazing up at the plaster ceiling? Finally, the memory had revealed itself, it had come back to her, all of it, in an unstoppable reel, the detail and the horror of that summer's day and its aftermath. Of what should have been a happy day, out in the fields with Constance. All it had taken to unlock memory was a name.

Constance's drowning will forever haunt her. If only she had been a swimmer, had not been shipwrecked, afraid ever after of water. If only she had been more attentive, discarded the lark-glass sooner, found some other means of saving Constance, thrown a lifeline, something for her to cling to, if only she had stayed longer in the water and tried harder, done all she could, if only, then the child might have lived. But with the haunting and the complicity come relief. Overwhelming relief and gratitude. She had not drowned the child. She was no murderess. Nor ever could be.

Simone gets up from her bed to pray, to give thanks to God for allowing the memory that had lain dormant, frozen in the winter of her subconscious, to finally thaw. When she finishes her prayer and is up from her knees, she thinks of Clara opening her letter. She has no doubt that Clara will come in haste. She will not delay. When Clara comes, she will tell her everything.

Medical Officer's Quarters

Blakely selects the key from his belt and opens the door to his quarters. He locks the door behind him, leans into it and sighs, a long out breath. At last, he is separate from the world, in particular from the Asylum. Time to think and rest. He pours himself a glass of port, takes both glass and bottle from the dresser and sets them down in front of him on his desk.

He settles into the button-green leather of his desk chair, reminding himself he cannot yet relax. Although the last bell has sounded, his day is far from over and his desk is littered with papers calling for his attention. There are reports and notes to be written up, not least now, an account of the unfortunate incident with the canary in the Day Room which he knows will displease Stafford.

Sundays are intended as days of rest, gentility and quiet contemplation, and it could have been so, a full chapel and a good sermon. A pleasant day, the women and men out in their Airing Courts and a small party of men taken beyond the grounds by the attendants for a river walk. It had all been going as a Sunday should. He had hopes of being at his desk early, until that damn bird had been let loose at the Magic Lantern Show and all hell with it. There was one consolation though, at least now he won't have to deal with the complaint that unknown persons had been dripping laudanum into the bird's water bottle. That would have entailed an investigation into the origins of such laudanum while everyone knows it's impossible to keep track of the stuff when it's so freely available outside and so easily smuggled in. They really should do something about it, the place is knee deep in the stuff, but as ever, when Blakely raises the issue, Stafford is disinterested.

He should begin by writing up the incident but instead he sifts through his papers and pulls out the invitation, gilded lettering on fine card, from Miss Vaisey requesting his presence at a Charity Ball to be held at her cousin, the Earl of Howard's, Cambridgeshire home. He will have to go. Perhaps he will even enjoy it, though for him she is little other than a pleasant and pretty diversion. She does not quicken his pulse, nor do her eyes fix his as Simone Gastrell's do. But one thing is for sure, Stafford will be all for it.

He prefers not to think of Stafford, away for a few days in Oxford, at a symposium of alienists and most likely availing himself of the college's generous hospitality. But he cannot ignore his parting gift. *The Proposed Use of Galvanic Current in the Treatment of Insanity at Long Meadow*, Cornelius Stafford. M. D., Long Meadow County Asylum, sits menacingly on his desk. He has read it and found its arguments not unfamiliar. After all, he does his best, despite the ever-increasing demands of his job, to keep abreast of the latest research and is well acquainted with the work of Reymond and Meyer. He also knows Remak's *Galvanotherapie* and his recommendation for the use of constant current in morbid conditions of the brain and disordered mental functions. Stafford's paper relies heavily on Remak, and on Newth's account of his work at the Sussex County Asylum. It concludes that if galvanic therapy were to be introduced at Long Meadow, the Asylum would fulfil its duty in employing the very latest scientific knowledge in the patients' interests.

The paper proposes daily stimulation of ten to twenty minutes duration, not on the skin but on the head or spine, the patient's hands or feet to be placed in a bowl of acidulated water with one of the electrodes dipped in the water to increase receptivity. This way, it will be possible to send a current up or down both extremities at the same time. Typically, notes Blakely, Stafford says nothing of the danger of convulsions. Nor of the skill needed in administering the treatment. A skill acquired by studious and repeated experience that some referred to as an art. A superficial knowledge is a dangerous thing and Stafford is not a man interested in particulars or fine detail. He lacks the true clinician's instinct and compassion for the task, being more concerned with the prestige it will bring and the establishing of his own professional credentials. Moreover, in Blakely's opinion, the whole field of research lacks rigor, the only evidence being that which is substantiated through observation by those invested in its success. And even then, the experts disagree. But what troubles him most about Stafford's paper is that Simone Gastrell's name appears foremost on a list of those he considers suitable subjects for such treatment.

Blakely pushes the paper to one side and pours himself another glass of port while inwardly bemoaning his luck in finding himself under such a Superintendent's command. He fears what is to come. He reaches for the fragments of paper that lie on the desk side. He gathers them up and lets them fall through his fingers.

whilst I was
My fainting fits
est of Everett and his
g among its sad and pitiful

123

nowledge of when I might
attends me,

w where I mig
gin I must by tellin
mong them, the drowning
attendance. There is much
have become more frequen
you to come at once to
and pitiable, I am not a madwo
  too. Please hurry my sweet
of what might become
ing sister

He pours himself another glass. Though he is pleased to have stemmed the tide of loose paper and to have spoken at length with Matron about the censoring of the women's mail, he is beginning to regret his actions. Yet how could he risk it? The mention of his name was too revealing. For both of them. Besides which, Matron had made Everett Gastrell's wishes that his wife did not contact her sister under any circumstances abundantly clear.

Anyone in his position would have done the same. Surely. He could not imagine what might have transpired had Stafford caught sight of the letter. Yet in hindsight, there was no suggestion of impropriety in her words. He had been hasty, hostage to his own guilty conscience or, dare he admit it, keen to keep her close by him at Long Meadow. No, that was nonsense. Nevertheless, he sees he has doomed her to Stafford's experimentations. Unless of course the Committee are not persuaded of the efficacy of galvanic therapy. Which is, he hopes, a possibility. The Chaplain has already declared himself against, no doubt others could follow suite. Stafford may not have it all his own way, though in the end his was a nature determined to override all opposition.

Could Blakely vote against him and keep his position? He doubted it. If it came to it, he would be forced to agree. God, but he was sick to death of the eternal compromise. He spent his life pacifying Stafford and constantly stemming the tide of the man's ambition. And for what? He gets no thanks. No thanks from any of them. He is little more than Stafford's lackey, compromised at every turn. He lifts his glass, empties it. A rush of anger and alcohol courses through his veins. His throat burns and his temples throb.

'Damn him, damn Stafford, damn the bloody lot of them.' He lifts his arm and sweeps the contents of his desk to the floor, shattering the glass. He is careful to stop short of the bottle. He picks it up and puts it to his lips.

The polyphony of the dawn chorus wakes him, the sissing of blackbird and wren, the chirruping of robin and sparrow, and the low boom of the bittern in the reed beds. It's not yet light when he lifts his head from the desk. He sees the empty bottle of port lying prone and the slow drip of what little remains trailing from desk to floor, staining the rug. He picks up the bottle and wipes away the spills with his handkerchief. He rubs his foot over the stain on the rug. He must rise now despite his thick head. He has work to do, but first last night's mess of glass and papers must be cleared away.

An hour later, he has disposed of the broken glass, washed and put on a fresh shirt and rearranged the papers on his desk in order of importance. He has written an account of the Lantern Show and the bird's escape and he is heating water for tea in the silver spirit kettle that sits on his sideboard. It had been his mother's and travels with him wherever he goes. When the tea is made, he takes his cup over to the window. The sky is changing its hue from ash to coral as an early morning mist dissolves and the sun rises. He opens the window to breathe in the morning air and help clear his head.

As he looks beyond the yew hedge out over the Airing Courts, he catches sight of her by the flower beds. Even from this distance, he knows it is her. He knows the shape of her, her shoulders, her waist as she bends to smell the roses. He turns from the window, puts his cup on the desk and knowing only that he must see her, hurries out and down to the Courts, along the path through the yew.

A light in the western sky. A rising sun. The garden shadowy, wreathed in a gentle mist that stretches down through the parterre, through the hedges and kitchen gardens to the meadow and to the river. She steps out along the gravel paths, breathing in the sweet scent of roses and phlox, of a philadelphus coming into bloom. Blackbirds and wrens sing hymn to the morning and she wonders if she will see the bird, Goldie, or if it will be long gone, as she would be, far away over the feathered top of Keeper's Wood. Perhaps she is hiding in the reed beds. But a bird such as Goldie could be frightened away by the boom of the bittern. No. Surely freedom will have given Goldie a courage beyond that of the caged. As it will her, for as soon as Clara hears of her plight, she will be rescued and with freedom Simone is determined to shape a new life for herself, far from the unhappy life of constraint she has lived with Everett.

But for now, here in Long Meadow, she steals time. Time to study and mark the small things, a silver bead of water on a leaf, a bee at the flower cup, a ladybird balanced on the tip of a fern, a cuckoo calling in the wood. As the mist rises and the sky lightens, she moves among the flowers beds, picking a stem of lavender and rubbing the newly formed head between her fingers to release its oil. She is breathing in the scent, a reminder of other gardens and happier times, when her reverie is disturbed by the sound of boots scraping on the gravel path.

She looks up. There is a familiarity in the shadowy figure caught in the arms of the yew. As the figure emerges into the light, she sees it is William Blakely hurrying towards her. She cannot imagine why. What can he want with her? Has he come to remonstrate, to tell her she should not be out at this hour? Will she be forced back inside and the door kept locked? Could it be a letter from Clara? Too soon, she thinks. She crumbles the lavender seeds in her closed fist and stands unmoving. As he approaches, she can see that he is smiling, and though there is something fierce in his demeanour, she cannot tell what. He slows and for a brief moment they stand together in a world of path and hedge, marigold and lily, in a golden light that conjures dream and make believe, in the silence of swallowed words.

Then he coughs and clears his throat. 'Good morning, Mrs Gastrell. I saw you from my window. I did not know if you were quite well or if...'

'Oh, I am quite well, thank you. I have come out to enjoy the quiet and to see the sun rise.'

'So I see. And why not? It promises to be a beautiful morning, the birds, the sky...' he looks around him.

'I take solace in it,' she says. 'It is what keeps me afloat in this alien world, while I wait for my sister to come. As I'm sure she will. My letter, thanks to you, should reach her any day now.'

He hesitates. 'Ah, indeed.'

'I know my sister. She will come post haste. Then I will surely be released for I have done nothing wrong. I can assure you of that now. You see my memory has returned and with it, thanks be to God, my innocence. Though I am not without fault, of course not, but I know now I did everything I could to save Constance. I do hope you will grant me the opportunity to explain it all, all that I have remembered, to you, who have been so kind.'

He swallows hard. The fragments of her letter float before his eyes and momentarily he is consumed with regret. But he cannot undo what is done now. Besides he had his reasons. He prays she cannot see through his subterfuge. Her gaze is direct, imploring, He cannot take his eyes from her. He wants to take her hand, he wants to place his hand on her breast as he did before. What has he done? What is he doing? He watches the rise and fall of her breath beneath the linsey of her dress. She is waiting for his reply, her gaze still fixed on him. She sees into all the places of his soul, dark and light. He is a drowning man. He struggles to regain a semblance of propriety. The morning bell sounds. 'Of course, all in good time, Mrs Gastrell. Now I'm sorry but I really must leave you. I have my duties to attend to.' He turns and is gone.

She watches him walk away into the arms of the yew until he is nothing but a black shadow. He is gone and yet something of him still lingers, alive in the air around her, charged, just as it had been when he'd come to her at dusk in her room. She had not imagined the intensity of his gaze, the way his green eyes fixed on hers. Nor the way her heart beat fast at the sight of him.

How she wished they were together in a garden of their choosing, far beyond the walls of Long Meadow.

Restraint and Seclusion

62. No patient shall be struck or kept in perpetual restraint or seclusion; and no Patient shall be restrained or secluded at any time except by medical authority or kept in restraint or seclusion longer than is absolutely necessary.

Rules for the Government of the Pauper Lunatic Asylum situate at Long Meadow – prepared and submitted by the Committee of Visitors thereof, by virtue of the 53rd section of the 16th and 17th VIC. CHAP 97

Alice Semple's Notebook

Upstairs

I am sent upstairs for attempting to unpick my stitches with a needle and a hatpin. If it hadn't been for Blakely's good mood that morning and Stafford's absence, they would have put the gloves on me. But I begged Blakely not, and I promised to be good. I swore to take the chloral draught each night. Thus, my hands roamed free but I slept more than I would wish. A whole week or more I have slept here in the place where cries and pleadings go unheard, fleeing up instead through chimneys and roof, smoking our messages of pain out into the world. Tis here, in Long Meadows treatment rooms, prepared and waiting, malignant and brooding, like black shuck come in a howling wind, that our greatest fears and deepest sorrows reside.

There are rooms set aside for bathing and restraint, for immersion, what we call a Long Meadow baptism. Wet pack, hot, cold, a compress to the head. A ducking til near dead, blindfold, icy water waiting under the trap door. A swaddling, a rolling in tight wet sheets, a mummification, straight jacket, camisole, muff, strap, chair, cuff, mitten, render us paralysed. Hours, weeks even. Rooms for the purging of bowels, ten or twenty times a day until collapse. Rooms for forcible feeding, bleeding and cupping, even in this time they have been known, as has the caging of genitals and the blistering of offending organs. Rooms locked and padded for seclusion, leather, linoleum, indian rubber, for our own good they say. And the nurse waiting to give you your morphine dose dissolved in beer. Not too much they say, for they know how the women will supplement with their ill-gotten laudanum.

Indian hemp, chloral hydrate, brandy, castor oil, senna, opium, bromide of potassium. I know them all and not one sufficient to disguise our melancholia, mania, visions of devils and angels, seizures, voices, the swallowing of hairpins, a noose about the neck, a deep cut thigh, lust, what happens in the cellar, in the coal dust.

I have heard it called *the moral treatment*. There is work in the laundry and kitchens, there is recreation, air to be taken in the Courts, there is the Chapel, a Lantern Show, a Lunatics Fete. They will make of us their angels of the house. So they think.

They wish to tame me. But I am ever wild, woman of dykes, and shimmering waters, Clare lifting my skirts to the drum of the pumps, to the sails in the wind. My name on his lips. How I healed his wounds with lavender, fed him the flowers of St. John's Wort to ease his suffering. Men of science would do well to know the Doctrine of Signatures. Bring me walnut and carrot, eyebright, hyssop, feverfew and lemon balm, gather them under the planets as I did with Clare, when we wandered among rushes and thistles, on sheep tracks, along the heath in the golden-blossomed furze. The fields were our church. Without him I am dust and I will join him soon but only when my work is done.

The Chaplain believes me for we have prayed on it. His eye is on them and he will bring it to the meeting. Miss Vaisey is smitten and cannot be relied on. He will investigate. He will watch over Phoebe Baines, poor child, whose history I have taken and written in the back of this book. Clare says there is pleasure in recalling past years in recollections, yet I doubt there can be much pleasure in hers.

They have taken their razors to Emma Brewer's head and shaved off her hair. All of it bar a few stray tufts. She is like a feral cat, her scalp bleeding from their cuts. When she cried out in protest and made to grab the razor, they put the gloves on her. They have not taken them off. They say her head was infested with lice, that such infestations spread and if we are not careful we too will be shorn. Matron says it is her punishment for letting Goldie loose and not a murmur of regret. Such hair it was, long and thick with curls, that I wonder who has had it? The Chief and Houndsworth I would tout, making money, hugger-mugger on the fly. The selling of hair. Tis their crooked cross. They say no woman is buried at Long Meadow lest she be well shorn.

Rumour has it Matron has fallen out with the men. Tis said they laughed at the loss of her bird, her pet which cannot be found. They say she has been scouring the woods for her. I grant that Matron might be more than the hedge whore I thought her to be, for she cares for small defenceless creatures. She has allowed that Phoebe Baines sit with Mrs Gastrell, even as night draws on, so that Mrs Gastrell may read to her and calm her voices.

133

If Emma Brewer is not calmed, they say she will be subject to the new fashion for galvanic current to the head, to the tongue. They wish to silence her. They want us mute and passive. No words, no pen. They want to take my notebook from me. But I defy them all. Needs be I will put it in safe keeping, perhaps with our murderess. Mrs Gastrell. A sly one her! I saw the pippin-flush on her cheeks at breakfast, a week past, ripe as a hothouse peach, she was. I spied them from my upstairs window, her and Blakely, out in the Airing Courts, meeting like lovers at dawn who would lie together in the murmuring grasses, by the rest harrow and fairy flax, in the margins where orchids hide. There is a heat between them that cannot be denied.

So it was once with us. All of us. In our youth we were loved. Pale and green as fresh milk from the cow, untouched, untainted, sweethearts. Daughters of the May, our blossoming stolen, our mothers dead, our sisters dying. We are caged and yet we grow, as she does, as gives us hope, as fruit luscious and red. Our stems reach up far beyond these bars. We will wear new bones.

The Visiting Room

'Ah, just the man,' says the Chaplain as he comes upon Blakely in the main corridor. 'I need to speak with you, but not here with all and sundry passing. Perhaps in here?' he says, indicating the door to the Visiting Room. 'It's Tuesday so we will not be troubled.'

Blakely nods and follows the Chaplain into the room where visits, should there be any, are held once a fortnight on a Thursday. The room is also used for meetings such as those held by the Committee of Visitors. It is not unlike a drawing room, being panelled in oak, with a white marble fireplace, and hanging above it, a portrait of Her Majesty. The long windows are draped in damask. Sets of small cherry wood tables and chairs replace upholstered couches. On the floor, a painted oil floorcloth as advised by Matron for cleanliness.

Blakely sits down at the nearest table. 'For God's sake,' he says, bringing his arm up and holding it across his nose. He follows it with a hasty, 'Apologies,' as the Chaplain sits down opposite him. 'But it's the smell of the place. It's off, sickly sweet. It needs a damn good airing and a proper clean. Remind me to tell Matron to get up a cleaning party.'

'I will, and while we're about it, might you also speak with the gardeners? The grass in the graveyard is up to my knees?'

'Yes, indeed. Now, I'm glad you've caught me, there's something I was hoping to discuss with you.'

'Likewise,' says the Chaplain.

'Well, you first, Chaplain,' says Blakely.

'It's about the young girl, in Dormitory Twelve, Phoebe Baines, the one who is prone to pulling out her hair.'

'Yes, I know her, go on.'

'I have concerns. There are whispers, gossip. As you know Alice Semple has made accusations. There is no smoke without fire, Blakely. The child is vulnerable and I fear there may be some truth in all this talk.'

'You spoke with Alice Semple?'

'I'm afraid it couldn't be avoided. It's my duty, whatever Stafford may say or wish. I want you to know it's my intention to investigate the matter, fairly of course and without prejudice. I'll say nothing for now, nor will I raise it unless I find evidence. Do not judge by appearances, but judge with right judgment. John 7, 24.'

'I won't stop you. As it happens you have my sympathy and support in the matter. When we spoke before it was the Superintendent's concerns I conveyed. I find my own are more akin to yours. Though I'm led to believe that Mrs Gastrell has taken the girl under her wing of late and that should provide some protection.'

'Quite. At least we must hope it does. Mrs Gastrell seems like a good woman. I find it hard to comprehend how she came to be admitted to Long Meadow and under such a cloud of suspicion. Is it true?'

'That she is held responsible for the death of a child?'

'Yes.'

'Well, there are those who believe it so but I cannot say. These things are never straightforward, matters of guilt and innocence. I have my doubts. I believe the girl is safe with her. Which brings me to the matter I wished to raise with you. You've seen this I presume?' Blakely waves a copy of Stafford's paper in front of the Chaplain's nose.

'Regretfully, yes.'

'It cannot be allowed,' says Blakely, surprising even himself at the strength of his declaration.

'I do not disagree,' says the Chaplain.

'These women are in our care. They are not monkeys with a barrel and pole, they are not caged pets to be treated at our whim, to do with as we wish. I am not convinced of the efficacy of the method. There are dangers, the evidence is far from conclusive. Mrs Gastrell, whose incarceration you so rightly question, is named on his list.'

'As is Alice Semple and the child, Baines. God knows these women have suffered enough at the hands of men.'

'We are in agreement then,' says Blakely, breathing out audibly. 'Stafford plans to raise it at the next Committee of Visitors meeting. There will be a vote. I need your assurance you will vote against, even if I am unable.'

'You have my word. And you in turn will leave the investigation to me?'

'That I will,' says Blakely. He proffers his hand. They shake on it. When the door closes behind them and he is out in the corridor Blakely takes a moment to steady himself against the wall. He is relieved to have begun her defence, but there are others to enlist, not least Miss Vaisey, who as luck would have it, is that very moment hurrying towards him along the corridor. As she approaches, he pulls his shoulders back and broadens his smile.

137

The Visitors' Book

June 16th

I have today spoken with the Medical Officer William Blakely concerning the cruel and unnecessary punishment of Emma Brewer, whose hands have been restrained for at least five days and whose head has been shaved bare. He has given me his assurance that the restraints will be removed and that he will investigate the matter of the head shaving with urgency, also that a suitable cap will be found for her forthwith.

M. Vaisey

Simone

Simone removes Phoebe's bonnet and lays it on the bed, she smoothes her pale hair with the palms of her hands, then takes the brush to it, lightly, as if in a caress, as she once did with Constance when her long hair became tangled after days of running wild in the fields about the house. She is careful to avoid the bald places.

Phoebe closes her eyes and hums softly to herself.

It had begun at the Lantern Show, when Phoebe, so alarmed by the restraining of Emma Brewer had reached out for Simone's hand. Simone had taken her hand, squeezed it in reassurance and seen the girl safely back to the dormitory, promising to come for her before breakfast the next morning.

Now Phoebe looks for her each morning and sits with Simone in her room in the afternoons, sometimes the early evening, while Simone brushes her hair or reads to her from the *Child's Guide to Knowledge*. Its litany of question and answer has a calming effect.

What is the World?
The Earth we live on.
Who made it?
The great and good God.
Are there not many things in it you would like to know about?
Yes very much…

Phoebe listens intently and sometimes tries to answer the

questions. Simone is reminded of reading to Constance at bedtime, the closeness and warmth of child and companion, but it is bittersweet, for with it comes the reminder of her pain and loss.

She mourns Constance, as she mourns her own stillborn child. It comes when she least expects it, out of the blue, it surfaces and clutches at her chest as if it were yesterday, bringing with it such despair that might drown a soul. Bringing fear, the fear that she will now never be a mother. That it is not her destiny. She is not fit. Fear that she will never escape Long Meadow, that it will draw on her like a poultice to the wound. That like Alice Semple, she will become a part of its very fabric, her spirit sucked into its brick and stone. Grief and fear, Simone battles them nightly and learns fast that if she is to survive, she must banish the past by whatever means she can find. She must think only of now, of here and now, of a world apart from anything she has known before.

She stops brushing, coils Phoebe's hair loosely and puts the bonnet back on the girl's head. 'There, now try not to pull at your hair. It is growing nicely. Leave it be,' she says.

Phoebe nods and remains sitting.

The evening bell sounds. 'It's time to go. It will be time for bed soon and for the night draughts. You want to sleep, don't you? I'll see you in the morning.'

Phoebe gets up, smiles at Simone and leaves silently.

Simone puts the brush away. She's pleased to see there are only a few strands trapped in its bristles. Already Phoebe's hair is stronger and she is pulling at it less. She goes over to the window. Will there be stars tonight, she wonders? Might she glimpse the frosty, spangled vault of which the women speak, the arc that leads the pilgrims to the shrine at Walsingham? Or will the stars sleep behind a curtain of cloud? She comforts herself in the knowledge that even if they are thus hidden, they will shine, even when their light is obscured. What is bright and good is not always seen.

It has rained most days this past week and the low thud of the Pumping Station can be more keenly heard. The gardens have been grateful, they grow verdant, the grasses grow tall and stifle the small crosses of the graveyard. The skies are overcast, a featureless grey, and Keeper's Wood is masked in a low-lying mist. Summer has stalled, it lies in waiting, hidden like the stars. Surely it will appear again once Clara comes.

When Simone thinks of her sister opening the letter, a flutter of hope and anticipation rises in her like a fledgling taking flight. Her release cannot come soon enough. Yet now, she finds she is troubled at the thought of leaving the girl behind. Phoebe cannot take care of herself. She needs a friend, a guardian. She needs someone to keep her safe.

The light is fading fast but Simone remains at the window in the hope of catching sight of William Blakely. She has not seen him since their dawn meeting though she hopes for it. Every day she hopes to see him, waits for the opportunity to tell him of her new-found innocence. She catches glimpses of him in the Dining Hall, the corridors, always busy, engaged, but he has not joined her in the gardens again though she goes every morning regardless of the weather.

Still she hopes. Anticipates the comfort his nearness will bring, his sandalwood scent, the trace of port wine on his breath, the bulk of him leaning towards her, the brush of his lips. It is forbidden, of course, patient and doctor. She knows this without the saying. She should dismiss him from her thoughts. And he her. Perhaps this is his intention. This is why he does not come.

Voices echo outside in the corridor. Simone turns away from the window and goes to the door. She pushes it open and sees Mrs Corey standing in the corridor talking with the Chaplain.

Mrs Corey turns, 'Good evening, Mrs Gastrell. Can I help you with anything?'

'I think I might take a chloral draught,' Simone says, suddenly knowing that more than anything she wants oblivion. More than anything she wants to slip unfettered into the dark night and wake with Clara at her bedside.

The Superintendent's Cottage

'Shuttleforth, there's a man. Keeps his own raven. Can you believe it? Damn thing has its own valet. If you can believe that. Got it from the nest half-fledged, so he says. Tame apparently, though it took a while, got into his study once, tore up his papers, stole one of his best cufflinks. Loquacious thing by all accounts, calls it Grip after Dickens, you know Grip in *Barnaby Rudge*. It seems Dickens kept a raven himself. Have to admit it's crossed my mind once or twice, keeping a pet. I fancied a monkey but I thought better of it. Bite you soon as look at you, nasty vicious little things. Anyway, back to the matter in hand.'

Blakely sips his burgundy and settles into the carved spoon back on his side of the fireplace. It's pointless to speak, there's no stopping the old man when he's in a mood like this and half drunk with it. Stafford had come back from the symposium high as a kite on a windy heath and awash with wine. It had been no surprise to Blakely. Observing him now, he sees how Stafford's nose is swelling with the drink to a bulbous, veined, purple and red.

The Superintendent paces back and forth. 'As I was saying, you can forget Connolly, the moral treatment cannot suffice, not with the numbers being admitted these days. Galvanism is the answer. We were pretty much all agreed. It's bang up to the elephant. Shuttleforth has already introduced it. I've ordered the Mayer and Meltzer, the battery's powerful and it comes with the induction apparatus all in one. I expect it to be delivered within the week and there's no reason, no reason whatsoever, for us not to proceed. You've read my paper?'

Blakely nods. 'I have indeed but I somehow thought we would wait for the Committee's approval before...'

'No. Definitely not, my mind's made up. I cannot see the need for informing the House Committee, it's really not a matter for them. It's a matter for us medical men, a matter of science. God's blood man, we cannot be ruled by clerks and clerics and women who ought to remain at home where their talents can be best made use of. No.'

'I take your point,' says Blakely, 'but I think we might be better served to take the establishment with us on a matter of such experiment.'

'Nonsense,' Stafford pours himself another glass of burgundy, draining the bottle. 'You lack grit man. It is up to us. Besides they don't even need to know about it.'

'Ah but they don't miss much, take the Visitors' Book, the entry concerning Emma Brewer.' Blakely had already tried to recount the events leading up to Emma Brewer's restraint and to discuss his actions with Stafford, but Stafford had shown no interest. Since his return from the symposium where the flames of his obsession had been well and truly fanned, all previous concerns were erased.

Blakely tries again, 'They are like hawks, the Committee, nothing goes unnoticed, and the women, you know how they talk.'

'Perhaps I will keep a hawk, instead of a monkey, what think you? Goshawk, sparrow hawk? Hawking, falconry whatever you call it. The men would love it. A new hobby for them. Outdo Shuttleforth. We can train it to attack the likes of our Miss Vaisey.' He laughs heartily and flings himself at the chair. In doing so spills half a glass on his waist coat. 'Damn.' He attempts to brush it off with a napkin. 'How are you getting on with her, by the way? Making progress?' Then before Blakely has a chance to reply. 'We'll start as I outlined, in my paper, with Mrs Gastrell. I'll get Eames to visit and approve. That way we'll have independent approval. Yes, that's the way forward undoubtedly.'

'Do you not think it might exacerbate her condition, the headaches, the fainting? Are we sure they are not seizures? I believe there are other better suited candidates.'

'I've no concerns whatsoever. I've discussed her case with Shuttleworth and he considers her eminently suitable.' He pauses to draw breath, 'I wonder what is with men that they need these exotic pets? Why a raven for God's sake?'

'Vanity,' offers Blakely. 'Status. Didn't Ovid keep one? Beautiful birds, of course, glossy and black.'

'Provocative if you ask me. And on the subject of Mrs Gastrell, say nothing, we'll let Eames do the talking. I'll speak with him myself in the morning.'

Knowing there is little point in arguing with Stafford in such a mood, Blakely drains his glass, makes his excuses and leaves. He has work to do. There are several new admissions to attend to, though he has asked the Chief to oversee these for once, but he will still have to sign off and then there is the letter. If he is not mistaken, he has the envelope intact somewhere among his papers. He will write to Mrs Clara Gibson in Paris and tell her that her sister, Simone Gastrell, has been committed to the Asylum and is in danger. He will ask her to come as a matter of urgency. He will post it first thing in the morning. He will sign it *a friend*.

He takes the shortcut past the Chapel among the small

crosses which mark the graves of those who have died at Long Meadow. The evening sky etiolates, lilac to grey, to white, the time when solid becomes liquid, becomes mere silhouette, time and space liminal. He looks up at the splatter of stars above him and wonders at the vastness of the heavens and where a man such as Stafford might fit into the great design, or for that matter, a man such as himself. Ape or angel? He inclines to ape and yet when he is with her, it is as if his faith is restored and he dwells in the realms of angels. There are good people, saintly even, for whom you strive to better yourself. Angel, it is not impossible. Science confirms the rational intricacy of God's creation, both ape and angel are credible. If it is so, then he is in no doubt into which category Stafford falls. He is not on the side of the angels.

It is left to him to warn her.

The door at the end of Dormitory Twelve is locked.

'The women are restless, Sir, we thought it best, says a night attendant, jumping up from her chair by the door. 'Are you looking for the Chaplain, Sir? He's about, came through a short while ago.'

'Yes, thank you, the Chaplain,' says Blakely, lifting his keychain from his pocket and selecting a key. The corridor is empty, the Chaplain having most likely followed it to its conclusion, to the double-locked side entrance. But he is not looking for the Chaplain.

He stops outside her door and listens intently for the rise and fall of her breath. He thinks perhaps to wake her, in order to warn her, though he is not sure what he will say. He opens the door and enters as quietly as one might enter the room of a sleeping child. He approaches the bed. On her table lie the remains of a sleeping draft, next to it a small crown, woven in green. He rubs his fingers on its leaves, releasing the sharp herbal scent he identifies as rosemary. Her hair spills onto the pillow, her soft, pale lips open slightly as she breathes in and out. He lowers himself gently on to the bed, sitting down beside her. His breath slows. If only he could lie beside her now. If only he could put his head on the pillow next to hers. He is overcome with tiredness, yet beneath this weariness and worry beats the small but insistent pulse of desire. He tells himself it must be resisted. He reaches out and places a hand on her head, draws it gently down across her ear, her neck and rests it on her shoulder. He sighs, lifts his hand and settles it back on her head. It is here that the apparatus will be placed. He has seen the diagrams. This is where the current will enter and who knows what it may do to an already fragile mind. He must do everything in his power to prevent it. He must do everything he can to save her.

Fatal or Dangerous Accidents

13. In the cases of fatal or dangerous accident or other emergency, the Resident Medical Officer and Superintendent shall immediately communicate the fact in writing to the Members of the House Committee, any one of whom shall thereupon be empowered to summon a special meeting of such Committee, as soon as practicable, if it shall be thought expedient.

Rules for the Government of the Pauper Lunatic Asylum situate at Long Meadow – prepared and submitted by the Committee of Visitors thereof, by virtue of the 53rd section of the 16th and 17th VIC. CHAP 97

Simone

She wakes to the slow and persistent click-click of the blind as it blows back and forth against the window. As with each waking, she remembers anew where she is. Long Meadow, a blade to her heart. It is no dream, she dwells here now, in a hidden world which she fears, without Clara's help, may become her home, as it has for so many women. A place she can be conveniently forgotten and left to rot.

Daylight presses through the linen of the blind and she knows at once she is too late for her stolen hour. The bitter taste of chloral lingers in her mouth and her head is thick and clotted with the remnants of dream. She sits up and strains to hear the daily noise she has grown accustomed to, Long Meadow's morning song: the bell, the coughing and calling of the women at their ablutions, the emptying of pots, feet shuffling in the corridor outside, the wheels of the trolley, the rattle of the attendants keys. But all is silent.

How long has she slept? She looks across at her table, at the coronet of rosemary and rue woven for her by Phoebe at the behest of Alice. According to Alice, a garland in the hair will stimulate the mind. According to Alice, if a man cannot smell rosemary, he cannot love a woman. Perhaps the rosemary had brought about her dreams. Dreams so vivid as to be real. He had come to her in her room and lay down next to her on the bed. Mingling with the fresh breath of the night, she smelled sandalwood and wine, the light around them silvery, soft and pale as a catkin on willow.

If she closes her eyes now, he is still there beside her. But she must not give into it. She must resist.

She shakes her head, gets out of bed and dresses in haste. Pulling up the blind, she sees there are only the swifts wheeling through the air, floating on the wind. There are no groups of men going down to the garden. There are no gardeners about the churchyard, no attendants hurrying across the grass. All is silent, as if the world and time itself have frozen about her. She turns from the window and ventures out into the corridor. There is no one there. The clock shows eight-twenty which is well past time for the women to be up and breakfasted. She tries the door to Dormitory Twelve but finds it is locked. And as she has no passage out, there is nothing for it but to go back to her room and sit and wait.

Silence weights the air. She tastes the rotten fruit of its dark heart, smells its mourning black, hearse black, and sees the laurel about the door. She knows enough of this place now to know something bad has happened. Something unalterable. She picks up the wreath of rosemary and holds it close to her, breathing in its aromatic scent. Rosemary and rue, *Grace and remembrance be to you both*. How much she needs His grace. She sinks to her knees and prays to God to keep them safe. She prays for those few, precious to her now, those who eclipse all others dwelling here with her in this underworld: Alice Semple, Phoebe Baines and William Blakely. She prays for him though she knows she should not. She prays for the good, for they are not all bad at Long Meadow, she prays for the Chaplain. Then a prayer for her sister that she may come safely but quickly.

150

Phoebe Baines

Dormitory 12

no bells
no rising but the wind knocking
stay abed they say, stay
all ladies in, all ladies in
they say mind yourself the bees
workers in the hive busy about and matron
queen matron hurrying white face eyes agog
gargoyle eyes in the cloisters screaming
down mouths agape stay
they say we must stay abed
they bring bowl sop milk bread
sugar atop crystal
swallow for the hunger
breakfast gone there will be later dinner
i ask to go to her
my sister, my mother of kindness and soft words
simone
heavens adorn her with a rosemary coronet
she will plait my hair like a pretty maiden
brush it out but i am forbidden
all doors locked silence
cannot think what except up too early
out with the dawn

dancing with the birds again
also forbidden
but hush listen in quiet the women come
shuffle from bed to bed whisper
words shush the hours past
last night what they heard
say Emma Brewer
has come to harm
say she is hanging like a fish on a hook
cut her down too late
too late cut her down too late
shush say attendants no such no such thing nonsense
eat your sop forget your wash rest then just as fast
like a swarm
up up and dressed unlock up up and dressed
go about your business they say
if anyone ask strangers stop
accost why
then say well
how well you are cared for
needs met all remember that says Matron
swallowing words the queen is dying
all needs met
on her death bed hair in my mouth
i cannot speak
i dare not speak for fear it is all truth

Alice Semple's Notebook

*Pale death, the grand physician, cures all pain; The dead
rest well who lived for joys in vain – J Clare*

Emma Brewer is gone. Departed two days since from this
world of trouble. When they took the gloves off her, she
plaited her bed sheets to rope and hanged herself from the
gas socket. They have been out all morning digging her
grave, black peaty soil heaped to one side and a small cross
for marking. I have asked the Chaplain for the words of
Clare written above to be inscribed on the cross. The
Chaplain is a good man who says she may have a cross
despite her sin. The robin and thrushes are out after the
worms. The wind is up.

We are eleven now – *Mary Ann Holdsworth, Amelia Grey,
Esther Knox, Anne Bickerdale, Phoebe Baines Katharine
O'Sullivan, Ivy Cole, Eveline Web, Gladys Carter, Dorcas
Fisher, Alice Semple.*

We alone are to attend the funeral. Only the women of
Dormitory Twelve, for Emma Brewer has no family beyond
Long Meadow except a husband who beat her half to death
and is disappeared. Mrs Gastrell, who the women call by
her first name, Simone, as she is one of us, is granted
permission to attend. There will be the hoi polloi, as always,
sorrowful after the fact, and the men who carry the cheap

painted coffin that has no furniture but a small brass plate. I rise early to polish the Chapel pews. Anne Bickerdale goes out to beg rosemary from the men in the kitchen garden.

The frogs are croaking. We take umbrellas for fear of rain, but the wind blows them inside out and our caps with them. It blows holes in the sky itself. We hold our caps close to our heads. Esther Knox cries. Katharine O'Sullivan is afraid the Devil may come out to dance from Keeper's Wood. Ivy Cole takes her hand to persuade her she is safe. Phoebe Baines stays close to Simone Gastrell.

In the Chapel we sing, *Weep Not for Me You Standers By*, Amelia Grey's voice the loudest and sweetest. I am silent for I do not know hymns and besides my voice is but a tattered, broken wing. The Chaplain reads from the Bible, *In my Father's house there are many mansions...* I think of Long Meadow, its many rooms, its corridors and hidden places, and wonder if God has forsaken us and left us to dance with the devil as Katharine O'Sullivan fears.

We sing as we process to the graveside, hands still on caps, our voices rise up into the wind and are carried down to the river to float far away to the world's end. We throw our sprigs of rosemary onto the black coffin lid. We do not look long or linger at the edge for we see our future in the grave's dark pit.

After, they think to soften us, to make us forget, with their sandwiches and sponges, with their cushioned chairs and curtains, in the Visiting Room that smells of fish and laudanum, for this is where the poison is passed between visitor and patient when the attendant turns a blind eye for a favour.

Dorcas Fisher and Phoebe Baines toy with the food on their plate. Mary-Ann Holdsworth collects their crusts and scraps of bread to call her babies. She will hide them in her locker until they are green with mould.

Matron's smile is a dragon's that could breathe fire at any turn. Her eyes signal danger. They are afraid, the likes of Matron and Stafford, the attendants, all afraid of what we might tell and say to the great and the good of the House Committee who are out in force today.

Miss Vaisey is at the fore, though she is distracted for WB is attending to her cup and plate. He stands close to her and they are engaged in who knows what. Who knows what they say for they stand apart by the window and Simone Gastrell watches.

If it wasn't for Emma Brewer and our respect for her, our sister, we would play the fool and the madwoman for all we were worth. There would be hijinks, lewdness, laughter, voices louder than they ever should be, skirts pulled up, skin bared. For we sense it, we smell it, when it happens, our advantage. But we do not take it because we mourn one of our own.

Miss Vaisey comes over from the window and WB and asks me how I am bearing up. She tells me she is sorry for our loss, that a death such as this does not go without investigation. The Committee has met. We may soon expect a visit from the Inspectors of the Lunacy Commission who are called the Masters.

I tell her women like Emma Brewer should never be locked away. She meant no harm. I tell her we have, all of us, all of our lives been robbed and ill-used.

We are nightingales, listen for us in the dead of night while others sleep, hear us pour forth the struggle of our existence into song. When the nightingale appears before you, listen well. And wonder as Clare did *that so famed a bird should have no better dress than russet brown.*

Simone

'Phoebe. Phoebe Baines.'

'Phoebe, Phoebe.' They are calling out her name and there is a hint of fear, a hint of desperation in their rising pitch.

The calling wakes Simone. As she sits up, she sees she is not alone. For standing at the end of her bed like a visiting spirit, shivering in her chemise, is Phoebe. As the voices grow louder, Phoebe shrinks back into the corner of the room, as if she would dissolve into its walls. Simone jumps out of bed and stretches out her arms.

'What is it Phoebe? Have you had a bad dream? Are you ill? Don't cry. Please. You are safe here with me. Come, come…'

But the girl does not move, her hands are clasped tight to her chest, black with dust, and Simone catches the grey scent of the hearth hanging about her. *Everyone knows what happens in the coal cellar.* The notebook. If she is to understand, if she is to help Phoebe, she must ask Alice.

Silent tears run down Phoebe's face but before Simone can comfort her, Mrs Corey is at the door, pushing it wide open.

'Found her. She's in here, Matron,' she shouts and with that they are all at Simone's door. Attendants, Matron, Houndsworth, and they take Phoebe by the arm and usher her out, fussing about her, shushing her. They whisk her away as if she never was. And it is just Simone and Mrs Corey left.

'It'll be a bad dream or such nonsense. The poor child. Cannot read nor write. Born in the workhouse, by all accounts a terrible difficult labour. The mother near dead, poor thing, and the girl well, an imbecile from birth, and nothing to be done about it,' says Mrs Corey bustling about, drawing up the blinds. 'Oh my, just look at that sun. It's going to be a fine day for your walk and no doubt.'

Simone puts on her freshly laundered gown and a new cap. The Lunacy Commission are due before lunch. By all accounts, they have been summoned by the Members of the House Committee, after a special meeting, to investigate the death of Emma Brewer. The women are instructed to take special care with their appearance. In the days preceding, there has been a frenzy of scrubbing and dusting and fresh whitewash adorns the walls. There are flowers in the Day Room and there is honey and fresh butter for the bread at breakfast and a slice of cheese. The women are to be taken for a river walk, accompanied by Matron and two attendants. Simone is glad for the opportunity to go beyond the Airing Courts and the Asylum walls, thankful for a brilliant sun and a cloudless sky. She has told herself she must try to banish sadness and fear, that for this one morning, she will walk out into the world and breathe the air as if she were a free woman.

As they gather in the Courts, spirits are high. A member of the Commission, a tall man with a red beard is to accompany them. Following Matron, they process down through the terraces, their skirts brushing at the phlox and the lavender, down through the kitchen gardens and out to the open fields. Phoebe, pale after her morning fright, walks beside Simone. Simone takes her hand. With their backs to

Long Meadow's sprawling wings and smoke-filled chimneys, they are awash in sky and meadow grass, meadow thistle and ragged robin. Gladys Carter raises her arms and pirouettes her way to the river like a damsel fly hovering above the water. Even the *silent women* applaud.

The air is different here and Simone's senses are alive with it. As they approach the riverbank, the pumps beat ever louder in her ears and the fishy, scent of river water assails her. All at once, the sun is blinding. She pulls back. Stops. The morning of the drowning comes at her headlong and fast. She can do nothing to prevent it. In a flash she sees herself striking out through the reeds, diving down, her head underwater, a thick black soup. The long-ago sensation of a sinking ship and a wild sea surround her.

She looks up at the sky. The sun is wreathed in violet. It sparks and blazes. She turns her head away, looking down instead at her feet. She seeks to steady herself, but it as if her feet belong to someone else. As if they stand separate from her, alone among the sharp, emerald blades of grass. She cannot move, her hands are sweating, her arm is numb, and the world is closing in around her.

When she comes too, she is lying in the shade of a willow, looking up into a canopy of leaves dancing in the sunlight. Phoebe is holding her hand and Alice is whispering in her ear. 'I have gathered groundsel. Later I will make you a decoction, with a little ale. It is good against the falling sickness.'

'How are you feeling, Mrs Gastrell? Perhaps the heat was too much for you?' says Matron, interposing herself. Indicating to the others by a waving her hands that they are to move away

'A little better, thank you,' says Simone.

'Good, good, because as it happens, I have just had word that there is someone who wishes to see you. You have a visitor, I believe. So, if you are well enough to stand and walk, the attendant here will take you back. He has a parasol to keep off the sun. We must take care of you. We do not wish any of our women to suffer unnecessarily,' she says the last with a smile directed at the Commissioner.

Simone is unsteady on her feet. Her head aches but she has known worse, and she is energised by the news of a visitor. Who could it possibly be? Who would want to speak with her? If Matron says she has a visitor, it must be true. Could it be her sister come at last? Please God, let it be her sister. Let it be Clara and with that thought in mind, she feels at once better, stronger on her feet and begins to walk back, an attendant at her side and a parasol above.

Blakely

According to Stafford, the fault was all his. *What in God's name were you thinking of man? This whole damn mess is down to you. You're the reason the Lunacy Commission are crawling all over the place. Thank the Lord I've got connections, Blakely, else we'd be in serious trouble.*

Blakely stares down at his feet. His shoes are in need of a good polish, he thinks, as he ponders Stafford's accusations. He is skirting the graveyard on his way to the Chapel, hoping for a brief respite from the Commissioners.

He doesn't disagree with the premise. He should have acted sooner. Who knew what Emma Brewer had suffered in those days of isolation and restraint. Who knew what part it had played in her suicide? He'd done nothing to stop it, he'd dropped the ball, guilty of neglect on all counts. As for the shaving of the poor wretch's head, he'd failed to even notice, and he deemed it unforgiveable. But to be blamed for informing the House Committee, to be blamed for following the rules, that was typical of Stafford who, true to form, had been desperate to hush the whole thing up. As if they could. As if word wouldn't reach the likes of Miss Vaisey. As if the House Committee would not act. No. He'd done the right thing in informing them. Nevertheless, he was full of regrets. He regretted an unnecessary death. He should have acted sooner. He admits he had been distracted.

As he reaches the Chapel door and looks up from his dusty shoes, he sees her, the very cause of his distraction, coming back from the walking party, beneath a parasol, an attendant at her side. A small electric pulse surges through him. Why is she returning early? He fears for her. Is she unwell? He fears for himself. What might she have said to the Commissioners? What is to be done? He's a farrago of self-reproach, contrition, annoyance, remorse, anger, guilt. When she disappears out of sight, he pushes open the Chapel door and steps inside.

At last, he can breathe out. Here he can find a moment of peace, a moment of quiet in which to think. He feels the stone flags of the floor beneath his feet and is grateful for their permanence, their solidity. It is blessedly cool. A pale light filters through the window glass, illuminating the walls in a Naples yellow, falling as rectangles and diamonds on the grey stone. He slides into the pew nearest the door. He cannot risk being away for long with the Commissioners about though, praise be to God, there are only four of them, all men, and Stafford appears to have them in his pocket. The Commissioners are perhaps the least of his problems.

He is thinking of leaving Long Meadow. It is the only way he can see to end the temptation. It is time for him to consider becoming a Superintendent of his own establishment. It is well past time to get away from Stafford and his dangerous regime. He sinks to his knees on the hassock in front of him, puts his hands together and prays. He prays for God's guidance. He prays for forgiveness, for the soul of Emma Brewer, for Simone Gastrell. He prays for all who dwell in Long Meadow. He prays with a fervour he hasn't possessed since he was a boy.

Alice Semple's Notebook

A woman dies and they send us men, only men, their so-called Masters in Lunacy. They say it is by invitation of the House Committee. Yet what may such men know of us, they who blame our sex for all their ills, who would cut out our wombs, shave our heads, feed us with funnel and tubes. Only what they determine we must be:

smaller than he, named for flowers and fancies
ladybird, sweetheart, bedfellow
laced woman of virtue
beaten and raped with no fear of prosecution
wise to never fail from his side
nor set herself above
willing to take bruises for love
be for hearth not field, needle not sword
never doctor or apothecary, there is no room for her among
    them
white rose of purity
without desire or longing
taking the knife not to others, only herself, the scratching,
    the cutting, the grazing kept hidden beneath her clothes
found and presented as idiot
sweet and long-suffering
imprisoned for refusing conjugal rights
Must have:
no fondness of finery, no showy colours

no love of reading

no wild wandering nature

no delight, pleasure, or wonder

all learning, all passions not serious, for her brain is but the
brain of an animal, closer to child and savage than to
him

she must never sing more than two songs consecutively

nor laugh too loud and long, nor dance too hard

she must wear her collar and sleeves neat, shoes and stockings
tidy

never trust her female acquaintance

never lie on the dyke or dwell in the clover with a man

nor question, nor raise a voice to complain

only comply

Our knowledge is not the learning of men but the knowledge of the heart. The wisdom of poetry. Theirs an otherness, invented by them. There are ways in which words fail, ways they tumble from mouths all sense lost. There are ways that writing down winkles out the truth. I cannot speak with the Masters of Lunacy. There is too much for my poor voice and where to begin? I offer them my words instead. I write as well and simply as I can. I make no accusation. I fear that to accuse, to make a fuss will render my words that of a madwoman. I make a copy on a piece torn from my notebook. I fold it and give to the Commissioner, the one with the red beard who accompanies us on our walk. I ask him to read. No more than this. I tell him this is who we are. Sprung from the same pasts, we may not appear as sisters, but we are stitched together by what is lodged inside, by what has been torn from us. We are various as the patches on a quilt, sewn together we are whole.

For the Masters of Lunacy

The Life of the Idiot Phoebe Baines

I have it on good account, from a woman who was an attendant here in Long Meadow but a short while ago, a woman well acquainted with Emily Baines, Phoebe's mother, that these facts are true and undisputed.

Phoebe Baines is the eldest child of seven. Born with the cord about her neck and near died at birth. The family, her mother and seven children, lived alone in Magdalen Street, in the city of Norwich, above the pork butchers. The men who sired the children, were various and all long-gone. Emily Baines took in washing in order to make a living and never once paid for a pork chop or a knuckle but in kind.

When Phoebe was eleven, the pork butcher declared himself interested in a different more tender cut of meat. Phoebe was given to the butcher as and when he wished and Emily took up with a sailor from Yarmouth who she met in the Adam and Eve, public house.

At thirteen years of age Phoebe was sold to a clergyman who called at the house distributing religious tracts. Emily Baines would not part with the child for under five pounds, for she was pretty and, Emily claimed, a virgin. The clergyman paid seven pounds and ten shillings, most of which went on ale in the Adam and Eve and on slips in the betting house.

Before long Phoebe Baines was a fancy-piece, a fuckstress,

165

call it what you will, out in the shadows and the cold, walking back and forth on Rosary Road. (This is where the attendant's account ends.)

I have it on Phoebe's account, though her words are few and small, that a man of God gave her to a fat man, to mind his shop in Elm Hill, but the bees stung him on his arse when he was fettling her up against the wall in the cupboard his trousers about his ankles, so he turned her out.

The women in Rosary Road showed her how to powder her face and redden her cheeks. The women on Rosary Road showed her how to rid herself of child. She took gunpowder mixed in a paste in a soap dish and suffered sickness for three days and nights and there was much blood and vomit. She wandered out of the city into the countryside. She did not know where she was. I have it from her that she stood in field from dawn to dusk in all weathers scaring crows with barely a bite to eat

Matron says she came to Long Meadow from the Workhouse. She has been here two years April past. The House Committee know well what she suffers and she is in danger of following in Emma Brewer's footsteps, though she may use starvation and not the rope. I ask you, good gentlemen, to consider her fate. To enquire of her well being. I ask for your help.

The Visiting Room

Simone

She'd known at once that it was not Clara, seated at the small cherrywood table with her back to the door. The figure was too small, the hair too pale, the bonnet too plain, the bearing less than that of a woman of means. It was not her beloved sister come to take her away. It was Maria, her housemaid.

Though she had longed for her sister, at the moment of recognition, Simone had been overjoyed at the sight of this familiar and loved face. A face of kindness, of someone who had always been there to take her side against Everett. There was pleasure and an unexpected relief too in meeting a face from the life she'd lived before Long Meadow. The face of someone from outside who had nothing to do with the Asylum. A keen reminder that another world existed still.

Maria for her part had jumped up out of her seat, embraced Simone, then shed copious tears which she dabbed away with her handkerchief.

Maria brought with her news of the household. Unsettling news. Everett was planning a wedding. The parlour maid had heard the word divorce whispered more than once. The staff had taken against Henrietta. Maria cited her superior ways, her lack of grief for her sister, Constance. She is nothing but a slip of a girl, Maria told Simone, a bossy-boots, 'Though I don't like to say it Ma'am, truth be told she is a brazen hussy, of the very worst kind.'

They missed Simone, every one of them, Maria said. The new mistress spent her days re-arranging the rooms, planning their re-decoration, and entertaining her French dressmaker, Madame Badeaux. They were all agreed it was the height of extravagance, the ordering of this silk and that lace and all manner of adornments for the wedding dress.

'But I have not come to gossip,' Maria said. 'I have come with a letter, Ma'am. I believe it to be from Madam Clara. I recognised the hand at once and the foreign markings, being the only letters that come from abroad. I knew I should bring it to you before the Master, or Henrietta, got wind of it. I trust I've done the right thing. I hope its good news, Ma'am. I will be only too glad to come again and do whatever I may for you. I have been as bold as to lock your valuables safely away until such time as you might need them, especially your purse of gold sovereigns, Ma'am, and the diamond butterfly brooch, the black stones, the Italian cameo. In no circumstances will she get her hands on them, Ma'am. I promise you. And should you need me, for whatever reason, for anything at all, you may contact me through Mrs Corey's cousin, Tom Makepeace, who delivers bread and vegetables to the house.' She paused, then taking the handkerchief again from her pocket and dabbing at her eyes, added, 'I do so hate to see you like this, Ma'am. It is not fair. We are all praying for you, we are all praying you will be back with us soon'. With that, she passed the letter to Simone and tear-stricken, hurried away.

As she'd watched Maria go, Simone had wanted to stop her, to cry out after her – *Wait, take me with you. Please I*

beg you, do not leave me here, alone among strangers, Please.
But she'd held back, for such an outburst, such protestation
would be taken only as proof of lunacy.

She watched her go in silence.

It had pained Simone greatly to hear of all that was happening
in her absence. It brought back her exile from the world, a
grim reminder that life carried on without her, with no
thought for her. It brought home the truth that aside from
Clara, she had only Maria and the women of Long Meadow
to rely upon.

And now it seemed, now that she had read the letter that
presently sat open in her lap, all hopes of Clara coming to
free her, to take her home, out of this god forsaken place,
were dashed.

Dearest Simone,
April 14th
S.S. Alba

*Forgive me but this letter will of necessity be short as
I find myself quite indisposed due to suffering from sea
sickness. Please do not ask how I ever dared set sail
again after our terrible misfortunes at sea but I assure
you it was out of necessity. Edward is reassigned from
Paris to the India Office in Delhi, and like a dutiful
wife I am accompanying him to his new posting. Once
we arrive and are settled, it is my fervent hope that you
will come and join us, for as long as you wish. I will
write as soon as possible with our address. For now, I
am all at sea and have no address but the ocean, though
a kindly woman, who has been a companion to me so*

169

far on this journey has agreed to post this for me when
she alights in Port Said.

Your dearest,
most affectionate sister
Clara

Simone

At supper Simone seeks out the *silent women*. They eat their bread. There is no honey and little butter. The Commissioners are gone. A day which had begun with the promise of a molten sun high in a summer sky had become a night without hope.

She cannot eat and thinks only of being outside. She looks across at Matron, standing alone among the tables, and notices now the sadness etched on her face. It has been there, Simone thinks, since the loss of her bird. Such a small thing, a bird flown, and yet Simone understands how well small things matter in a place like Long Meadow. Though Matron may leave at the end of the day, though she may wear belt and keys, she still breathes the air of containment, just as her patients do. She too lives a life in exile, behind the Asylum walls and cannot escape its deprivations or its harm.

As the women clear their plates, Simone approaches her. 'Excuse me Matron, but I wondered if I might go out into the Airing Courts before bed? Just for a brief while? Just to take some air and clear my head. Much has happened today, and I believe it will help ward off a headache.' She has surprised herself that she dares ask, and certain now that Matron will never agree to such a request.

Matron sighs, pauses, and as if her thoughts are somewhere else far away, says, 'I don't see why not, Mrs Gastrell. I believe the vestibule door is open still. As long as you are back before the lights go out. You really must be back before then.'

'Thank you,' says Simone, 'thank you,' and she leaves quickly before Matron has a chance to change her mind.

A thin mist, like breath on glass lies beyond the Courts, veiling the kitchen gardens, running down across the meadow, following the course of the river. The air is still warm, the sun low in the sky. She walks quickly as if she fears being discovered, fearing that Matron will change her mind, come looking for her and order her back inside to join the women preparing for bed. Should this happen, she will not be able to bear it. She needs this brief respite, this momentary escape from a partial, haunted life, a life where all daily activities are conducted in the company of others, where movement is in numbers, a dormitory's count. A pack, a herd, they are sheep, they are cattle, corralled into obedience. No choice or influence, their fates caged in the hands of their masters. Their hopes locked away. And what of Simone's hope that she might be released? Who will come to her rescue now? With Clara far away at sea, it will be months if not years before she dares anticipate that salvation. She stands in the place where hope is lost, and what is survival without hope? But she tells herself she must not give in, she cannot, will not countenance a life spent imprisoned between the walls of Long Meadow. She will devise a plan. She has no idea yet what that plan will be, but she clings to the knowledge that Maria is on her side and who knows, there may be others. If it takes years, then so be it, she must believe there will be a letter from Clara one day. Maria will bring the letter and hope will be resurrected.

Simone sits down on a bench on the lower terrace, out of sight. She feels the day's tensions ebb from her. How rare it is not to be observed, surveyed, how rare to find a moment of privacy away from a room that is little more than a cell. A moment of peace, of quiet, entirely to herself, unshared and unsullied. She understands why the *silent women* have so little to say, for even agreement, politeness, conversation in a place such as this, renders a woman powerless. Agree, exchange pleasantries, offer help and you are at one with the Asylum, complicit with its keepers. Argue, dissent, fight and you are branded a troublemaker, likely to be restrained and taken away out of view where they will be sure to find a punishment that ensures compliance.

Simone closes her eyes, imagines herself travelling abroad with Clara in the calm that it is surely possible to find on the vastness of the ocean, surely not all seas are for drowning. Maria's visit has prompted a spill of memories, falling in random one upon another like the coloured glass in a child's kaleidoscope: she and Clara side by side stitching clothes for their dolls, their needlework basket, the silver thimble engraved with her initials given to her by her aunt, those afternoons when Everett was away in London, how she relished those, a fire in the grate, delicate slices of bread and marmalade, a few salted almonds, a glazed pear, snow falling silently and gently covering the lawns, weighting the leaves of the hornbeam, scattering crumbs for the birds, her mother's hands, even though she knew so little of her mother she recalls her hands, she is sure of it, folded in her lap, their pink fleshiness. She thinks too of the small slippery body that she pushed into the world, that they took from her, that they would not let her see or name, the worst pain. Eames had been kind to her then with his cold hands and instruments of steel, had told Everett he was to stay away from her and let her rest a good few months. How different it might have been if her child had survived. She thinks of Constance's body laid so pitiably on the bier. But she cannot dwell there. She closes her eyes and thinks instead of open meadows, wide skies, a lark soaring into the blue, anything but her life here at Long Meadow.

Footsteps, sudden and insistent, disturb her reverie. She opens her eyes, her breath catches in her throat as she sees William Blakely making his way towards her.

'Good evening, Mrs Gastrell. Matron said I might find you here. I came to enquire as to your health. I hear you had an unfortunate fainting on the walk today.'

'I did, yes, but I am quite recovered, thank you.'

'Still, you look pale. Are you certain you are well?' Then in the pause before she answers, 'May I sit here?'

She nods.

He sits down beside her. She breathes in his masculine presence. In a world of women, such a presence is affecting, exotic almost. He is tall, so much broader than her, and she is aware how she has shrunk, how loose her linsey dress has become, whereas his chest fills out his wool coat and the deep red of his brocade waistcoat. His dark hair curls at his collar, his scent, as always, the scent of sandalwood mingles with the grass-sweetened air of the summer evening, a grass that lends its colour to his eyes.

'I am certain, thank you. I believe my paleness may be more to do with the fact that I have had some bad news today brought by a visitor from my household. A letter.' She lifts the letter from her pocket and hands it to him. 'You may read it if you wish,' she says.

He reads the letter then folds it back into its envelope. 'I'm sorry. I see that must be very disappointing for you,' he says, handing it back to her. Inwardly, he is pleased to be absolved from his cowardly act in destroying the first

174

letter and relieved of worrying about the second, which despite his best intentions, still lies in his desk drawer. He hopes his relief does not show. 'But you will get news to her eventually once she is settled,' he says.

'Eventually is too long, I fear. I cannot remain here indefinitely. I cannot live like this as if I am a criminal, as if I am a mad woman when I am not, when I have done nothing wrong. Surely you see.' The events of the day overwhelm her, tears well up. She had determined not to give way but they are falling into her lap and there is nothing she can do to stop them.

'Of course, I see, but do not despair, please,' he says. Then taking a hand from her lap and clasping it in both of his, 'I will help. Let me help you. I will do my best to secure your release, after all I have some sway with the Superintendent and with the House Committee who I'm sure would be sympathetic to your plight.'

He does not release her hand, only turns towards her. He looks at her then, his gaze searching for hers.

She dares not meet his gaze, for if she does, she will be found out.

He leans in towards her. He means to kiss her.

The flush of desire rises to her cheeks.

His lips are pressing on hers. He pulls away, his face only inches from hers, 'I will help you,' he whispers. 'I will help you, Simone.'

He stands then, and keeping hold of her hand, leads her down to the gate that opens into the kitchen gardens. He reaches for the keys on his belt and unlocks it, then draws her through, locking it behind them. He hurries her past the herb beds, her skirts bruising the mint and bergamot grown tall in the sun, her feet crushing the thyme sprouting on the brick paths. He leads her beyond the neat rows of peas and beans, onions and salsify, until they are out of sight of the house to the garden's edge where the grasses are long and the flowers wild. He stops by a stone wall and pulls her down to lie beside him. He kisses her face, and her neck, then reaches round and unbuttons her dress, peeling it from her shoulders, so that her bodice is exposed. He loosens it and cups her breasts.

She has wanted this, she cannot deny it, wanted his kisses, his mouth on hers but now she is uncertain, she had not expected it. She pulls away, sits up, pulling her dress around her. He sits back.

'I do not think...' she begins, but it is as if her voice loses intention.

He lowers her back down to the grass. She does not protest but reaches up for him. He lowers himself, laying his weight across her, pressing into her thigh. He reaches his hand up beneath her skirt and petticoats, whispering at her ear, 'Shush. Hush, now, there is nothing to worry, no one will know, we are hidden here.'

He parts her thighs and bloomers and finds the wetness there.

His touch is nothing like Everett's, it is as she touches herself. She is looking up, lost in the blue where a moon like a communion wafer prints itself on the sky. When his fingers move inside her she cannot help but cry out.

The Superintendent's Cottage

'All to the good. All to the good,' says Stafford with a smugness Blakely is beginning to find abhorrent. 'Thank God they're gone. I was afraid I was in for a night of it, but their train leaves at seven from Cambridge. We can breathe out now. Fortune favours the brave, Blakely. I am quite sure we will be left alone now to get on with our work.' He pours two large port wines and offers one. 'Anyway where the devil have you been? I expected you here for the Masters' report back. Had to make all kinds of excuses for you.'

'Sorry about that,' says Blakely, 'I got caught up with the Chaplain. It seems there are some concerns about the Baines girl, Dormitory Twelve. They've put her in the padded cell.'

'Good God,' says Stafford. 'Who? When? Who put her in the padded cell? Was that really necessary, especially with the Masters still about.'

'Late on, apparently, after the women's walk to the river, the Chief I believe, something about her being distressed, believes she must eat the sins of the Brewer woman. A danger to herself.'

Stafford sighs, 'Always something with these women. Did you know Semple handed them a life history of the girl? Scratched out in pencil. Said it was a copy. Has one in that damn book of hers. God preserve us. Anyway, as for Baines, if it was the Chief who put her in the strips, then I don't doubt it was necessary. As a matter of fact, I told them I thought that's where you'd be, with the Chaplain or some such, concern for the patients' welfare and all of that. Altogether they seemed happy enough. The report will be out in a month or so. Brewer's death will be deemed unavoidable. Privately, between you and me, they had their reservations about a certain attendant on duty that night, a Mrs Corey, and of course Matron's oversight. I've assured them I will discipline them both. Interview Corey, dock her wages, nothing more, attendants are hard to come by these days. A slight rebuke for Matron should suffice. Thank God, Powell was in charge, I can rely on him, we go back a long way, all the way back to Edinburgh in fact.'

Blakely nods in agreement. He is only half listening, for the greater part of him, mind and body is not in the room but outside, beyond the Asylum, lying in the long grass of the kitchen gardens with Simone Gastrell. Her smell lingers about him. He feels at once more alive than he can remember in a long time. He is itching with desire still. As ever he is conflicted. The seed kept buried in the ground, that he intended to remain dormant, has taken root. It has pushed up through the earth and blossomed.

He had wanted to possess her there and then. Though he'd restrained himself, he knew he'd gone too far. Tenderness, steadiness, proper composure, noblesse oblige, *the precise and acknowledged principles of urbanity and rectitude,* as cited in Percival's *Medical Ethics,* this was the conduct a man such as himself, a man assigned the care of others, must aspire to. His behaviour had fallen far short. If the Commissioners got word of it, he'd be finished. He'd wrestled with it all the way back, in the shade of the yew, her vulnerability, his advantage, their desire. For he was certain she felt as he did. Their connection went beyond that of friendship, beyond mutual respect. It was intuitive, physical and impossible to resist. For a moment they had lived in a small world composed entirely of themselves and nature, harmonious and at ease. He wonders if there is a future they might share. If he is in fact in love. Love, lust, togetherness. Even if it is not possible, surely he tells himself, it is better to let the flower of their desire bloom and die away.

'Are you listening man?' asks Stafford sharply.

'Yes, of course, I'm sorry, just a little distracted, it's been quite a day.'

'Indeed, but we've weathered the storm, if there ever was one. The committee seem satisfied the report will be favourable. I'm grateful to you, Blakely, you've played your part, and with that in mind I have a proposal to make. It concerns Edinburgh. As you know, I still have contacts there and it seems likely that a position will very soon become vacant for a Superintendent at Saint Martin's. Powell informed me. I have the papers, the details and such somewhere about.' He gestures at his desk piled high with paperwork. 'I'll ferret them out, get them to you. Anyway, short story is I've recommended you. I still have some influence and Powell is on the board. They want to meet you as soon as possible.

A trial of a week or two might be in order, get to know the place, let them get to know you, mutual satisfaction and all of that. What do you say, you won't get another opportunity like this falling in your lap any time soon? What do you say? Shall we drink to it? Here, top us up man, let's have a toast to the new Superintendent of Saint Martin's, drink up we've got a lot to celebrate. A good day all round I'd say, wouldn't you? Wouldn't you?'

Matron

A Village two miles from Long Meadow

He says he must speak with me. I am to come to his cottage in the grounds early evening when the patients are preparing for bed. He says we will take a glass of port wine together and in my foolishness, I believe it to be an invitation of the kind a suitor might make. I rise early to wash my hair in rosewater. I warm the water in pans on the range, and mother comes in sleepy-eyed and says, 'What's going on here? And at this time of the morning. It is barely past dawn.' But I know my hair will take its time to dry, being thick and unruly, though I have learned well how to tame it and pin it beneath my cap. 'Nothing,' I say, 'other than I have observed several of the women scratching at their heads and I am determined I will not be infected with the cause, or with whatever mites they harbour.' She is satisfied with my explanation and sets about brewing tea for us and griddling oat cakes for our breakfast which I do not eat due to a nervous excitement in my stomach.

I take my tea outside and watch the morning rise over the vegetable patch that mother tends. It sits across the path, having it's own small wicker gate, and rows of bean and pea sticks stripped from willow. The wind is warm. My hair dries. I hold my tea at arm's length, careful not to spill a drop that might prove impossible to remove and might stain the white starch of my apron. Though I will take a spare with me in case. I have already thought of this. I watch the sky, another foolishness of mine to cherish the hope that my darling bird will somehow reappear out of the blue, fluttering down to rest on my shoulder and whisper in my ear and peck at my chin, a hope that she will know by instinct this small terrace where I live, not so far beyond the grounds of Long Meadow.

This is how my day begins, and all day spent in anticipation, an unknown folly. I cannot help smiling, all through breakfast so that the women notice. Not much gets past their noses. And Anne Bickerdale says, 'Who put a smile on your face? A penny for them, Matron.'

'Cost you more than that, I'll warrant,' says Gladys Carter. 'It's a juicy one and no mistake.' They laugh. Even Dorcas Fisher laughs from behind her mask. I shake my head and smell rosewater. I laugh with them.

'Why, that's the first time I've seen you smile since that poor bird was let out,' says Anne.

I smile again. I cannot help but smiling at what is to come, at the prospect of what may bubble up between us like an underground spring finding the air.

The day is never ending due to the waiting. When at last it's time, and I arrive at his door, he is eager to greet me, laying his arm on mine, ushering me in and bidding me sit in one of the spoon back chairs either side of the fireplace. There is no fire, it being summer, though the parlour is cool and I am glad of it, else my cheeks would bloom redder even than they do now in the heat of anticipation. I take the wine he hands me, careful not to spill. He regales me with stories of the Masters' visit, of the success and how he is in the mood to celebrate, a weight lifted from his shoulders.

He is almost giddy with it. Yes, that is the word, giddy. He looks me up and down from head to foot, he lingers on my breasts and my ankles. It is not the first time he has looked at me thus. He is in the habit of seeking me out and standing closer than he should.

It is then, after his silent appraisal, that he comes out with it and it takes all my efforts not to tip my wine. It is not a declaration of affection or admiration as I had thought. No. It is nothing of the sort. It is, believe it if you will, for I find it hard to countenance, a reprimand. He prefaces it with a nervous clearing of the throat, says he is reluctant but there is something he must raise with me. It has to be done. It seems I took my eye off the ball, so to speak. I was negligent. I did not supervise as I should. I did not check or admonish. I allowed the night attendant to fall asleep on duty. He is disappointed but I have the opportunity now to put it right.

I am speechless. It seems I am held, in part, to blame for the death of Emma Brewer. That my record has been nothing but spotless, exemplary, is overlooked. It is almost as if he finds pleasure in marking me down in this way. Let it be a lesson he says, we are none of us without fault.

God help me. My glass tips. It takes all my will to steady my hand to fix my face in a rictus smile. And then it happens, I spill my wine, red drops splashing and spreading across my apron. He offers his handkerchief. I refuse. I cannot speak. I watch the wine soak into the cotton like blood seeping from a bandage.

He tells me my actions do not warrant dismissal.

Dismissal. If you will. 'Run this place without me,' I want to shout. 'It will go to hell in a handcart and in no time. Watch the standards slip, cleanliness, orderliness, organisation, at my fingertips, all of it.' But I am silent, looking down at my apron.

'A warning,' he says, 'written, according to the Masters' wishes,' going over to his desk and picking up an envelope. It's purpose, to remind me of my duties according to the Rules of Governance. 'That is all,' he says, handing me the envelope, written in his hand and addressed to me.

That is all.

That is all.

God save me.

How dare he.

I choke with rage and humiliation, though I will not cry. And will not give such satisfaction as to offer a reply.

'Finish your wine, my dear,' he says.

But I have had quite enough. 'Thank you but I must take my leave, there is work to be done,' I say as I get up from my chair and turn away.

I pull off my apron and walk quickly from his cottage. I do not make for the main entrance but instead take a side door near the Boiler Room and coal cellar. As I pass I cannot help but think of Phoebe Baines and what I have heard whispered about the cellar. It is no surprise to me that such deeds may take place in a world where women have little or no purchase, where we are at the mercy of puffed up, pigeon-chested men who have no regard for our work, our dedication, for what we do.

I hope to slip in unnoticed. One look at me and any fool will see my distress and might wonder if I have taken leave of my senses, grown momentarily mad as the women of Long Meadow. If I had a knife or a gun who knows what I might do, or where I might end. That he thinks so little of me that he allows it. He betrays me without a second thought. All his flirtations, his ogling, have been for the purpose of his own arousal and vanity and nothing more. I do not want him near me, the casual hand on my arm, my waist. I will not allow it. I cannot bear him to even look at me. No. It is the end. The end of it.

Only when I arrive home, back in the safety of our little terrace, with its chimneys smoking into the summer sky, water boiling in the pans for the men and women coming home from work, some already out on the stoop, in the gardens tying up beans, picking greens for the pot, only then in this humble world, this poor, safe place, with mother snoozing in her chair, am I able to stop, breathe, discard my spoiled apron and open the letter.

I gather from its contents that I am to admonish Mrs Corey. The women are to shoulder the blame. Those who work the hardest and longest are least valued. We are paid less, thought less of, where the men hold each other in the highest esteem. They may be ignorant, lazy, they may be out for their own advantage, but still their pathway to success is assured. They are a club. They pat each other on their backs, dine together, drink together, overlook the worst in each other, turn a blind eye to cruelties and abuse

I unpin my hair. The scent of rose water lingers in the air about me. I put my elbows on the table and my hands together in prayer, only I do not pray. Instead, I make a solemn promise before God, though I doubt he would wish to receive such a promise, but I make it nonetheless. I will have my revenge on Stafford, one way or another. I will have my revenge on all of them. They are all cut from the same soiled cloth. Not forgetting the Chief and what he did to me. No. I never forget that.

But all in good time. All in good time.

And in the meantime, I will smile as I go about my work. For I want none to suspect that a splinter of ice has lodged in my heart that will not melt.

Mrs Corey's Kitchen

Mrs Corey sits with her son, Michael at a small table where there is barely room for two, him having grown so tall his knees no longer fit under. The kitchen smells of fish. A frying pan of freshly trapped eel, dusted in flour and fried in butter sits between them on the table. Michael forks an eel from the pan to his plate, takes his knife to it, picks up a cut piece with his fingers and eats. His mother looks on. Her plate is empty.

'Tis slander,' she says, while he sucks the butter from his fingers. 'The bloody cheek of it. Docked me a fortnight's wages into the bargain. I ask you. Work my fingers to the bone and this is the respect I get. I could see she wasn't pleased mind, to be the one to have to tell me. I am sorry, I says, but it is all lies, Matron. I cannot accept it. I was never asleep. I might have closed my eyes for a moment no more. And bye the bye who says so? Who says I was asleep? Where's the proof? That's what I'd like to know. Matron just shook her head, mark my words, she was as unhappy as me, for I reckon she got a good telling off too, though being Stafford's favourite, perhaps he spared her. Excuse my French Matron, I says, but he is an arsehole that man. A pig in fine clothes. And the funny thing, she did not disagree, not one bit, didn't turn a hair. She got my meaning all right. If it weren't for my Michael, I says, and the paucity of eels in the river just now, I'd up and leave and I reckon there's one or two might follow. Oh, don't do that, she says. I wouldn't want to lose you Mrs Corey, you're one of my best. The women would miss you and that's a fact. Well, he hasn't heard the end of it, I says, and make no mistake. Wait til my Michael finds out.'

Michael looks up from his plate, with alarm, wipes his fingers on his breeches. Surely his mother doesn't expect him to do something, say something to this Stafford she likens to a pig. A man with clout and learning, he would warrant. 'Best left for now,' he says, 'no good going upsetting folks. Bide your time, mother. Tis good money not to be turned down lightly. Eat your supper.' He goes back to the eels.

Mrs Corey forks an eel onto her plate and leaves it there uncut. 'I'll swallow it alright, got no choice have I. Didn't even have the guts to tell me himself, sent her in his stead.'

Michael pushes his chair back from the table. The pan is empty, he picks it up and puts in the sink.

'Bloody pig, thinks he's God's gift and it's his kingdom. Some kingdom, rooms full of mad people, poor souls, come to think on it, half of them saner than he'll ever be. Thy will be done and all of that. Just you wait. They haven't heard the last of this.'

'No doubt,' says Michael.

'Why should we be blamed for the death of Emma Brewer, God rest her soul, and loose half our monthly living to boot? So she takes her life. I know tis a sin and all of that, but what life I ask, locked up day and night? Can't say as I blame her and that's a fact. But us poor attendants cannot win, anyway round, cannot do good for bad, right for wrong. No pleasing some people and there it is. Let that be the end of it.'

Upstairs

The Padded Cell

he says, here
come here and you may eat your sins
better still he says eat mine
salt on bread pain and penance
if a soul is to pass
salt on bread
they must hang the hives with black
knock with pole, the bees must know
it is not done instead i lie
in a hive of my own dirty and grey
no honeycomb light
but a window high square
day night and a peep hole
no sound but the pulling
hair from scalp
no sound but his filthy grunt
i am mink, teeth sharp points
minks bite dare i bite
when he stuffs it in my mouth
i would bite and none to hear the scream
no stranger here i count the stars
i can pass through walls
turn ceiling sky
hear the bees swarm in the oak

trees furrowed and sown
how i am to keep them in rain and wind
scarecrow
keep the crows come stealing corn
and not a bite to eat
hunger always hungry in the fields and cold
he keeps me here for his convenience
coal to rubber
here is white the cellar black
bring me salt and bread
and pole to knock the hives
sweet winds bear the first
and last of summer
pollen and rose petal softness of puddles
feet breath path criss-cross
i am leaf smooth side up
ribbed underskirt
i lie on a bed of thistles
in the purple shadow of blackberry
hush hark hush hark

a key turning in a lock
out says the chief, out says he, some sorry bastard wants
you free, besides I am made deputy now William Blakely
is off to Edinburgh, I have much to do, fun and games
my little one, thin as a needle skin and bone, new
treatments if I'm not mistaken and you among the first

dark when i climb into my bed
dormitory twelve
home
too late for Simone to brush my hair

189

Simone

She had hurried back from the garden through the dormitory to her room, noticed only by the women. A knowing look from Alice, a smile from Eveline Webb. Certain they knew, sure that the fire between her legs was written on her countenance, shame on her lips swollen with his kisses, her creased skirt, the hair escaped from her pins and her cap. They knew, she was sure of it, yet even so, she was sure they would say nothing, for beneath the ordered surface of lives run to the routine of bells lay the secrets the women shared. These were secrets never to be revealed, shoring up their determination as patient to outwit staff. Secrets that shrugged off their powerlessness, the way they were shaped to obey, the ways in which they were violated. The women of Long Meadow were armoured in their secrets.

Once in her room she had stripped to her chemise and hurried to the washroom. Alone there, she'd doused the heat on her neck and arms, all the while thinking of him, of what had passed between them, of what she was sure was forbidden. Forbidden, yet how her spirit had soared, how alive she'd been in that moment. The pleasure in his touch. His tenderness, his breath on her neck, the words whispered at her ear. For the first time since alighting from the carriage and entering Long Meadow, Simone has woken as if from a bleak and frightful dream. She has touched hope in the grass stain on her skirt that refuses to be washed away, heard it in his voice, the words that echo in her head. It is all feeling not thinking, bright like a small flame that will not be extinguished.

But it does not last. She expects him the very next day but he does not come, nor the day after, nor the day after that. Until a week has passed and another, and the flame grows ever weaker. Try as she might to remember everything, the smallest, most intimate detail, try as she might to conjure the evening, a summer mist, a low sun, the keys at his belt, the gate unlocked, the pale moon watching, it alludes her more with each passing day.

She sees him once in the vestibule deep in conversation with the Chaplain. She looks for a glance from him. He must have seen her there. Surely his eye will catch hers, but he is firmly fixed on the Chaplain, and he does not look at her once. Neither does he appear in the Dining Hall or the Dormitory, and she learns from Alice that he has left for Edinburgh where he is to take up a new position, and rumour has it the Chief is soon to be appointed in his place, until a new deputy arrives.

How could he lie with her, look so deeply in her eyes as he touched her and brought her to pleasure, how could he promise to help her, how could he do this and then leave without a word? How could he take her broken heart and break it once more? The questions abound. There are no answers.

Simone sleepwalks through her days, a new grief added to the weight of those that already haunt her. When the lamps are extinguished, she stands sentinel at her window, the night her familiar, its shadows as uncertain as her future. She listens for the hollow cry of the owl, flying out of Keeper's Wood, the yelp of the small creature captured in its talons. The slow heavy beat of the pumps, that repeat, he is gone, he is gone. By day, she sits with the silent woman. Her clothes grow looser still, the bread sticks in her throat. How to eat? How to swallow when her body is stuffed full of grief and measured in shame? What a fool she had been to believe him.

There are times, momentarily, when she thinks perhaps he might return. Perhaps he has already put her release in motion. She oscillates back and forth, thinking the best of him, then the worst, that he is like all the men she has known, selfish and weak. She spends her days longing for Maria to come with a letter from Clara. She prays sometimes three or four times a day. She would like to ask the Chaplain for absolution, but she dare not.

Alice brings her water steeped with lemon balm and rose, crushed hawthorn berries, their bitter taste matching her mood. Alice says they will bring ease, they will temper pain. Simone must mend herself, she says, they will all need their wits about them if the Chief is to become the new Deputy, especially Phoebe, though thanks be to God she is out of the padded cell where he did not keep her more than one night due to the Masters being about.

Phoebe spends her days with Simone. They sit together. Simone brushes Phoebe's hair and although they are mostly silent, she reads to her from time to time, taking consolation in their companionship and in Phoebe's growing need of her.

Long Meadow catches the mood. The women are subdued and watchful. Something has gone from this place, Simone thinks, and it is more than him. It is a spirit, a soul. The Chief has none. Matron is aloof, lost in her thoughts, only half-present, she does not inspect the rooms, the laundry, the kitchen, so say the women who work there. In the laundry, they talk of an apron stained with wine.

Mrs Corey is short-tempered and not inclined to help. The Chaplain spends a great deal of time in and about Dormitory Twelve, but he says little. Miss Vaisey from the Committee of Visitors has been taken ill and has not been seen since William Blakely's departure. Stafford and the Chief strut about the place and the rumours of a new treatment are rife. They say the women of Dormitory Twelve will be the first to receive it.

Alice Semple's Notebook

The Treatment

I am a toad in winter. My memory lies crouched beneath stone. Even Clare and our time together as distant as a half-remembered dream. Time has slipped from me and I have slept a great deal. I would begin with an inventory but my mind is not as ordered as it once was. Though I am determined to keep record for didn't Clare teach me the power of words. I write for myself and for the women of Dormitory Twelve who undergo the Treatment, so that what happens here cannot be denied. I will keep it simple and plain.

They have set aside a room especially for it. It is named it The Galvanic Treatment Room though we call it to Hanwell and back and no return, though Ivy Cole who was once in Hanwell swears that the Superintendent, Conolley, is a gentleman, whose boots Stafford is not fit to lick. The room has no window. It smells of vinegar. There are four chairs set out along the plaster wall and a chair in the centre, made from rough wood liable to splinter with leather straps on the arms. Beside the chair is a table on which sits a wooden box, Stafford's machine. The instrument of our torture. Tis where he stands when treatment commences. Inside the box, a mess of wires tangled like coiled snakes, and on the ends, the gubbins, whatever you call them, my memory fails me, these are the pads that they place on our skin and through which the shocks come. There are dials on the machine which Stafford fiddles with constantly. On the side of the box is written *Mayer and Meltzer*. The words etched in my mind despite my loss of memory, for I see them each time I am bid to sit in the chair, when it my turn to have my arms strapped down, to be wired up to the infernal machine.

Twenty minutes a day for ten or twelve days now or thereabouts. Each of us the same, Simone Gastrell, Phoebe Baines, Ivy Cole and me. We are the chosen from Dormitory Twelve, chosen to be the first. Such privilege bestowed on us. I know not why. They shave our heads in preparation. As if we have a fever of the brain and need cooling. As if we are adulteresses or harlots. They delight in it, Houndsworth hacking away with blunted scissors, Farrell with soap, blade and strap. We watch our hair fall at our feet, we watch each other's hair as it is shorn, for they have a fondness now of making us share in each other's humiliation. Of bearing witness to their new abominations. It is for the good of all that we should watch each other thus, so Stafford says.

We wear only a chemise and a thin shawl, our bodies exposed for all to see. Stafford allows the shawl for modesty, he says, though it barely covers our shoulders. Twice now, perhaps even more, visitors have come and watched the treatments, men from Cambridge, lining the back walls. They come with their notebooks and their pince-nez to record the experiment. We shuffle in barefoot, an exhibition of poor creatures, a zoo of shaven heads, like sheep in a pen waiting our turn. Little, lost baa lambs.

There are always others present, most often the Chief, Amos Farrell, who is now the Deputy, and a new attendant, her name escapes me but she is named for an animal, I will remember before long. To go back to the vinegar which never fails to catch in my throat and nose, it reminds me of the gypsies, the nights Clare and I sat with them by their fires, making merry and eating badger meat and hedgehog. T'was not the finest of meats I grant you but much improved by washing in vinegar. When I sit in the chair with the wires about me, I put my mind back to those evenings and the warmth of the fire and his body next to mine. Ah! I have remembered, her name is Fox, how could I forget? Fox by name, Fox by nature. She is sly enough, always whispering in corners with the Chief or Stafford himself. She barks and snaps at us like a vixen. She has red hair and a long snout.

One by one we take our turn. At the foot of the chair is a basin of water in which we must place our feet, tis where the smell of vinegar is strongest. We sit with arms bound by leather straps to the chair, our feet in the basin and the gubbins on a wire from the machine hanging in the water and another such stuck on our heads or spine. Electrodes, that is the name by which they are known.

Stafford does his speechifying. Every time for visitors. Telling of the machine's origins, the men of science who have thought fit to devise it. Something about trials and Long Meadow and the University. Then he addresses us, which I will try to render authentic, here, 'Just a little electricity, ladies,' he says, as if we are paraded before him in our finery, as if we are about to take afternoon tea in a fine hotel. 'The best remedy science has to offer. All the rage in the United States

196

of America, and catching on fast here at home, in the parlours of England. Mark my words, we may be the first at Long Meadow but there are others. It is becoming fashionable you might say. And we are at the forefront. The best way to rid you of your debilitating afflictions, your melancholia, your visions. A grand force, a natural restorative...' this is how he proceeds for the benefit of those who come to gawp. I have heard it many times now.

At first, when we were wired up and the machine switched on, it was but a ticklish and warming sensation that did not much bother my thick skin. But as the days passed, it became ever stronger. There is discomfort, pain, something intolerable, alive and crawling in our veins from head to foot. Twice now, Simone Gastrell, who takes it badly and suffers most, has cried out and taken a fit, bringing to mind Clare's afflictions, his blue devils, his fen fever. She slumps forward in the chair and would fall over were it not for the straps. They pull her head up, her face as white as snowfall on leaf, and bring a jug to pour water over her head. After she is revived, they bring tea, make her drink, then take her from the room. Both times this happened, I watched Stafford with his dials, turning them up and up, a madness, yes, a madness in his eyes. I cannot say if it is this obsession, or something other, but Stafford looks like a man who has slept in a farmer's barn among the livestock. And smells like one too. He has spots of wine on his cuffs and belly. His nose grows fatter and redder than ever it was. Tis a drunkard's nose and no mistake and the whiff of it often on his breath.

The treatments are written down in a book. I know not what detail is kept in it, bar the numbers, for Stafford calls out numbers as he fiddles with his dials and Fox writes them down.

Phoebe cries out the loudest. I survive it best. Simone the worst as it brings on her fits, whatever they be. Ivy Cole has not been present for the last two treatments as she is in the Infirmary. I know not why. Phoebe and Simone have open sores on their scalps, where the wires and the gubbins are fastened.

When Phoebe is in the chair, the Chief is in charge. The dials are his. 'Now my little one, my skin and bones, it is your turn for the fire,' he whispers, his eyes ripe with lust and power to rival even Stafford's. He is a monster and no mistake.

When I am able, God willing, I go out to the Airing Courts and gather what there is to make a decoction to protect us, sage, thyme, nettle, boxwood and lavender. If I am indisposed, the women help, bringing me what they can. I mix unguents for our scalps, but there is no salve for our souls. God save us.

Violence Towards Patients

54. Any Attendant or other Servant who shall see or be aware of any violence offered to a Patient, who shall not immediately or within six hours at the furthest report the same to the Resident Medical Officer and Superintendent, shall be dismissed, and every such report shall be included in the statements made by the Superintendent in his journal

Rules for the Government of the Pauper Lunatic Asylum situate at Long Meadow – prepared and submitted by the Committee of Visitors thereof, by virtue of the 53rd section of the 16th and 17th VIC. CHAP 97

Simone

The days merge one into another without distinction. It is as if Simone has flown from her body to inhabit another. Her world shrinks to that of the treatment room and her own, cell-like space, with little else between. Her jaw aches, she has pain in her arms and legs. Fatigue is her familiar, so that she hardly wants to get out of bed and when she does she is nauseous and cannot bear the smell of food. She thinks constantly of Everett forcing himself upon her, trapping her beneath his weight. The reek of his sour sweat and his grunting as he voided himself in her. The shame of it. She tries to divert her scattered thoughts, to dwell instead in happier times, in Paris with Clara. But her recollections fade. There are gaps in her memory that she cannot fill and they worsen with every treatment. Phoebe's head is a mess of sores and she suffers nightmares and crying fits. Alice does better but sleeps a great deal and lives as if behind glass. Ivy Cole is taken upstairs.

She fears it will kill them. They have no defence against the instrument of misery and persecution that is Stafford's machine. His rack, the cruciation, from which there is no relief. He is a mad man, and the Chief, not much better. The new attendant, Fox, appears to be without human sympathy. Their faces haunt her dreams and her waking, as does the room, its acid smell and the sound of Phoebe crying out. She cannot separate them, her thinking is confused, a fog has descended in her mind. The smell of hyacinth hangs about her and more and more the threat of darkness closes in.

The room is warm, the air close. It is not her room. It is padded all around, the only furniture a mattress on the floor on which she lies. It is partially lit from high up, a kind of aperture you might call a window, glazed and patterned with fallen leaves. Outside the muffled sounds of feet and then the bell, for what she is not sure, for in the darkness that overcame her she had lost all sense of time. Then the calling, 'All ladies in, all Ladies in.'

Her head aches. Her fingers explore a sticky patch in a tuft of newly sprouting hair. It is moist with blood. A key turns in the lock and two attendants enter. One of them she recognises as Fox, tall with flame red hair. She is newly appointed at Long Meadow, a friend of the Chief's, known for her cruelties. In her arms she carries a garment of ticking and leather straps. The other attendant, unknown to Simone, holds a cup. Fox orders Simone to get up and undress. When she is naked, they force her back down onto the mattress and into the canvas gown, lacing it tightly with her arms crossed about her, and fastening its leather straps.

'Hold her down, Fanny.'

Fanny passes the cup to Fox and kneels down over Simone's chest. Her thin, bony knees press into Simone's diaphragm. It is hard to breathe. Fox prises open her mouth and pours liquid from the cup down her throat. She cannot swallow, she is choking, the bitter taste of chloral bubbles up, flooding her mouth. Fox puts her hand around Simone's neck and works at her throat, forcing the liquid down.

'It is just as well her head is shaved,' says Fox. 'Fetch the plasters.'

They lay mustard plasters on the wound on her head and the soles of her feet. She cannot move, bound in canvas, arms held fast, legs strapped together. Like a mummy in a tomb. She convulses inside the straitjacket. A trembling from head to foot that she cannot stop, overtakes her. Pain, sharp, burning, as if her feet and her head have been held to the fire. Her body is alive with the pain, she longs to move, to curl like a foetus in the womb, to hold herself, but she is trussed like meat for the oven. The weight of the world is on her head and she wishes to die. She prays for it. Please God to take her, to join her Mama and Papa.

The chloral draught begins to take effect. It weights and quietens the trembling in her limbs. Her mind begins to wander, the mirrors of the lark-glass shine and flutter about her, the room is filled with the high, thin song of the larks. As she falls in and out of sleep, they come to her, in procession, her Mama and Papa rising up from the deep ocean, her sister Clara, her lost baby, the child, Constance. She smells the salty sea, her baby's skin, the river weed, otto of rose, and candle smoke. Then he comes with sandalwood and wine on his breath, William Blakely, and he settles his lips on hers.

When she wakes, she has no sense of time lost, of how long. The Chief is beside the mattress and Fox is standing next to him. He peers down at her and tells her that according to Stafford, she has had a severe attack which has nothing to do with the treatment or the cold bath. Forget the bathroom. The cold bath. They loosen the straps and remove the straitjacket. They help her up and into her clothes. Forget the cold, they say again. 'Forget the jug. No harm done.'

'Forget the cold, forget the jug.' It comes to her uncalled. As the words slide from their lips, she remembers. For once her memory does not fail her. She knows why she has woken in the padded cell.

Phoebe had refused the treatment. She could not bear to have the electrodes placed yet again on her shaven scalp. She said her head was full of bees and she held tight to Simone's hand. Houndsworth and Fox dragged Phoebe from Simone, holding her by her small, thin arms. Stafford ordered that she be taken from the room.

'May as well take the others with you while you're at it,' Stafford added in pique, slamming down the lid of the box. 'Out you go, the lot of you.'

The women followed Houndsworth and Fox, Phoebe's body slumped between them, her feet dragging the floor, to the bathroom. The Chief followed.

The bathroom was divided into three cubicles, each with a bath and a sink, all tiled in white and black. Fox and Houndsworth began to undress Phoebe while the Chief turned on the cold tap and filled the bath. The women stood by, Simone, Alice, and Ivy, huddled into the curtain that separated one cubicle from another.

When the bath was full, Houndsworth lowered Phoebe into the cold water, pulling her backwards by her shoulders so that her head was submerged. The Chief looked on, a faint smile spreading across his face. Ivy Cole cried out. Alice turned away. Simone stood fast. The memory of Constance, disappeared beneath the surface of the river flashed before her and she knew she must stand fast. Above all, she must remember and bear witness.

Houndsworth pulled Phoebe up, spluttering and coughing, fighting for air. Then before she could catch a breath, Fox poured a jug of water over her head and she was forced back down. Each time they dragged her up, a jug was emptied over her shaven head. Each time, Houndsworth looked to the Chief who nodded and mouthed, 'again.'

Then Fox filled the jug at the sink and held it out to Simone. 'It is your turn to pour,' she said.

'I will not,' said Simone, stepping back, hardly knowing from where her defiance came. 'It is cruel beyond belief.'

'I said it's your turn,' said Fox continuing to hold out the jug to Simone.

Simone refused again. 'No. I will not,' she said.

Fox, red-faced and fists clenched, looked to the Chief. He shouted at Houndsworth to pull Phoebe up from the water. As he did so, as Phoebe's head came up, Fox dashed the jug against it, cutting open her scalp. The water in the bath ran red with blood.

'For pity's sake,' pleaded Simone, 'I beg you. You will kill her. For God's sake, please stop!'

Fox turned then and lashed out at Simone.

The crack of porcelain against her scalp and then a stab of pain, blood running down her face. The blinds pulled down on her vision. She was sightless and falling. The words, 'padded cell,' echoed about her.

July

The Chaplain

Daniel Hawkins is grateful for the month of July which has so far been warm and dry so that the dampness that creeps slowly up the Chapel walls makes no progress. He leaves the Chapel door open to let the drying breeze and the scent of fresh mown grass drift down into the nave and across the aisles. Sunlight shines through the glass windows, through the bodies of the evangelists, staining the stone floor in fading yellow, indigo, crimson. He busies himself with the tidying of hymn books and prayer cards which he knows is an unnecessary task but provides a distraction. When he can distract himself no longer, he heads to the vestry, a panelled room not much bigger than a large cupboard where there is room enough for a small table and chair. He closes and locks the door behind him. He needs time to think. He does not want to be disturbed. He sits down at the table and rests his elbow on the chenille cloth. He opens his Bible at Ecclesiastes 8:7. and reads, Even still, in the end we must keep our eyes and ears open to God and trust His wisdom over all else! Since no one knows the future...

Next to his Bible sits a plate of cold meat and bread fetched from the kitchen, and a pot of beer. About him, hanging from hooks on the walls are his vestments, the surplice and the cassock he wears about his daily work in the institution, the stoles, and a chasuble he has never used. He is not one for dressing up. He closes the Bible and puts his head in his hands. He has much to ponder, and his head hurts with the weight of it.

He had no knowledge of the two newly appointed visitors from the House Committee, the Hon. Peter Ramshaw, town councillor, and Eunice Nightingale who had replaced Miss Vaisey. He had not expected to meet with them, but they had sought him out and come upon him in the kitchen, carving a slice of pork.

'Ah, Mr Hawkins, Chaplain, just the man we've been looking for. Might we have a word?' said Ramshaw, introducing himself and Miss Nightingale. Then adding, 'In private that is.'

'Certainly. Certainly, perhaps the Chapel? I was on my way there with my luncheon, rather late I'm afraid. We will not be disturbed there, if you'd like to follow me.'

Hawkins put his lunch in the vestry and came back to his visitors who sat in a pew near the front.

'Now, how can I help?' said Hawkins.

'It is a matter, I fear, of some delicacy,' said Ramshaw, throwing Eunice Nightingale a worried look, 'we have some concerns as to what we find and hear as we go about the place on our rounds and though we have asked for a meeting with the Superintendent or at the least with his Chief Mr Farrell, who I believe is now acting as his Deputy, to air such concerns, so far we have not been granted an audience.'

'I see,' said Hawkins.

'I assure you they are not of a minor nature, not small matters at all. To the contrary, we consider them quite serious, don't we Eunice, and we are intending to raise them with the Chair of the Committee, unless we have some answers, unless you, Chaplain, or someone else, can put our minds at rest?'

Eunice nodded in agreement.

'I'm listening,' said Hawkins. Sometimes he thought listening was all he ever did. 'Please, go ahead, continue.'

'Well, there are a number of matters but most urgent are those relating to the women in Dormitory Twelve. You know of them?'

'I do,' said Hawkins.

'Well now, what I'd like to know,' said Eunice Nightingale, butting in and sitting up very straight, despite the ache in her back, not helped by the wooden pew, 'is how long it has been the accepted practice to shave the women's heads. Caps can only disguise so much you know. Frankly I am aghast at what I see. It is a barbaric practice, an echo of the very worst of the Workhouse and I was led to believe that an asylum such as Long Meadow had an express purpose in providing good and moral living, quite the opposite from the Workhouse, wouldn't you say?' Then before Hawkins can reply, 'I asked Matron, do they have lice these women, is there an infestation? But I was assured not. Absolutely not, not on her watch, it would not be tolerated. Matron said any infestation would be stamped out immediately with baths and powder and combs. Quite right, I said, after which Matron led me to understand it is the new treatment that requires it, the galvanic treatment I believe she called it, electricity being involved. What kind of treatment is that, I said, that requires such harsh measures? People use these new electrical gadgets in their parlours and they do not shave their heads. I have to tell you, Mr Hawkins, that I got the very distinct impression that Matron did not approve

208

of it either. She told me the women were falling ill as a result of the daily doses that were administered. Ivy Cole is a case in point, in the Infirmary I believe. We will be visiting her shortly. So you see, we have concerns and the treatment is not the only one.' She looks to Ramshaw and cues him back in.

'Quite. We have been talking with the patient, Alice Semple, who alleges a very serious matter involving an assault on two patients by an attendant named, wait I have written it down.' He takes out a pocket notebook and pencil, and thumbs through. 'Yes, here it is, Fox is the name, and the patients are Gastrell and Baines.'

Hawkins nods.

'You know something of this?' asks Ramshaw

'I know the patients you name, but I assure you I know nothing of an assault.'

'Well, I must warn you we intend to investigate further. It is all most disturbing, most disturbing, and very difficult to match with the recent report from the Masters of Lunacy which was shared with the Committee. It might be describing an entirely different place, if you get my meaning. I sense an air of despondency about the place. I see no reference to activities, walks out, dancing, the summer fete. I was told there was a summer fete every year.'

'So, Chaplain, can you throw any light on any of these matters?' asks Eunice Nightingale. 'And if not, then we suggest you make representation to the Superintendent so they can be properly assessed before we present our concerns to the Committee. You are after all God's representative here, surely a man of God such as yourself wields considerable influence.'

'Not as much as you might think, Miss Nightingale, not

at all, but it would be disingenuous of me not to confide that I too share your anxieties. Leave it with me for the time being, will you? We can speak again in a day or two.'

On reflection in the quiet of the vestry, having eaten his lunch, Daniel Hawkins considered it could have been worse. They could have come to him with the rumours about the Chief and the Baines girl. Rumours he continues to investigate without turning up proof enough to make a charge, though he thinks it likely to be true.

He understands their concerns. He shares them. He is far from happy. It seems to him that in a matter of weeks, the place has gone from bad to worse, and now he is without his ally, William Blakely, who at least appeared to share similar standards as his, a certain unwritten code of conduct one might say. A basic respect for one's fellow man. And in this case, woman. Whatever Blakely was, and there were rumours about him and Mrs Gastrell and the flattened grass by the wall in the kitchen gardens, Hawkins considered him a decent sort. You could not believe everything you heard in the corridors and the dormitories, though Mrs Gastrell had been at pains to seek absolution of late and had asked him to pray with her on more than one occasion. At heart, he was sure she was a good woman and he had been as appalled as Eunice Nightingale to find her head shaven. Hadn't he been opposed to the treatment from the beginning. A pity Blakely wasn't coming back but the word was he was finished with Long Meadow and was to take up a new position in Edinburgh immediately.

It was time to stop praying for guidance and take a lead. God had put him here for a purpose. From the beginning, he had seen himself as a champion of the women. After all, it was the women who came to the Chapel more than the men. It was the women who picked flowers for the sills and the altar, who swept the floors and polished the wood.

The assault was alarming news and before he meets with Stafford and confronts him, he needs to know exactly what happened and who was responsible. Assaults on women such as Gastrell and Baines were unforgiveable. These women were life's victims and as such, deserving of care and sympathy. Long Meadow could learn something from the way Gastrell cared for the girl with such tenderness, as if she were her child.

There are those who said that God forgot the women of Long Meadow, that he was gone from the place. But Daniel Hawkins saw God in Long Meadow clear as the light of day. God was here for all to see, residing in the care and the loving kindnesses the women showed one to another.

Simone

Simone looks at her reflection in the washroom mirror, her face unrecognisable, the sunken cheeks, her features grown large and bony, lips swollen. Who is she? She takes her cap off but can hardly bear to look at her head, shorn of hair, with its wound and sores. She is the feral cat, half-starved and homeless, its skin broken, its fur moth-eaten and tattered. A cat with only itself to rely on. She sees that now. As she looks in the mirror, it comes to her, she sees her mistake in believing others might care for her. Might protect her. Such care is to be had only from the women around her, who share in her predicament and who have no power other than a small gesture or a kind word.

What choice then but to be the cat, wild and watchful, a huntress who must sharpen her instincts for survival. She must be at one with the elements that Long Meadow's walls cannot confine, as stealthy as the draught at the window, as cold and unrelenting as a wind from the east. She will be as the small creatures that slip in and out unobserved, the fly, the bee, an echo of the never ceasing, determined thud of the pumps. She will be as smoke and fire, as things without shape or form, that live in the mind and in the soul and reach out far beyond hedge and stone.

She stares hard in the mirror, breathing this new, feral, self into life. She whispers to it, 'You must prevail, Simone. One day you will leave Long Meadow, and this will all be in the past. Until then, you must watch and prevail.

When the time comes, you must seize your chance, however small.'

When Houndsworth and the Chief come for Simone in the Dining Hall, at breakfast, to take her to the Treatment Room, she refuses. Though she shakes inwardly and her heart races, she is determined she will not go. She is unwell, she says, and she demands to see her doctor, for she is sure even Eames who put here would not approve of such treatment.

Phoebe and Alice are next. Alice says she has brought the matter to the attention of new visitors from the House Committee, in particular a Miss Eunice Nightingale, and Miss Nightingale has promised to take it up with the Superintendent. Such refusals come with great risk, not least the risk of being hauled upstairs and thrown in the padded cell. The blood rises to Simone's cheeks, her palms sweat with fear, but in her heart there is a newfound certainty. She looks down and attends to the black bread on her plate. Phoebe and Alice do likewise. The women hold their breath as one.

Matron comes over, their ears prick up as she stands next to Houndsworth and the Chief, and announces with a distinct note of disdain, 'Enough. I will not have my patients used day after day, Mr. Farrell, for the purpose of this experimentation. Are you blind? They are not fit for more of this galvanic nonsense. It will kill them, and I believe my brother, Doctor Eames, would concur with such observation. They will not be attending treatment today. They will instead be out in the Courts taking the air and if Mr. Stafford disagrees, he can speak with me on the matter. Thank you. Your presence is no longer required in my Dining Hall. Now please let us be to get on with our breakfasts in peace.' With that she sends an attendant to the kitchen to fetch honey for the bread and slices of cheese. Houndsworth and the Chief slink away.

The women in the Dining Hall break into a spontaneous round of applause. Matron cannot help but smile, though she turns away to attend to plates for the cheese. Esther Knox and Gladys Carter bang their cutlery on the table and the others join them in what becomes a thunderous crescendo. Matron tells them to shush, but all the while she is grinning from ear to ear. And so are they, each sharing in the victory, the audacity, and the provocation bringing with it untold joy and cause for celebration.

In this moment, Simone knows she truly belongs. She is a part of this community of women and the community of all women: women incarcerated, women who are free, women who cry and grieve, who celebrate small mercies and victories, who laugh too loud, who suffer at the hands of men. Women who gossip with friends, arms entwined, whose lips loosen in wine, who sing to their child in its crib, who know kindness and joy despite ill-use. Women who pray and whose prayers are sometimes heard.

They eat their cheese and their honey and clear away their plates and cups. They leave the Dining Hall in a happy procession, making for the vestibule and the door to the Airing Courts.

For the first time in what feels like a lifetime, Simone steps out into the morning, stopping in the parterre to look up into the sky and give thanks. She breathes in the scent of heliotrope that perfumes the air, walks down through the rose beds, to the borders where bees are busy among the snapdragons, to the lower terrace where the fruit ripens on the apple tree, finally coming to rest on the corner bench. She sits here, shielded by the dark yew, in the place where he had come for her. She breathes out and her breath tunes to the slow heartbeat of the pumps.

She is relieved at the temporary cessation of the treatment, proud of her refusal and thankful for Matron speaking out, but her thoughts are jumbled and restless and she cannot still her mind. The effects of the treatment render her such. So that she drifts in and out of Long Meadow, floating through a fragmented world. One moment she is back in her Aunt's house, with Clara playing shipwrecks in the nursery, the next she is in the water meadows with Constance who clutches her Dutch doll for fear of losing it. Then she is with her child, stillborn, a moment so far beyond grief, she is outside of herself. She is sky, wind, breath, the lark glass. At sea in a ship going down. It is dusk, here in the gardens, her hand is in his. He leads her to the long grass, seeds catch in her skirts, and in her hair, for she had hair then. It is as if her memory is dreaming, refusing her the comfort of order. It has become an ever-changing shoreline she cannot mark, in and out, the ceaseless ebb and flow of a tide.

Before long, Phoebe joins her, reaching out for Simone's hand, grounding her in the present. Then Alice appears, notebook under her arm. They sit together. They smile but do not speak. Each as lost in thought as the other.

Phoebe

on the bench by the yew
her hand warm
holding mine no hair to brush to calm
gone
taken shaven sold says Alice
taken shaven sold
scissors leather strap carbolic soap
the bees gone no sign of them
death moth on the sill, my head open
blood in my mouth
on my tongue i cry out i cry but they do not stop
i will die by water
choke
pour over my head over my head
gasping for breath the day gone black
rag in my mouth
pain at my chest i might burst
suffocate like his hands at my throat
which he is fond of
the jug
the water
stop it must stop
she is shouting i will not, i will not
god bless Simone she my saviour
she will not obey
she will knock on the hives

tell the bees and scarecrows
how our bodies are shaken
how their marks live in our skin
burns bruises sores burns bruises sores
damaged wings rest in a cobweb morning
sparkling in our yew nest
here together heal

Alice Semple's Notebook

In a clover field, in the graveyard, beneath the oak, on a mother's bed unknown, embankment, dyke, ditch, hidden only to the skies, to finches and larks, hide away, do not tell, eat the apple, your lips redden, his breath spilling on your neck. I am everywhere we were together. I am here. I am past and present. I do not think of the future only as release. I barely breathe. My mind moves too fast, galloping, mysterious, but here, on the bench in the shadow of the yew, with the two beside me, it begins to still. To settle. I remember where I am.

I know what they have done to me, to us, and what they may still do, for I am threatened but an hour ago. On my way out here to join my companions, he caught me, Stafford, with his wine breath and his wicked nose. Said there were rumours that I was the cause of trouble again, that I had been a perpetual thorn in his side, that if I did not cease, if I did not refrain from talking with the visitors of the House Committee, he would see to it that I was removed from Long Meadow and sent elsewhere, perhaps as far north as Edinburgh. And when I laughed and said, 'What have I to fear, where I am makes no difference to me, for I am always with Clare.' He said he did not believe that I had ever known John Clare, let alone been his love. He said it was a figment of my diseased imagination, old hag I was, that no man could ever have desired me. It is water off my back, running down into the stream. The storm in which I was born. I will do what is necessary. And I will not stop until they listen.

The Superintendent's Office

'Come in Chaplin, come in, man. To what do I owe the honour? Mind you, it will have to be quick,' says Stafford sitting behind a desk piled high with papers. 'I have a report waiting here somewhere, well more than one to be precise, so to the point if you will.'

'I'm afraid it is a rather delicate matter,' says Hawkins. 'Might I sit down?'

'If you must,' mutters Stafford under his breath.

'I have some concerns, you see, and I suspect there may be trouble afoot from the Committee no less.'

'Trouble? I find that hard to believe, Chaplain. We've just had an exemplary report from the Masters. Have you not had sight of a copy? I have one here, somewhere,' he says, moving the papers around on his desk.

'I have seen it, Superintendent. Yes, I am aware,' says Hawkins, hovering about the chair on the other side of Stafford's desk, still uncertain as to whether to stand or sit. 'Nevertheless, these are important concerns.'

'Well, you better sit down then,' says Stafford, waving at the chair, 'but make it quick.'

Hawkins perches on the edge of the chair. 'I had a visit yesterday from a Mr. Ramshaw and a Miss Nightingale both newly appointed to…'

'Yes, yes, I know all about them, from Farrell you see, he has an ear to the ground, nothing gets past him.'

'I see. Then you will be aware from Farrell that they are

unhappy about the new electrical therapies, the new, treatments.' Hawkins swallows hard, then takes a deep breath. It's not easy facing Stafford across a desk like this. There is something about the man that he cannot help but find intimidating. For one thing, he reminds him of his father when he was displeased, which was often. He takes strength from God and knowing it is his duty, he ploughs on, 'I am afraid to say that I too share their concerns. I have had reason to converse with the women in the trial though Mrs Ivy Cole is now, as I'm sure you know, in the Infirmary. In my opinion, they are not well served by this practice, and as for the shaving of heads, Superintendent, these are not novices, not witches or women of ill-repute, we do not live in the Middle Ages.' There he's said it. He settles into himself. He does not take his eyes off Stafford.

Stafford coughs, clears his throat, 'I grant you the removal of the hair was perhaps a little extreme, yes, but initially a matter of safety to prevent the possibility of burns. As for your other opinions, Hawkins, and as for the opinions of Mr Ramshaw and Miss Nightingale, they are of little or no interest to me. To be frank, this is not your domain. Your domain is God and the soul, mine the body and the mind. You would do well to remember that. We are engaged in serious scientific work here which may change the course of medicine. I am not alone in my belief that galvanic therapy is the way forward. I grant you we have yet to refine the details of the application. These matters take time and patience, but I guarantee in the future you too will be convinced of its efficacy.'

'It is not me you need to worry about Superintendent,' says Hawkins. 'It is my understanding that if the treatments do not stop forthwith, the visitors will raise it as a matter of urgency and who knows where that may lead. Added to which, Mrs Cole appears to me, having seen her just this morning, to be gravely ill. Our reputation, your reputation, can surely not afford another death so soon after Emma Brewer's.' Emboldened now, he continues. 'We have a duty of care. We have a duty of care to these unfortunate women, and in my opinion, we are falling far short.'

'For pity's sake, man, it is nothing but a storm in a teacup,' says Stafford, 'and the better part of it having been stirred up by that wizened old hag, Semple. I have warned her I will move her out. It is well within my power. She is nothing but trouble.'

'But there is more, an alleged assault, I believe, but then you will know all about that too, from Farrell? I trust you will think about what I've said,' says Hawkins. He watches Stafford closely for a flicker of recognition. Stafford's mouth is hard set, his lips tight. 'Also, if I might, while I am here, and on another matter entirely, I trust I have your permission to go ahead and organise a summer fete. I believe it will provide an antidote to some of the more recent unfortunate events. The calendar would not be complete without Long Meadow's summer fete. It is eagerly anticipated by the communities round about.'

'I have no interest in fetes, Chaplain. However, if you wish to organise such an event, I suppose I have no objection.'

Hawkins nods and gets up from his chair. There is a knock at the door. It opens slowly. Stafford turns around, 'Why here he is. Come in. Come in, Blakely. Good to see you,' says Stafford. 'Good to have you back, man. That will be all, thank you, Chaplain. We have a great deal of business to attend to.'

Simone

It is late in the afternoon and Simone is alone on her corner bench. Phoebe and Alice have gone, soon the bell will ring, and they will shout, 'All ladies in, all ladies in.' Until then, she sits and listens for the birds, catching the sweet, sonant piping of the blackbird in the lilac. Below her, in the kitchen gardens, she hears the rasp of saw on wood, the men cutting logs and when the sawing stops, their voices mingle with the hum of foraging bees returning to the hive. She does not want to go in. She wants a moment more to celebrate the reprieve, however brief it may be. For she is no fool, she knows their refusal will count for nothing should Stafford be determined. She knows now, too well, the confinement of the straitjacket, the way a woman might be rendered helpless, unable to move. She closes her eyes and lets the sun, still warm, fall on her face. She takes off her cap and lets its healing power anoint her scalp. She drinks in the air, the rich scent of summer.

The bell rings and the voice calls them in.

She opens her eyes and puts her cap back on her head. It is time to go. She glances up, towards the parterre and sees him. He is on the path through the yew, coming just as he had before, that evening. She shakes her head, her eyes are playing tricks, her memory is befuddled. It is a mirage such as is seen in the desert by those who thirst. She closes her eyes again and entreats God to save her from such cruelties. She opens them but he still there. He keeps coming. Before long he stands in front of her, solid, immutable.

'I saw you from my window,' he says.

'I was listening for the birds, for the blackbird in the lilac. But it is gone,' she says.

'The birds are all around us, look,' he says putting a hand up into the air.

They look together at the swifts flitting in and out of the eaves

'You left and I am a like a bird flown into glass.'

'But I am returned,' he says, 'for a brief while at least. A bird can mend its beak and wing.' He sits down beside her.

'Not if she is shorn of her feathers,' she says, taking off her cap.

He gasps.

'Not so pretty now,' she says.

He lifts a hand to her head but then pulls it back. He must not make the same mistake again. He has forbidden himself to touch her. But what have they done to her? Damn them, damn them to hell and back. He is glad to soon be out of it.

He gestures to her hand in her lap, 'May I?' he asks, attempting, despite everything he has promised himself, to take it in his.

She feels the fluttering of desire in her chest. She swallows it down. To prevent heartbreak, one must swallow and disappear. That is how it is in Long Meadow. She shakes her head. She will not let him take her hand. She puts her cap back on. She must defend herself. Prevail Simone, the face in the mirror. Prevail. She does not know him. She cannot know such a man, a man who can lead her into the long grass and then abandon her.

'I am going away,' he says, 'taking up a position in Edinburgh. It is decided. Perhaps in time you might be transferred there. It is not beyond the bounds of possibility.'

'I am not leaving. I will not leave Phoebe,' she says.

'Phoebe? The girl who does not eat, whose hair is falling out?'

'Yes, though she eats a little better now, when I persuade her. And as you see all our hair has fallen out. I shall not leave until I can take her with me.' The words come from somewhere deep inside. She had not known or expected them and yet she recognises the truth. Their fates are bound now. Hers and Phoebe's. She will not abandon her.

'I have something for you,' he says taking a piece of folded paper from his trouser pocket. 'I believe this is where your sister's husband is to be stationed, their address in India. I have a friend who helped me procure it.' He offers it to her.

She opens it, reads the address, then folds it again and puts it in the pocket of her dress. 'Thank you,' she says.

'Remember, it is within their power to censor your letters, to deem them unfit. In which case, they may never be sent but lie on a desk until they are buried under a sheaf of papers. Remember also, it is in the Superintendent's interest to keep you here. Your husband pays good money and is a man with influence. Stafford will not want you released.'

She nods.

'God go with you, Simone,' he says.

She says nothing.

He rises and takes his leave.

She watches him go, his coat fading into foliage, his body subsumed in yew. No doubt the treatments have rendered her numb, but she feels little other than a faltering sadness. And as he disappears from view, the notion occurs that though he may be weak and selfish, he is not all bad.

The men are coming in now through the kitchen gate, their day's work done. The voice calls again, 'All ladies in, all ladies in.'

It is time to go.

The Superintendent's Cottage

'What a day. Fox will have to go,' says Stafford to Farrell
as he lowers himself into an armchair, 'after what's happened
we cannot afford to keep her. The Committee won't sanction
it, they'll want an investigation and that is something to be
avoided at all costs. I know she's a friend of yours, and I
have no doubt she is a good attendant, apart from this
inclination to, shall we say, the more violent methods of
control? A jug to a patient's head, for God's sake, man, what
was she thinking of? What were you thinking? No, it's
brought things to a head, pardon my pun. We cannot ignore
it. This new woman, Nightingale, she's all over it. You've
met her, I presume? What's she like, ugly spinster I would
warrant?'

'I have met her. Yes, Sir,' says Farrell who remains standing.

'Well, she's out for blood and I won't let her have it. I'll
outwit her. Old biddies poking their noses in what doesn't
concern them. I'll call her bluff. First things first, I want Fox
out, and before the next Committee meeting, that'll take the
wind out of Nightingale's sails. I know someone at Marsden
who might have a position for an attendant. Send Fox to
me and I will give her the details and a letter of
recommendation. Now, as for the treatments, Farrell, we are
changing tack, yes indeed. These women are nothing but
trouble. Like the majority of their sex, they are not capable
of rational thought. They belong in the separate sphere, in
the domestic, and yet unnaturally, they have turned their

backs on it. Turned their back on a proper life. They are incapable of fulfilling their destiny. How on earth we are expected to manage them, I don't know. They are not women as women should be, in my eyes. But the men, Farrell, the men are more compliant, it's as simple as that. I don't know why I didn't think of it before. We'll offer them an incentive, to take part in these groundbreaking electrical trials, a small increase in wages or in the tobacco allowance.'

'A gate pass, perhaps?' says Farrell.

'I think not, no,' says Stafford. 'At least not while they're undergoing treatment. Afterwards, perhaps. We'll see. I guarantee we'll have a waiting list. A waiting list, think of it, man. No recalcitrant, obstinate women. Hello to the obliging man. The men are always more obliging, don't you think, in comparison to the women? Prone to fighting amongst themselves I'll admit, but what's a little fisticuffs when all's said and done. They do not gossip and they do not rebel like the women. The more I think of it, the better I like it, Farrell, and now Blakely is gone and you're the Deputy, it falls to you to draw up a list of the willing. You must speak with the men, get them on side, hint at the incentives. Then once the list is drawn up, I will take account of the histories and the suitability. I'll say it again, Farrell, I don't know why I didn't think of it before. It's better by half, it will get these women out of our hair. They're fit for tupping and little else. Did you see the size of Ivy Cole's nipples through her chemise, like saucers. Remarkable. How is she by the way? I find I've so little time these days to devote to my rounds. I rely on you, Farrell. Don't let me down.'

'I won't, Sir.'

'Good man. So, you've met this Nightingale woman, you say.'

'I have, Sir.'

'And?'

'Some would say ugly, Sir, as you suspect, though she has a comely waist and a plump arse. A bit old for my tastes.'

'Hmm. That reminds me, Matron does not seem herself these days, do you think? A little quiet, a little standoffish I'd say, definitely not her usual accommodating self. What think you?'

'I don't know, Sir, hard to say. She seems all right to me but perhaps a little quiet, like you say.'

'These women are a bloody mystery, likes leeches at our blood. But I have a further plan to alleviate this blood sucking which involves getting rid of the fattest and worst of these parasites. I'm thinking of Semple for one. I've already spoken with Dryden, over in Yarmouth, says he'll take her in exchange for one of his lunatics, a troublesome woman no doubt, but you will cure her of that. She cannot be as bad as Semple, and it will be all to the good to be rid of her and her jottings. Cole too, before she kicks the bucket, though that might prove more difficult. No one's going to want a half-dead, deranged woman on their hands. We need to see some improvement there. Is she eating? Get her fed to the gunnels, man, fatten her up. We might stand a chance if she looks half decent. Weed the worst out, a rout is what we need. A change of scenery will do some of these women good. They have been here too long. And we have been too tolerant. I have been drawing up a list. I am minded to include the Baines girl, for I hear there is some improvement in her condition.'

'Oh, I wouldn't say so, Sir. She's best left where she is. Where I can keep my eyes on her. She's very unstable still and prone to the wildest of fantasies.'

'As you wish, Farrell. But a good clear out is what's in order. Bear it in mind. As for the rest of the women and that dormitory in particular, make it known we weren't happy with Fox, that we won't have our women ill-used, that's the tack, we're on their side when it comes down to it. About time they started to show some gratitude. As for Miss Nightingale. I have a plan, a charm offensive you might call it. Leave the woman to me.'

Farrell is right, thinks Stafford, as he shows Eunice Nightingale to the chair opposite his, so that they sit facing each other either side of his parlour fireplace. She's chicken-chested but she has a plump arse all right and he is not averse to pointing at the back avenue.

He has offered her a glass of wine but she has refused. He pours one for himself and puts the bottle on a small, leather-topped console next to his chair.

'Well now, this is nice,' he says. 'I'm so pleased you have taken up my invitation to join me. I feel we have been like ships passing in the night. I'm sure you understand I've been very busy of late, so I'm especially glad to have this opportunity to meet with our Miss Vaisey's replacement, face to face. We were very fond of Miss Vaisey and regret her illness. If you should see her, please give her my very best wishes and tell her we are so very grateful for her work here and for the work of our House Committee visitors in general. You keep us on our toes, Miss Nightingale, and that's all to the good. All to the good.' He puts his wine glass to his lips and drinks, then smiles. He flashes her what he considers his best, most charming, winning smile, some might even call it flirtatious, but she appears immune. She sits motionless, her hands clasped in her lap, her face inscrutable. He takes out a handkerchief and wipes his lips, rubbing at a spot or two of wine on his chin. He is doing his best to keep up appearances. He has to admit he'd let himself go somewhat and it wouldn't do, not for a man in his position. A little less to drink and a little more attention to collar and cuffs was called for.

'I too am glad of the opportunity to meet with you, Superintendent,' says Miss Nightingale. 'You may be aware, I have visited Long Meadow several times now in the company of Councillor Ramshaw, you know of him I presume?'

'Indeed I do,' says Stafford nodding, 'a fine fellow.' He picks up his glass, looks at the wine and puts it back down, reminding himself he must go easy on the liquor. He needs his wits about him. There will be time enough for a good drink when she is gone, when he has ushered her fat arse out of his door. He smiles to himself and raises his face to hers. He is all ears.

'In that time, Superintendent, I, or should I say we, have come upon a number of matters that have given us cause for concern. I would be more than happy to share them with you, our conclusions, our apprehensions, now this evening if you will. But if you prefer, we can of course raise them at the next meeting which is perhaps a more appropriate setting.'

'Let me stop you there, Miss Nightingale or may I call you Eunice?'

'I prefer Nightingale.'

'Very well then, Miss Nightingale, I am all ears as to your concerns, but I believe I may have anticipated them, nipped them in the bud as we say. May I outline my thoughts, my anticipation to you?'

'Please do,' says Miss Nightingale.

'Well, I believe there are two matters that will be concerning you most. Let us begin with the conduct of a certain attendant, Fox, in respect of the bathing of prisoners Baines and Gastrell. Would I be right in thinking this matter has come to your attention?

'You would. Please, go on,' says Miss Nightingale.

'Believe me, I was horrified to hear of it. Quite unacceptable, Miss Nightingale. I will not tolerate violence or abuse from my staff towards patients at any cost, and for yours and Mr Ramshaw's information, she has been given notice and you will not see her again in our corridors or our dormitories. I hope this will allay your fears.'

'I see,' says Miss Nightingale, nodding in approval.

'Now to a trickier matter, the new electrical therapies. I will be presenting a report on them to the Committee, but between us, I have decided that the women are unsuitable for this particular treatment, though I am sure you will grant that we do need to make progress in our understanding and treatment of matters pertaining to the mind. However, the shaving of heads in preparation for this trial was, in hindsight, overzealous. I regret it, Miss Nightingale. It will not happen again and nor will the treatment, certainly not in the immediate future, for we will be trialling these methods with our sturdier male population, and we will be taking only volunteers, you understand. Now have I allayed your fears, my dear?'

'I believe you have,' says Miss Nightingale.

But something in her manner leaves Stafford wondering if he has been entirely successful, for the woman is poker faced. He picks up his glass.

'There is something else, Superintendent,' she says.

Ah, he thought so. Had he missed something? He was convinced he had it sewn up, heading her off at the pass as it were. Against his better judgement, he takes a slug of wine. He puts his handkerchief to his lips, 'Indeed, do go on,' he says.

'As I'm sure you are aware, Superintendent, my concerns and sympathies are very much with the women at Long Meadow, and I am of the opinion that they would benefit greatly for an increase in educational and artistic opportunity. You have some wonderful lacemakers here, and quilters and knitters, and I believe more of such activities, as well as reading and writing, should be encouraged. The Chaplain, Mr. Hawkins, tells me there is to be a summer fete. I would like to volunteer my help in organising it, and bringing some of the women's crafts to bear on the decorations for the stalls and a sale of work perhaps?'

He nods as she speaks, relieved.

'I have a number of women from the town who would be only too happy to assist me in this. And I'm sure you will agree, the women are best employed in work that is meaningful and, dare I say, enjoyable. Idle hands make mischief, Superintendent. I'm sure you can see my point.'

'I can,' says Stafford. 'Splendid, quite splendid. I concur, and I can only repeat that we are most grateful for your efforts. I'm sure the fete will be a great success. You will liaise with the Chaplain?'

'Gladly, Superintendent. And one more thing, if I may?'

For pity's sake, what now, he thinks, but nods, 'Please?'

'Walking, Superintendent, walking in nature. I believe regular accompanied walks, beyond the bounds of the Asylum, which I understand have been allowed previously, would revitalise these women. A change of air, new locale, new objects, new miracles of the natural world, all waiting for their attention, a little pteridomania even. New passions can work wonders to restore body and mind. We cannot take them to Nice or Menton, but surely there is no reason why they cannot go walking in the countryside round about, and I have naturalists and botanists more than willing to accompany such ventures, to share their knowledge of God's great gifts.'

'Well, thank you, Miss Nightingale, an impassioned plea if ever I heard one. I see no harm in it. I will let my Deputy, Mr Farrell, know and Matron of course. They can make the necessary arrangements and provide you with attendants. I suggest you take the women from Dormitory Twelve. Now, thank you for your time. It's been instructive and helpful and much appreciated,' he says, thinking let the old crone have her way, it will keep her out of his hair and those troublesome women in Dormitory Twelve to boot. Two birds with one stone. A good day's work.

He rises from his chair. She follows suit. He ushers her from his parlour resisting the temptation to put a hand on her waist, on her arse even. He senses such a gesture would not be well received. He shuts the door behind her and breathes out audibly. Walking indeed! Botany. Enough of such women. Now, to the bottle, a plate of cold meats and cheese the cooks have sent over, and a well-deserved night's rest.

August

Alice Semple's Notebook

There is heat enough to drink the meadow dry, the earth beneath our feet shrinks, bees feed on the purple loosestrife, on fescue and thistle, the grass alive with all manner of winged insects. We walk out, past the Airing Courts, through the kitchen gardens, beyond into the fields in the direction of the river. We take off our caps where there is no one to see. Miss Nightingale strides ahead, leading her charges, oftentimes accompanied by Mrs Corey. There are others besides who join us, known to Miss Nightingale, come from the University, who are keen to help us identify the birds, the meadow flowers and grasses, though I need no such help for I have dwelt here all my life, until my incarceration.

Walking in nature has become a regular pastime for the women of Dormitory Twelve, which is where Miss N – I have determined to call her this for short – has concentrated her attentions. Our skin is browned in the sun, our cheeks blush like the wild rose, our spirits lift skyward, opening like wings. We do not live by the bells. Clare sees us, watches over us, I am sure of it. He looks down from his vault and pens such lines, as I cannot, of which true poesy is made. My poesy being a matter of mere record and practicality.

Inventory for Walking in Nature

Stout boots – men's being best – our boots belong to the gardeners, hence they are too big, so we stuff the toes with brown paper, better still, and softer, our drawers. While we are about it, we hitch up our petticoats and skirts to ensure they do not hinder us or drag in the mud. Miss N says we are following in the footsteps of women who have gone before us, women such as Margaret Gatty, who wrote *The Book of British Seaweeds*. Who collected over two hundred species and who advised the wearing of men's boots and the taking up of hems.

Socks – once again men's, borrowed for the purpose, and procured by Miss N.

Sticks – Miss N uses a peasant's stick for walking, such as shepherds do. There are canes for the those who are less able and benefit from something to lean on.

Knapsacks – carried by the strongest to contain our picnic lunches of bread and cheese, like the ploughman, made by the kitchen women and in good quantity as is necessary for the expenditure of energy and breathing in of fresh air. There is an apple for each of us, she insists on it. I hide mine in my pocket. I keep it for later when I am alone and can savour it. Before I take the first bite, before I taste its sweet flesh, I roll it in my hands and marvel at its beauty, its russet hue, its scent. I do not remember when I last ate such fruit. Even Phoebe eats her lunch, here out of doors, where it tastes a thousand times again better than in the Dining Hall. To wash it down there is water. Miss N does not believe in ale at lunchtime.

Binoculars – brass, with leather straps, brought by the gentlemen and gentlewomen who come from the university. Field glasses which make the far seem near. The gentlemen show us how to adjust them, how to bring the birds close, so we might better identify, might see each feather.

Caps and Parasols – to prevent sunstroke.

Books – small, such as, Mavor's Botanical Pocket Book for knowledge and identification.

Quizzing glass – a hand glass to make the small seem large, with which we can peer into the very heart of the flower.

Tin box – which I believe they call a vasculum, for collecting plants and leaves.

Notebook and pencil, kept by Miss N – to record what is found.

In truth, this is the happiest I have been in my fourteen years here, for I am out with his wandering spirit, out with my Simpler sisters, the wise women, and men, the web-fingered and web-footed, the poler and rush cutter, eel-catcher and lock keeper, fowler, farmer, boatman and bone man. Awash with sky, under its dome, I find peace. Only the shadows, unwanted thoughts cast on the land by transient clouds, bring moments of sorrow, when we remember the worst. But for now, much has changed here for the better.

There is no talk of the treatments for Dormitory Twelve. His threats to have me turfed out and shipped off elsewhere have come to nothing though I do not count my chickens. I take these new-found pleasures where I can and thank God for them. Rumour has it that Stafford now practices his black arts on the men of Long Meadow, poor souls who have been persuaded with the promise of tobacco for the pipe, or money in a pocket which cannot be spent. I pity them but rejoice that we are left alone. The Chief is not much seen in the corridors. I have been so bold as to tell Miss N of my suspicions of the Chief and Phoebe which she says, if true, are a serious charge indeed. She says she will not forget but let us not upset the apple cart just yet, when such progress has been made, when we have been granted our walks in nature. I for one agree as I would not wish to spoil our new-found freedoms.

For the women who stay indoors, there is a good deal of craft such as sewing and knitting, some even make lace. It is not to my liking, as you may glean, but they are happy and gainfully employed making items to sell in the summer fete. Their work has meaning, unlike the shredding of paper and the mending of men's farty britches.

In the evenings we gather in the Day Room to make paper garlands and flowers to decorate the stalls. The Chaplain says the fete will be the best ever held at Long Meadow, with hoopla and tombola and donkey rides for the children.

He says it will attract interest as far away as the town, as well as the villages round about. And we will mingle with them, it will be impossible, he says, to tell the sane from the committed. I do not say what I know to be true, that they come to gawp and stare, that for them we will forever be on the other side of the fence, like the animals in a zoo. I have seen it often, visitors to the Asylum who come purely for their entertainment. At best they pity us. I have no wish or need for their pity, though I discern the kindness in the Chaplain's words. He is a good man.

Speaking of good men and bad, I am inclined to tell Simone what I know of the Chief and Phoebe, for if I am whisked away like a ghost in the night, as they are wont to do, she should know. I do not believe the girl will ever tell. Simone will not hear it from her. None can persuade Phoebe that the shame is not hers. She keeps her secret hidden. She clings to it as women do, who are used in this way by men. It is the tragedy that they do not see it for what it is, which is man's wickedness, his lordliness, his abuse of power. It is his fault entirely and there is plenty such fault, such power on show here. But for now, with Miss N at the harrow, the women of Dormitory Twelve, sprout forth like a newly sown crop.

Simone

He had gone, disappeared into the slanting light of a summer evening, under a cloak of yew. Their parting had been bittersweet. Simone would not see him again. Now, when she thinks of William Blakely, there is sadness still, and a loss that compounds all other losses, as if she is destined for nothing more. But there is fondness, despite the injury. For he has left her with the gift of hope, and a hope no longer dependent on him. Even so, she is careful not to clutch at it for fear that it will be dashed again. There are times when it is easier to bear the life to which she has become accustomed at Long Meadow, than to look out beyond its walls. And it is such a time now, for there has been a marked change in all their fortunes.

An angel has appeared in their lives.

At the time of their worst degradations, with all hope for reprieve or salvation lost, the God, who appeared to have abandoned them, had woken. He had seen their suffering and he has sent them Miss Nightingale.

How quickly it happened, a trio of voices raised in protest and Matron triumphant, defiant, as if she were one of them. The treatments had ceased and Miss Nightingale had surely played her part behind the scenes. Her respect knew no bounds, treating them as if they were her daughters. Here was a woman to emulate. Who was not the appendage of a man but had her own mind and had acquired considerable learning.

They walk out most days, when the weather is fine and even, on occasion in the rain. Simone wakes now without the clutch of fear and dread in her chest. Her headaches have abated, her mind has cleared. Her hair grows and the sore places on her head have begun to heal. It is the same for Phoebe in whose countenance Simone sees a marked change. There is colour in her cheeks, a willingness to eat and a newfound confidence. It is the miracle that is Miss Nightingale. For not only has she introduced the walks in nature to restore their health and well-being, but she encourages them to fully delve into the natural world, to know and understand it better.

For this purpose, she brings books, two of which are in Simone's possession now, loaned for as long as she wishes, the first, Priscilla Wakefield's *Introduction to Botany*, the second, Lindley's Ladies Botany which, according to Miss Nightingale, allows for the serious engagement of women in a science and not a mere amusement for ladies. It is possible, Miss Nightingale says, for a woman to become proficient in the field of botany, in identification and recording, in classification, and without the disapproval that so often accompanies women's attempts at learning. To illustrate such beliefs, she invites others to accompany her, women from the university, from Girton College, and a vicar's daughter, Miss Benson, who is engaged in compiling her own fenland flora using the natural system devised in Paris by Antoine-Laurent de Jussieu. According to Miss Benson, the Linnaean system is becoming outmoded among educated botanists. Due to her kind and patient instruction, Simone is learning the new system, though there is much to grasp in classification not simply the three categories, Acotyledon, Monocotyledon, and Dicotyledon, but fifteen classes beyond and over a hundred families.

'You see,' says Miss Nightingale, to Simone, 'once you are proficient it will be entirely possible for you to begin your own catalogue of the meadows round about, or to at least assist Miss Benson, and with Phoebe at hand for the drawing, who knows what might be achieved.'

Simone does not yet share Miss Nightingale's confidence in her newly acquired skills, but she is convinced of Phoebe's talent for drawing the flowers and grasses they collect, which they take back to the Day Room to catalogue and press. All are agreed, Phoebe has a special talent for it. Since Miss Nightingale's arrival, there is a flood of paper of all kinds, for writing, drawing, the pressing of flowers. There are pencils too and a box of water colour paints for Phoebe. Some of her paintings will be sold at the summer fete. Together, Simone and Phoebe have become known as 'the flower collectors,' and the women, as well as men from the gardens, sometimes even attendants, bring them specimens to identify and draw. Their work gives new meaning and purpose to life at Long Meadow.

When her head is bent over her books and papers, over seed head or meadow flower, Simone can forget for a time where she is. More than this, she has come to believe there are ways of living, of being a woman in the world, other than as wife or mother, daughter or mistress, ways she is only now learning for the first time.

But there is a newly formed cloud darkening her horizon, a cloud that overshadows their walks and this newfound freedom. It is something she has learned from Alice. In truth, it is something she had suspected. Thoughts of it had lingered at the back of her mind only to be pushed away when they presented themselves. She had not wanted to believe it, despite the evidence around her.

They had been walking in Keeper's Wood, looking at ferns, when Alice told her. In the shadows cast by the filtered sunlight, she had whispered the secret, her words swallowed in the rustling leaves. How he came for Phoebe on the pretext of collecting coal for the Kitchens or the Day Room, dragging the empty trolley with him. How he took her to the Boiler Room where the coal was stored. How he forced himself upon her

'They all know. Gladys Carter claims to have come across them once, says she tried to tell but was silenced, first by Farrell and later by Matron. Oh yes, they turn a blind eye when it suits them. But Phoebe, she will never tell. Which of us would? Which of us bear the shame? I tell you, so there will be another among us who knows. There is nothing to be done. I have already brought it to the attention of the Visitors.'

Alice's words haunt Simone. There is nothing to be done. She had suspected all along and she had done nothing, despite knowing how power at Long Meadow sat in the hands of men. How they were willing to use it to meet their own needs and flights of fancy. What chance did women like Phoebe have, what chance did any of them have, unknown, invisible, women that the world preferred to forget? What chance against a Superintendent who by all accounts dined with Justices of the Peace? What chance against even the lowliest attendant in cap and apron, in the uniform of respectability? Now, more than ever, she knows she must secure her release from Long Meadow and with it the release of Phoebe Baines.

Her sister's address, given to her by William Blakely, remains folded, tucked away inside, *The Child's Guide to Knowledge*, with the pansy in the handkerchief and her

244

precious cutting from *The Liverpool Echo*. She has sent word to Maria, via Mrs Corey's cousin, Tom Makepeace, asking her to visit. If she is to write to her sister a second time, then she must know for certain it will reach her. She composes the letter in her head, over and over, the letter on which hers and Phoebe's futures depend. She will not leave without her fellow 'flower-collector,' without the girl who despite their likeness in age, has become the daughter she must save.

Phoebe

A Paint Box

a box a key a key
in my pocket hidden
think of nothing else
the gladness of this
made from mahogany simone says
brass hinges smooth wood
open and close, lock unlock
key belonging only to me
show the world show the bees
show the world show the bees
draw first, pencil first, kept in the drawer
copy to learn that's the way
draw first
miss nightingale's books
flowering plants of great britain
grasses sedges ferns
anne pratt that's who
i copy
club mosses, pepperworts and horsetails
wild arum, cuckoo pint, berry red poisonous
devils and angels, stallions and mares
kitty-come-down-the-lane
lords and ladies, alice says is good for ruptures

scurvy and wind
copy to learn, draw, paint
washes of colour
rinse brush in cut glass
clouds overlapping
colours change
think of nothing else
thoughts settle no bees no hum
all sleeping peacefully in the hive
saucers to mix in
one with a chip on its rim,
twenty-one cakes of colour
no one else to touch nor me do not touch
me, no jug no Boiler Room coal cellar
he cannot harm, my soul locked in a paint box
think only is this right
simone says my tongue sticking out while i paint
and hum my song lavender green lavender blue
dilly dilly
if i should die dilly dilly as it may hap
simone says do not sing such about death
alice says she will make the inventory of everything
in my box of treasure
names of colours and all else besides
if they should take it from me
i will still have it

Simone

Rain threatens. Black clouds hang like a furrowed brow over the fields and the air is bruised with the ceaseless throb of the pumping station. At breakfast, Matron announces there will be no walks as Miss Nightingale is otherwise employed. There is much still to do for the fete, she says, and hopes the women will work hard at their tasks. Please God the weather will be much improved by then.

With no walk in prospect, Simone returns to her room with Phoebe. They take off their boots and despite the poor light occasioned by the storm-laden sky, Simone opens her books to study while Phoebe sits at the desk, as she so often does now, with her paint box open and a brush in hand.

Phoebe hums, *Lavender blue, dilly dilly*, and rinses her brush in the water glass as she prepares to mix paint in a small white saucer with a chip on its rim.

Simone puts her book down. It is hard to concentrate, wondering as she does what other employment would keep Miss Nightingale from their daily outing, for the weather would certainly not deter her. She worries over snatches of a conversation she overheard yesterday between Miss Benson and Miss Nightingale on the walk back through the kitchen gardens.

Walking a step behind the two women, Simone had heard Miss Nightingale tell Miss Benson that the Chairman of the House Committee had asked to see her and that she could not think what it might be about. She had spoken of a sense of foreboding, though said it was probably foolish. Miss Benson had replied that she was sure it was nothing, or that perhaps he wanted to thank her for the work she was doing with the women in Dormitory Twelve, of how much improved they were in spirits and how gainfully occupied. *Perhaps*, Miss Nightingale had echoed, though she had not sounded convinced.

Simone prays there is nothing that will prevent their new routines, nothing to stop the new sun on their horizon that is Miss Nightingale lighting the dark corner of their hidden world. It would be too cruel. But she has little time to dwell on such a misfortune as she hears a cough, a clearing of the throat, looks up from her book, to see Mrs Corey standing in the doorway.

'Excuse me, Mrs Gastrell,' she says, stepping inside. 'I'm sorry to say but I have unexpected news, a bit of bad news I'm afraid, concerning your housemaid, Maria.'

'Come in, Mrs Corey, please.'

'Well, my cousin went to the house as you asked,' she glances at Phoebe and lowers her voice to a whisper, 'you know, to deliver your note. Well, he called at the kitchens, being discrete and all, and was told she is no longer there, she is no longer employed in service in the house. When he enquired as to when she left and for what reason, the cook, Mrs O'Hara, you will know her of course, said she had not been there these past three weeks. No reason given for her departure, just paid off by the master they reckon, though for what, well I'll have to leave you to guess, Mrs Gastrell, all the rest being gossip and supposition.'

'No, surely not. It cannot be. Did he enquire as to where she might be found?'

'Apparently nobody knows, is what the cook said, done

a moonlight, maybe off to see her aunt in Dublin. Said she was well paid, enough for a passage. So, I'm sorry but there was no more to be done. He has returned your note. Here it is,' she reaches in her pocket, takes out the note and hands it to Simone, and checking there is no one behind her and that they are still alone, apart from Phoebe, whispers, 'He says if he can do you any other favour, he is more than willing. He's a good lad and can be trusted. There is the matter of payment, Mrs Gastrell…'

'Of course. I will see to it immediately,' says Simone, with no plan of how she will recompense Mrs Corey's cousin. She had been depending on Maria to sell the jewellery she had in keeping for her, for she has no other source of money. How else can she pay him, how else can she find the postage for her letter to Clara, and who will post it for her now Maria is gone?

'Thank you, Mrs Corey, and please thank your cousin for me,' says Simone. Tears prick the back of her eyes as she watches Mrs Corey leave. It is surely impossible, hopeless, the simplest things cannot be achieved, she has no self-determination, no power, and she has lost her only friend in the world beyond Long Meadow, other than a sister who has no knowledge of what she has come to. If only Maria had visited before leaving, had brought her the precious bundle. Where to turn now? Who to trust? Items were smuggled in and out of Long Meadow daily: laudanum, Dover's Powders, Bailey's Sedative, tobacco, strong liquor, gin and stamps were among them, but only by those with means. She has none.

Simone puts her head in her hands. Phoebe stops painting and comes over to stand by Simone's chair. She places a kiss on the top of her head.

Simone lifts her head from her hands and smiles. 'Let me see what you've been painting,' she says, getting up from the chair. 'I'm sure it's just beautiful.'

They do not go to the Dining Hall, ignoring the call of the bell, neither woman being hungry or wanting to eat the grey meat and black bread. While thunder rolls away in the distance, Phoebe hums and paints. Simone, fearing the onset of a headache, lies down on the bed where she falls into a restless sleep.

She is woken by a knock at the door which is pushed open.

She sits up. 'Matron.'

'Mrs Gastrell. Miss Baines. I gather you have no appetite ladies. I did not see you at dinner.'

'I'm afraid I fell asleep,' says Simone getting up off the bed and smoothing down her hair and her skirts.

'Well, that's as it maybe but now you must come with me. Miss Baines, pack away your paints and go and join the others in the Day Room. It will not be long before evensong. You, on the other hand, have a visitor, Mrs Gastrell, although it is most irregular, for as you will be aware, visiting is on the second and fourth Thursday in the month and today is Wednesday. However, it seems she has permission. She is waiting for you in the Visiting Room. Off you go, Miss Baines. Follow me, Mrs Gastrell.'

Simone's heart races in anticipation as she follows Matron along the corridor to the Visiting Room. Thank the Lord for he is merciful. Maria has come after all. Simone is certain of it. An attendant is waiting outside the Visiting Room and when Matron leaves she opens the door and tells Simone to follow her.

The visitor is seated at a table by one of the long, draped

windows with her back is to Simone. She is wearing a maroon silk bonnet and a matching cloak. It is not Maria. She can tell in a glance that the woman at the table is not her housemaid. She is too tall and too finely dressed. There is nothing about her presence or bearing that Simone recognises. The woman's head is bowed and her face hidden by a bonnet. As she approaches, Simone catches the faint scent of otto of rose.

'Sit here, Mrs Gastrell,' says the attendant, indicating the chair opposite the visitor, then leaves to go and sit at a distance by the fireplace.

As Simone lowers herself into the chair, the visitor raises her head.

'Why, it's you Henrietta!' says Simone, leaning back as if receiving a blow to the chest. 'Of all people I did not expect to see you here. I wonder that you have the time, being so busy with preparations for your marriage to my husband, Everett. What could you possibly want with me?' She leans back in her chair. 'How dare you...' she begins.

Henrietta interrupts. 'Please, Simone, I did not expect you to welcome me, but I come in good faith and with sorrow in my heart. I come to tell you I am truly sorry for what I have done, for what has happened to you. I know you grieve Constance as I do. You loved her like a sister, as I have loved her, and you deserve no blame for what happened. I regret so much, Simone. I regret I wasn't there to help, that I wasn't there sooner, that by the time I offered you my hand and pulled you from the river, you were half-drowned yourself.'

'You offered me your hand? You pulled me from the river? I do not remember,' says Simone. 'I only recall the diving down, going under, the blackness, searching and searching for her in the river weed.'

'You were practically drowned yourself by the time I got near enough to hold out my hand. You did all you could to save her. You risked your own life. More than many would. It was I and Everett who were at fault. You have nothing to admonish yourself for, whereas I have everything. What has happened to you is unjust. A crime. I confess I should have realised then what Everett's true nature was. Hadn't he been the one to encourage Constance to bathe that morning? Then, when you called and we came, he stood on the bank and did nothing. I was blinded by his affections and promises which I now regret deeply, with my whole heart. I do not expect your understanding or your forgiveness, Simone. But I come to tell you that I will not be marrying Everett. I am leaving on Friday for Northampton where I will be joining a friend of my late mother's who has kindly agreed to put me up while I decide where my future lies. Everett does not know and must not know that I am leaving. Most important of all, I come to bring you this.' Henrietta lifts from her lap a small parcel wrapped in brown paper and string. 'I believe your housemaid, Maria, was keeping these personal items and had intended to bring them, but her leaving was sudden and unexpected. She brought them to me instead and asked me to see that they reached you.'

'But what has happened that she is gone?' says Simone. 'Why is she no longer employed in your service? And why, why would she entrust my possessions to you?'

'Everett sacked her after she discovered him in the kitchen with the scullery maid. I leave it to your imagination as to what they were doing there. Or should I say what Everett was doing to her. Maria's mistake, if you can call it a mistake, was to tell me. As I'm sure you know, Everett expects his servants to keep his unpleasant little secrets. She was given a fortnight's wages and told to find work elsewhere.' Henrietta passes the brown paper parcel across the table.

Simone takes the parcel. 'I trust you do not expect me to forgive you for I find it is impossible. I have been rendered a prisoner through yours and Everett's doing with little or no hope of release. I am a dead woman, as dead as Constance, while you are free to do entirely as you please.'

Henrietta pulls a handkerchief from her pocket, twists it in her hands and dabs at her nose. 'If there is something I can do, Simone, anything to make amends to prove that I am truly repentant, then please ask me now and I will endeavour to do it.'

Simone thinks of Clara and the letter she must send. 'As a matter of fact, there is. I have a sister,' she says. 'She has travelled to India with her husband who has taken up a posting in Pondicherry. I have recently come into possession of their address. As my next of kin, I must contact her for she is the one person who can ensure that I am released from Longmeadow. I am certain Everett will never sign my release. I have not had the means to write or the money for postage but more importantly, letters have a way of going astray here so that they do not reach their intended destination. I beg you now, write to my sister on my behalf and tell her of my predicament and request her help as a matter of urgency.'

'I will do it and gladly,' says Henrietta, 'if you can furnish me with the address, I will write as soon as I get to Northampton.'

'I have the address but I do not have it here with me now. It is in my room. I will get it to you via a cousin of one of the attendants here who goes by the name of Tom Makepeace. I will have him deliver it to the house before Friday.'

254

'Very well, then tell this cousin, this Mr. Makepeace, he must ask for me and put it direct in my hands. It would not be wise to leave it with anyone else. I leave Friday, first thing in the morning. Goodbye, Simone.' With that, Henrietta stands, turns, and makes her way out of the Visiting Room. She does not look back.

'I'm not sure you're allowed a parcel such as that,' says the attendant, having left her perch by the fireplace and joined Simone.

'There may be something in it for you, half a gold sovereign perhaps,' says Simone.

'Oh well, better keep it out of harm's way then. Tuck it under your arm where no one can see it and follow me.'

Their footsteps echo in the empty corridors. The women are at evensong. When they arrive at Simone's room, the attendant hovers in the doorway. Simone, turning away from the door, undoes the brown paper parcel, takes a half sovereign from a purse and hands it to the attendant who disappears.

Simone closes the door and spreads the parcel's contents on her counterpane. The purse is black and beaded and heavy with sovereigns. She unwraps a strip of blue velvet and reveals the diamond butterfly brooch, a gift from Everett on their engagement. The black stones are there and the Italian cameo, as well as the seed pearls and her emerald brooch. How fortunes may change in a matter of hours. How hers are changed. She is suddenly a woman with means and more than this, she has Henrietta's promise to write to Clara on her behalf. There is light at the tunnel's end and yet, as she bundles the parcel up and puts it in the back of her locker, beneath her clean petticoat and stockings, she is overcome with a sense of foreboding. She is reminded of the proverb she and Clara were made to transcribe in their Latin copybooks: *Fortuna vitrea est: tum cum splendet frangitu – Fortune is like glass, the brighter the glitter the more easily broken.*

The Chaplain

There is something about a said evensong, entirely spoken as it is, that brings peace and tranquillity, a solace and stillness. It is the service from which his flock benefits most. No sermon for one thing, no pontificating, a nod to the monastic tradition, 'oefen-sang,' Vespers, the seventh of the eight daily offices, a time of quiet contemplation. This afternoon, as he watches the men and women, mostly women, file from the Chapel, the Chaplain finds it is less so for him. He cannot deny he has been somewhat troubled, perhaps he should admit, excited even, by the presence of one, Miss Nightingale, who has not moved but is seated still in the front pew.

She leans forward and whispers, 'Might I have a word, Chaplain?'

'Indeed, Miss Nightingale, you may.' He eases into the front pew to sit beside her as the last of his worshippers leave. She is tall but elegant, a tiny waist he has noticed, though he has tried not to, soft brown curls that escape her bonnet and gentle eyes. A word from her and his heart is a flutter. It is not something he is used to or comfortable with. He is brim full of admiration for the compassion and interest she shows in the women's lives, for the difference she has made in such a short time, but she unsettles him.

'It concerns the young woman they call Phoebe Baines, I believe you know her?'

'Certainly, I do,' his heart flutters again but not for sight of Miss Nightingale, but for what he fears she is about to say. For what he might be accused of failing to investigate properly or act on.

'It is a private matter, Chaplain, and I wish to speak in confidence.'

'You may speak in the utmost confidence, I assure you, and please Miss Nightingale, call me Daniel.'

'Very well, Daniel, forgive me if I speak plainly but I have heard it said with some authority, though I do not have definite proof, that Mr Farrell, the Chief and acting Deputy, is well... is abusing the girl. That he is known to take her to the Boiler Room where the coal is stored in order that he might, how shall I put it, well, to be blunt, have intercourse with her, against her will. I don't mind telling you, Chaplain, Daniel, that I am shocked to my core. If it is true then it must be brought to the attention of Mr Stafford. And I am more than willing to do so. But should it be a malicious rumour, well, I do not wish to sully a man's reputation. But then shouldn't Stafford be made aware of such rumours? I am in a quandary.'

'Indeed. I appreciate your dilemma. I have to admit I too have been privy to these allegations and between us, for I wouldn't like it to go any further, Miss Nightingale, I have tried to investigate, to see if there is any truth in them. I have done my best but so far, I have unearthed no evidence.'

'I see. So you are also in a quandary?'

'You could say so, yes, but until I can obtain, or am shown clear evidence, I'm afraid I have concluded I must keep my counsel, and as Farrell has been little seen in the women's corridors of late, since he has taken on the role of Deputy, you might want to consider doing likewise. You have made such great strides with the women, especially in Dormitory Twelve and we have the summer fete to think of. All steam ahead now, we wouldn't want to give the Superintendent a reason to cancel, would we?'

'But the girl, the damage…'

'If you'll excuse me, your compassion is to be applauded, but the damage, the damage is already done, done long ago and no undoing.'

'I do not think that a good reason for not acting, Chaplain, and besides, the girl makes good progress, she is eating, she is painting, she has a talent for it and with the help and encouragement of Mrs Gastrell, she blossoms. And while I am on the subject of Mrs Gastrell, she, above all, strikes me as saner than any at Long Meadow. If that woman is a lunatic, capable of drowning a child, then I am Mary, Mother of Jesus, forgive the blasphemy, Chaplain, but God sees all and knows all. There has been a miscarriage of justice here. I hear say her husband is divorcing her and wishes to take a new wife. Very convenient, wouldn't you agree, to have a wife in the Asylum?' She sighs. 'But, to get back to the matter of Farrell, it behoves us to keep an eye out. Wouldn't you agree? We must get to the bottom of the matter one way or another. And if we make no progress, then I will take my concerns to a higher authority.'

'Absolutely, Miss Nightingale, I couldn't agree more. In the meantime, there is a whole raft of things I would like to discuss with you concerning the fete. It is only ten days away after all. Would you care to take tea with me tomorrow? In the vestry? Nothing grand I'm afraid but…'

'I cannot, Chaplain, I am otherwise engaged, but later, early evening, might be possible.'

'Well, early evening it is, a glass of port perhaps, instead of tea?'

'Tea will do just fine, thank you. Now, I must be off.'

The Superintendent's Office

'Don't dilly-dally. Come in, man. Come in!' shouts Stafford. He stands before the window, waving a brass letter knife in his right hand.

Farrell keeps his distance and takes up position by the desk with the door behind him. On the desk is a half empty bottle of Burgundy and a used glass.

'I'm hearing all kinds of nonsense,' says Stafford, pointing the letter knife, 'about what's going on down there, in Dormitory Twelve. Women gallivanting about all over the place, out in the fields, lying about under trees, picnicking. I don't call that walks in nature. Do you? Lunatics running wild, consorting with Girton girls, and not a chaperone to speak of in sight.' He throws the letter knife onto the desk. 'Well, not on my watch. The place needs a thorough shake up. Look at it from my point of view, the embarrassment, the humiliation for a man in my position. I can't have it, Farrell, and though it pains me to say it, you're not without blame. It's your responsibility to ensure standards are upheld. You're my Deputy. When things go awry, I expect to hear it direct from you. You should have been the first to let me know what was going on. Too busy consorting with patients from what I hear. Too late to rise, too soon to drink. The devil makes work for idle hands, Farrell. How's that wife of yours by the way? Never see the woman. You should bring her to Chapel on Sunday, it would do your reputation no harm.'

'Afraid she's not well enough for Chapel, Sir.'

'Well, I'm sorry to hear it but as it happens you'll have more time to look after her from now on. From next week to be precise, when the new Deputy arrives. Brought it forward. I did tell you, didn't I? Quinn, George Quinn, from the West Country, Bristol, comes highly recommended, a man of some experience. The Chairman wants to see him in place as soon as possible. We've come to an agreement, the Chairman and I. Quinn will take over and Miss Nightingale will be moved on, to proffer her services to the fortunate inmates of another asylum. I appreciate all you've done, Farrell, but I have the Dean to think of and the Committee. I have people I need to keep in my pocket and people I need rid of. Time we shook this place up, and Quinn and I are the men to do it. Indeed.' He stabs the desk with the letter-knife. 'In the meantime, I want you to see to the arrangements for the transfer of Semple, Baines and Cole. Yarmouth, the lot of them. They're nothing but troublemakers. I wouldn't be surprised if Semple is the source of all this gossip. The place is like a sieve, leaking everywhere and Semple never far from the heart of it. As for the Baines girl, I hear she's taken to painting now. Painting my arse. Huh! I warrant a blind monkey could do better. Tomorrow morning at the latest and I want them to take nothing with them beyond the barest necessities. Inform them no more than half an hour before they are due to go. No time for stirring up trouble. I want them gone, ghosts in the night as if they were never here, do you understand?'

'I do sir. I understand perfectly.'

'Good, we are in agreement. Make sure it's done properly. I don't want to hear anything other than all has run smoothly and Dormitory Twelve is in good order and operating as it should. As for these so-called walks in nature, they will cease when Miss Nightingale moves on by the end of this week. Quinn will come and Nightingale will go and we will all be happy. Yes?'

Farrell swallows hard and nods. His lips tight, his fists clenched, he can feel the blood rising in his head.

'That will be all. Off you go now. You've got work to do and I have papers to sort,' says Stafford, settling his hand on the neck of the Burgundy bottle.

'Shake the place up indeed. Bugger him. Knows nothing about the place. Nothing. Hardly ever here, spends his days supping with his cronies in the Senior Common Room. The old sot. The bacon-faced blab.' Farrell mumbles to himself through gritted teeth as he makes his way along the corridor. 'Too soon to drink, ha! That's the pot calling the kettle if ever I heard it. Where would he be without me, that's what I'd like to know. Jesus Christ, that's gratitude for you. Is it my fault, the women are off in the countryside, lying in the meadows, skirts above their ankles, plaiting hair, making daisy chains, laughing like lunatics? No. Not my fault. The fault is Stafford's and Nightingale's. A plague on their houses, both of them.'

'Everything all right, Mr. Farrell?' asks the Chaplain, coming up behind him.

Farrell stops and turns.

'This weather's most disconcerting, don't you find? Was that a roll of thunder I heard just now? You look somewhat hot and bothered. Not your usual self, if I might say. Are there problems afoot? Off somewhere in a hurry? It's a hard job you have now you're Deputy, that's for sure.'

'Indeed, Chaplain. Though it is not always appreciated.'

'I fear someone has upset you.'

'You might say.'

'Oh dear, how unfortunate. If there is anything I can do? Always a listening ear and a resting pew to be found in the Chapel. At any time. God welcomes us all, no matter our sins. You should think of bringing your wife on Sunday.'

'Hmm. Yes. Well, I'll remember that, Chaplain. Now I must be on my way. ' He hurries off. What is it with everyone, this sudden obsession with his wife and Sunday Chapel? The world's gone mad. Farrell's chest is tight, his legs weak. Stafford's words reel about him. How easily he has been written off after but a few weeks. Stafford has used him as he uses everyone. Now some ponce called Quinn will breeze in and take over. And it will be, 'Yes, Sir, no, Sir, three bags full, Sir.' His palms sweat. His head is a hive of angry bees fit to burst. He turns on his heels and makes his way in the direction of Dormitory Twelve. It's been a while now, needs must, his last chance to have her. Oh, he'll show her where the bees swarm all right and no stopping short this time. What does he care if her belly swells? She'll be gone in the morning. The thought calms him and he smiles inwardly. It may be a while before such bread and butter comes his way again. He must take it where he can. An opportunity for revenge, on Stafford. On all of them.

Simone

Phoebe is singing, *lavender green dilly dilly, lavender blue,* her voice soft, barely above a whisper. The tip of her tongue protrudes from her lips as she dips her brush into the water glass, rinsing the remains of Raw Sienna in preparation for mixing Chrome Yellow and Sap Green in the saucer with the chip on its rim.

Simone is sitting in the upholstered chair, a book balanced on her knees with a sheet of paper on top, got from Miss Nightingale. She's writing a note for Henrietta, with Clara's address, intending to give it to Mrs Corey before the night bell, but when she hears the wheels in the corridor and the heavy tread of a man's boots she puts down her pen. She looks across at Phoebe. Phoebe puts down her brush and closes the lid of her paint box. They turn towards the door. It opens slowly. His body fills the frame. It is Farrell and he is angry, thinks Simone, she can see it in his face, she can smell it on him. She stands up. She knows this anger only too well, an anger so often taken out on her. There is sweat on his brow, small glistening beads of it and on his nose too.

He is in a hurry. He does not bother with niceties. 'Hey, you, skinny one, time to shovel some coal. The kitchen boiler is short. Now,' he says, looking at Phoebe.

Her eyes widen. She does not move but looks to Simone. 'Never mind her,' says Farrell, 'I said now. Hurry up.'

He is inside the room, grabbing Phoebe's arm. 'Put your

pretty paints away and come with me.' He pulls her to her feet. 'Won't be long,' he says to Simone.

Simone steps forward. 'No. Leave her be.'

'Oh, it's like that is it,' he says and before Simone can do anything by way of stopping him, Farrell has pulled Phoebe from the room, slammed the door and turned the key in the lock.

Afterwards, Simone will swear she did not know where the voice she summoned came from. In Long Meadow, they had their ways of silencing you and she had complied with them all. But something had changed that day with Fox in the bathroom, compounded by Alice in the woods whispering Phoebe's secret. There was no going back. She knew she must act. She must protect Phoebe.

Simone grabs her walking boots from under the bed and bangs them on the locked door. She screams for Mrs Corey, for Matron. Bang and scream, bang and scream, and before she knows it, the door is unlocked and Mrs Corey is there and and, behind her, Matron.

'Whatever is the matter, Mrs Gastrell?' asks Matron.

'It is the Chief,' says Simone. 'He has taken Phoebe. He has taken her, against her will.' She pushes past them and looks down the corridor in the direction of the Boiler Room.

Matron and Mrs Corey look at the empty corridor.

'Believe me. God is my witness. He came with the trolley and pulled her out, then locked me in. He means to, he means to...'

'There, there, calm yourself, ' says Matron. She turns to Mrs Corey. They exchange a knowing look. Matron shakes her head. 'I've had just about enough of this. Time to put a stop, I think.'

Mrs Corey nods in agreement and straight away sets off

down the corridor with Matron and Simone at her heels.

The door to the Boiler Room is ajar. Mrs Corey hesitates. Matron pushes it open and steps inside. Mrs Corey and Simone follow. Their eyes take a moment to adjust to the shadowy interior, lit only by a small skylight but there is light enough to see the brick walls, the hanging ropes for lowering the coal trolley which stands empty on its platform, and Phoebe. Phoebe is pinned against the wall at the top of a small flight of stone steps, her petticoats lifted. Farrell's trousers are slack about his ankles.

'Mr. Farrell, for pity's sake,' says Matron.

'Getaway,' shouts Farrell, 'it's none of your business, leave us be, you'll regret poking your nose in. Away with you. All of you. Else...' he puts his hands to Phoebe's throat and begins to squeeze.

Phoebe whimpers.

'I will not,' says Matron. 'Here, help me, Mrs Corey.' Matron reaches out for Phoebe's arm but Farrell knocks her back, a fist in her face. She falls at his feet.

Mrs Corey rushes forward. 'How dare you?' she says, as she and Simone help Matron up from the floor.

Matron is on her feet, a thin trickle of blood runs from her mouth.

'Let the girl go. I'm warning you,' says Mrs Corey. She lashes out at the Chief, pushes at his arm. 'Let her go. You're not fit to be Chief let alone Deputy, you wicked man.'

Farrell pushes her away, but he hasn't reckoned with the attendant's strength.

'Don't touch me you pigeon-livered scoundrel,' warns Mrs Corey. 'I'll have you and no mistake. Had a husband like you, knocked me about, blinkered me once. But no more. Let the girl go.'

Farrell does not move. Mrs Corey lunges at him and before they know it, he is stumbling backwards down the stone steps. He lands in the coal heap like a spilled sack. Still, slumped, unmoving.

The women peer over the platform at the lifeless figure of Farrell. They look in alarm from one to another. Phoebe pulls down her skirts and reaches for Simone's hand. Matron brushes off her apron and adjusts her cap. Silence echoes around them and then the night bell sounds, signalling the patients to the washrooms and their beds. Mrs Corey peers down again at Farrell's body in the coal. Matron ventures down the steps but is quickly back up, shaking her head. 'Listen...' she says but gets no further when the door to the Boiler Room pushes open and the Chaplain appears.

He steps back, 'Oh. Good evening, ladies. I did not expect to find you here. I was looking for Mr Farrell, as it happens.'

'Indeed,' says Matron, sucking in her lips for she can taste the blood from the blow to her face and she does not want the Chaplain to see. 'I believe he is with the Superintendent.'

'I don't think so, Matron. I met him in the corridor just minutes ago, coming from the Superintendent's office. Is there a problem?' he asks, craning his neck and attempting to look beyond the three women.

'No, everything is fine, ' says Matron. 'I'm sorry we can't help but if you'll excuse us, we need to fill the coal trolley. The kitchens have run short and Houndsworth is nowhere to be found.'

'I see,' says the Chaplain. He looks from one to the other and does not move.

He does not believe her, thinks Simone. Any moment now he will be further inside and see the body lying in the coal. She is trembling as she steps forward. She clasps her hands together tightly to stop the shaking. 'I wonder if I might speak with you, Chaplain. It concerns my housemaid, Maria. I understand she's been sent away and I would very much like to find where she is living. I wonder if you might help me. Perhaps we could go to my room, and I can explain the circumstances. Though it will need to be straight away for I believe I heard the night bell.'

'If I can help, I'll be glad to, but…' says the Chaplain.

'Thank you,' says Simone interrupting before he can find reason to stall. She ushers him away.

'On second thoughts,' says Simone, as she stands with the Chaplain at her door. 'It might be best left until the morning when there is more time. I can hear the women already in the washroom and now that I am no longer engaged in helping Matron with the coal, I must make my preparations for bed. Perhaps you will walk with me on my way to the washroom.'

'But it is no distance, Mrs Gastrell.'

'Ah, but one step beside a man of God is worth many alone.'

'How kind, my dear. I will of course escort you if it is your wish.'

She smiles at him. They walk to the washroom. A pulse of pain has quickened over Simone's eye and down the righthand side of her face. Not now, she says inwardly. Not now.

As the Chaplain finally takes his leave, she feels her breath begin to slow and her heart to quieten. When she is sure he is out of sight, she turns away from the washroom and hurries back to her room. On her way, she passes Mrs Corey pulling the coal trolley down the corridor. They nod in each other's direction but say nothing.

Once inside her room, Simone falls to her knees and prays God to have mercy on them, for she fears Farrell may be dead. And if he is, what then? It is murder, and though by accident and not design, a terrible sin, a crime punishable by hanging. What will become of them? She dares not think. She gets up and busies herself tidying away Phoebe's paint box, picking up her book and writing paper from the chair but as she does so, the edges of her vision blur. She longs to lie down on the bed and close her eyes, yet she dares not, for fear of seeing his body, unmoving, lying among the coal.

There is a knock at the door. She turns.

Matron enters. 'I have put the girl to bed. No harm done,' she says, her eyes glittering, her mouth tight. 'I have given her a chloral draught. She will sleep long into the morning. It is quite possible she will even forget what has happened.'

'But what of Mr Farrell?' says Simone, hardly daring to anticipate the answer. 'Has a doctor been called?'

'No need,' says Matron. 'The Chief is up and off. He came round quick enough, just as you left, as it happened. We fetched a jug of ale to revive him further, and partial as he is to ale, he drank it down as if it were his last. We mopped the blood from his head, no more than a superficial wound, and told him to be off and thankful that we didn't involve the Superintendent.

'Oh, he disappeared like a dog with his tail between his legs, through the Boiler Room door, out into the evening. Good riddance, I say. He'll think twice now before he comes here looking to sate his lust. The girl is safe. Mark my words he'll be hanging his head like a scolded child come the morning. Knowing him he'll have another bellyful of ale in the Pack Horse tonight and come carousing home to his poor wife in the early hours of the morning. But...' she pauses here, as if to give emphasis, 'I do believe that our little encounter with Mr. Farrell is best kept to ourselves. I find it is always the case in matters such as these. I trust you agree.'

Simone hesitates. She clutches her prayer book but decides there is nothing for it but to concur. 'I see, between ourselves. I understand.'

'That's right. Between the four of us. It's much simpler that way. He has learned his lesson, I am sure of it, and we do not need to bother the Superintendent or the House Committee with it. Goodnight, Mrs Gastrell. I trust you will sleep well.'

'Goodnight, Matron.'

The light is fading and the moon rising. Moths gather on the sill. Simone stands at the window, pressing her head to the glass, hoping to still her thoughts and relieve her headache. The moon disappears behind the clouds. There are no stars, and the room grows dark. Away in the woods a fox barks. The air around her smells of hyacinth. She steps away from the window, takes a cold draught of Alice's decoction and lies down on the bed. She drifts into a fog of sleep and remembering. The sea is black and wild as a crow's wing in wind. The river rises about her. She is tangled in river weed searching for a child's hand. She is leaning against the brick of the Boiler Room, brushing away the cobwebs and listening for a dead man's breath. She is lying with William Blakely in the kitchen gardens, his hand pushing up beneath her skirts, when Doctor Eames appears before her and Blakely fades away.

Alice Semple's Notebook

I would know it even by touch, thick ribbed underside of leaf, bell flower turning to berry. By sight, black-smooth and shiny as a small cherry, *atropa belladonna*, deadly nightshade, this the proper name, commonly called, dwale, banewort, devil's berries, the flying ointment, believed by the superstitious to be used by witches for fuelling their flight. Fatal even in small doses.

Matron knows it too, being a woman of the villages and fields at heart. And that is why she came to me. To stir the powdered leaf into a jug of ale. I did not ask for whom. I did not need, I had an idea, for she said, think of the girl, of Phoebe. But I am not one to misuse the virtue of a herb, or the wisdom of God in its creation, and so I took but a gnat's pinch of dwale, barely enough for harm, and a good deal of valerian root in a decoction I had ready prepared. By the next morning, I knew for certain who the recipient had been.

It is by chance that I am still here. I learned this morning that I had been destined for the Asylum in Yarmouth. I was woken in my bed at dawn by Matron and told to gather my effects. I could not take my infusions with me, she said, and she took away my tin cups and old bottles, my packets of herbs and roots, which I kept under my pillow and beneath the bed, though I managed to secrete small amounts on my person, beneath my skirts. Then an attendant arrived and informed Matron there was no carriage, and none expected, for it had not been arranged. She did not seem surprised. Now the hour is long past, and his lordship, that fat, ruddy-nosed pig, Stafford, is not best pleased. Not one bit, for it seems Farrell, whose job it was to arrange the transport, has gone missing. Now there's a thing, indeed. He has not been seen since early yesterday evening when he spoke with the Chaplain. It was all the talk at breakfast this morning. Houndsworth told the attendants gathered about him that Farrell had not turned up for his morning meeting with Stafford and was nowhere to be found. Houndsworth had gone to his cottage in the grounds but not a sign of him and, 'Guess what,' he'd said, and the attendants were all ears, as were the women, 'no sign of a wife either, and as far as he could tell never had been.' They gasped and gossiped. Word has it the place was a pigsty, empty beer jugs, dirty pots and pans, no sign of clothes or belongings packed and taken. If he'd gone, then it was in a terrible hurry and he'd taken nothing with him.

This was the word at breakfast and after in the Courts. The women miss nothing. The women who do not speak, hear everything. It is the strangest of days, not at all as our routines. Phoebe still asleep at morning bell and Matron not waking her, says, 'Let her sleep, she is in much need of rest.' Simone troubled with her fainting fits is deathly pale at breakfast and sits alone. Mrs Corey and Matron are in a huddle of whispers, meaningful looks back and forth. What meaning to take? There is but one for me which is there may be those here who know more of why Farrell is disappeared and though I am not one of them, I believe I have played my part.

By dinnertime, rumour has it that Mrs Corey's son, the eel-catcher, saw the Chief last night when he went out to set his hives, Farrell was drinking, down by the river. Pray God, Mrs Corey said, he had not fallen in and drowned.

I pray otherwise. I pray he is dead, face down in the water. I would fall in myself given half a chance. It seems that three of us, me, Ivy Cole and Phoebe Baines were to have been ghosted out at dawn. This according to Anne Bickerdale who heard it in the kitchens, though why Matron did not wake Phoebe is something of a mystery, she says. Not if she knew the Chief was gone, I think but do not say. Not if she was the woman who came looking for a deadly powder to stir in ale. Not if she risked all, placing her trust in one she has known longer than many. Who dwells in the same place, under the same roof. Who believes women should be safe.

We do not miss him. By supper there is a lightness in the air. On the contrary, though we do not, dare not, say it aloud, we are glad he is gone and hopeful he will never return. It is as if a darkness, a weight in the air about us, a noxious rotting scent, is dispersed. The devil who dwelt among us is cast out. There are and will be others. By God's grace, it seems Houndsworth is not one, but for now we rejoice. This evening, we smile one to another. As we take to our beds, we allow ourselves to dwell for a while in past pleasures. We dream of better lives, of spires and sails rising high above the cornfields, life beyond the walls where we walk in the company of those we love. We hold hands.

I give thanks I am not away in some strange, new place, for this is my home, whether I like it or not. Tis the place I am best known. I pray tonight to dream of another home, the kingdom above, which though it eludes me still, draws closer with every passing day. I feel it. I long for it, to be re-united with those I love, my mother and my grandmother, my one true love, John Clare.

I write the inventory for Phoebe. I do not forget.

Phoebe's Paint Box
An Inventory

One mahogany box with ebony edge and brass hinge a tasselled key to unlock
    inside, a lid of blue baize, written in gold, Winsor & Newton, by appointment to HER MAJESTY and to H.R.H. the PRINCE & PRINCESS OF WALES, 38 Rathbone Place, London
    a paint tray that may be lifted out, with 21 cakes of paint, their names known by heart to Phoebe Baines who does recite them even in her sleep
    3 ceramic mixing pans, one with a chip at the rim, each stamped with the name Winsor & Newton and a blue winged dragon
    a water glass, cut like a diamond
    a lower drawer, released with a brass pin, housing four brushes, one with a point so fine it is barely seen, six pencils and two black ink sticks.

Tis second hand, made first by Phoebe, as if it were only ever hers. No doubt bought by some gentleman, though they say that women are now instructed in painting, and why not, for it is said that even Her Majesty herself is seen out with easel and paint in the countryside.

To think, Phoebe Baines, had but a pencil before and never paper bar the scraps I gave her, and stubs of pencil. Though she begged them for both, they took no heed. Her talent now unlocked like the colours in the paintbox when the lid lifts and they reveal their secrets. Oceans of Indigo, Black Lamp, the darkest reaches of a well that barely catches the light. Prussian Blue of eyebright. Sap Green, the fields of spring and Emerald, new leaf on the willow. Burnt Umber, Raw Sienna, our feet walking the earth. Ochre and Chrome Yellow, the ripening of corn. Indian Red, Brown Pink and Orange Chrome, a sunset. Vermillion and Crimson Lake, a gypsy's fire at night.

I met a man once by such a fire who called himself a colourist. He was chiefly employed in the making of brushes and bought badger hair from the gypsies, and horse tail for the finest work, in miniature, such as Phoebe's, painted in the most refined and exquisite detail. Who knew salvation was shaped in a polished box, made in colour and water, a tongue peeping out in concentration, the swirl of brush on a glass, the lavender song.

Phoebe

sleep i sleep forever
colours swirl in my mouth when i wake
gamboge, raw sienna, yellow ochre, orange chrome
burnt sienna, vermillion,
light red, indian red and crimson lake
chrome yellow, neutral tint, scarlet lake
emerald, sap green, new blue
and purple lake
prussian blue, indigo, lamp black
hooker's green and brown pink
i paint
no princess no fairy story waking
past the bells past the calling
all ladies in all ladies in
remember the whisper forget forget
i do not forget
what she says pigeon livers
for a man, bruises and blinders
come to rescue me all three
pull down my skirts
from now i weight them with stones
for no man
shall ever again, shall ever again use me
i paint them all away in flowers
deck my hair strew my body with garlands
honey for the bees the hive protects me

the colours save me
the women save me, the three,
he has blood about the head
a sack spilled on a coal heap
then up sudden
they bring ale in a jug
mop the blood and be gone
they say else
be gone else we will tell
he is out through the door into the night
they fuss over me no anger no blame
their touch tender
shame smoothed, be gone
a spell
a mothers touch unknown
yet i taste what it should be
smell, it is not the smell of coal or dust
or brick or feral breath
it is rose petal soft wind from the south
shush rock shush rock
eyes, the touch of eyes
this their touch
tucking the sheet corners pillow nest
hand smoothing head shush now shush, rest
bird feather nest safe in the trees
breathe out, breathe he will not come again
scrub him out black ink stick
paint him in dragon's blood
pick up the brush wash him away gone erase
alice brings me an inventory i keep it under my pillow

Report to the Meeting of the Committee of Visitors of the Long Meadow Lunatic Asylum near Cambridge, in the County of Cambridgeshire, held therein on the 19th day of September in respect of the Disappearance of Amos Farrell, Chief Attendant and Acting Assistant Medical Office

Sir

In accordance with the rules for the management of this Asylum I have the honour to submit for the consideration of the House Committee the following report concerning the disappearance of the above stated Chief Attendant on the evening of September 15th.

Before I deal directly with the matter of his disappearance, I trust you will allow me the latitude of certain general observations concerning the man's character and service. Until such time as the evening of the 15th, it was my considered opinion that Mr. Farrell was a worthy and well-respected officer of the Asylum, one who had devoted himself to its interests and had been vigilant in all details of its management. He had carried out his duties with creditable efficiency, always with the patients' welfare at heart. Such was my testimony to his worth and the value I set on his service that I promoted him temporarily to Assistant Medical Officer, when a sudden vacancy occurred on the departure of my former Deputy, William Blakely.

In hindsight, I find I now have cause to question my judgement in respect of his appointment and to express my sincere regret as to the events outlined below which have occasioned the submission of my report.

On the afternoon of the 15th, I spoke with Mr. Farrell in my office and requested that he arrange transport for the transfer, arranged by myself in the manner approved by the Secretary of State, of three patients the following morning: Alice Semple, Phoebe Baines and Ivy Cole. He agreed. He was made cognisant by me of the need for discretion in this matter and for the discharge to be completed at the earliest possible time and in liaison with Matron. I also informed him that a new Assistant Medical Officer had been appointed and was expected within the week. I told him he would be relieved of his extra duties when the new Assistant arrived and I thanked him for his service.

It is my understanding, having spoken with the Chaplain Daniel Hawkins, who came across Farrell shortly after in the main corridor, that Farrell was disgruntled, seemingly unhappy about his treatment and the new appointment. The Chaplain reports he was distracted and in a hurry.

On the morning of the 16th, Farrell failed to report for work and for his morning meeting with me. As a consequence, no transfers took place. I asked Attendant Houndsworth to investigate Farrell's whereabouts. He visited Farrell's cottage in the grounds but found him absent and the place in some disarray. When Farrell failed to appear by lunchtime the Constable was informed and an investigation instigated.

The Constable reports that Farrell was seen late on the evening of the 15th at the river by one Michael

279

Corey. He was said to be intoxicated, stumbling and singing. The Constable is willing to present his findings to the Committee should they so wish.

Mr Farrell has not been seen since the sighting on the evening of the 15th and is officially designated a Missing Person. There is some supposition that he may have fallen in the river and drowned. It is not for me to comment. I will confine myself only to facts.

Consequential to these events:

The transfers of the three aforesaid women are to be re-arranged as a matter of urgency. This, in order to maintain our reputation as partners worthy of trust.

The re-arrangement of Medical Staff thus rendered necessary will be effected, with the Committee's approval, by the temporary appointment of Cyril Houndsworth as Chief Attendant and by the arrival of George Quinn, newly appointed, Assistant Medical Officer, within the week.

Whilst I have sought to protect the Patients of Long Meadow from the disruptions and upset this disappearance has caused, it has not been possible to shield them from it in its entirety. I find they are much disturbed by the rumour and gossip that surrounds it, and it is mine and my Staff's considered opinion they need a period in which calm can prevail. They need the solace of intercourse one with another, without interference from the world outside. Therefore, with much regret, I have cancelled the Summer Fete. The Chaplain has been informed.

In conclusion, I would beg most gratefully to acknowledge the kind and considerate support I have received from the House Committee in the discharge of my duties at this most difficult time

Your Obedient Servant
Cornelius Stafford
Superintendent
24th August 1875

Simone

'What news of Mr Farrell, Matron?' Simone asks. They are standing in the vestibule by the door to the Airing Courts. It is four days since the incident in the Boiler Room and there is still no news. Stories abound. There are whispers even of a poisoning. Surely, they cannot not keep the events of that night entirely to themselves. There is the matter of conscience. His wicked deeds should have no bearing on the facts. Tell the truth and such deeds are exposed. But Simone cannot deny it is unlikely that truth will triumph in a place such as Long Meadow and coming to this realisation, and in the knowledge that neither Matron nor Mrs Corey are inclined to spill the secret, she has begun to formulate a plan. A plan to turn Farrell's disappearance and the events of that evening to hers and Phoebe's advantage.

She is not sure she trusts the account Matron has given her. She senses something in the air between Matron and Mrs Corey, the smell of secrets, something caught in the glances they exchange, the confidences shared in low voices, hushed tones. Is she the only one to notice it? Or perhaps her lack of trust lies in the way others accuse Alice Semple of employing her dark arts.

'No news, Mrs Gastrell, other than gossip of which I'm sure you are well aware,' says Matron, in a voice unusually bright and high. 'It is a fine day out there I believe. Are you taking the air? And Phoebe with you? I recommend it.

Especially now we no longer have Miss Nightingale with us. No more walks in nature.'

Simone is taken aback. 'No more Miss Nightingale? I had begun to fear it. I do hope she is come to no harm. May I ask what has happened to prevent her coming?'

'No harm. As far as I know, she is fit and well. No. She has been reassigned to another Asylum. The Vale, over on the County border, perhaps you know it. It seems they are much in need of her help. I'm afraid we are unlikely to see Miss Nightingale again. We will miss her of course.'

'She will be sorely missed,' says Simone feeling the weight of such news heavy on her shoulders. She sighs inwardly because without her, their days will be all winter and frost, no matter the weather, such a difference she has made to their lives. But she will not be distracted no matter how significant the news. She has a plan, perhaps only half a plan, but she has thought of nothing else for several days now, since the idea came to her, since she began to suspect all was not exactly as Matron had claimed. Now is the perfect opportunity to put it into action.

'I am very sorry to hear that Miss Nightingale will be with us no more. I am surprised the Chaplain did not say anything. Perhaps he is the one we should speak to. I feel certain we must tell someone what happened in the Boiler Room.'

'Ssh. I would ask you to keep your voice down. Please. In any case this is hardly the place to discuss such matters.'

'I think it entirely the place,' says Simone, all the while reminding herself of the mirror. You must prevail, Simone. One day you will leave Long Meadow, and this will all be in the past. Until then, you must prevail. It is possible to resist. She had done it with Fox. One day you will leave.

She senses her opportunity. 'I will speak with the Chaplain myself. I will tell him the truth regarding Farrell and Phoebe and our part in his disappearance. After all, we are hardly to blame if he set off drinking and wandered too close to the river. And it should be known what he has done, to prevent others from doing likewise.'

Matron pulls her to one side, out of earshot of the women leaving through the vestibule door. 'Have you taken leave of your senses? What possible good will that do, Mrs Gastrell, apart from involve us unnecessarily in his disappearance? It will change nothing. It will not bring him back and I am certain you would not wish him back considering the harm done to Miss Baines. The Constable has been informed. He has been designated a missing person. The Superintendent has today presented a report to the Committee, outlining all of this. I do not think it would look well to contradict him. It is best left between us. We have done the girl, and the world at large, a favour. Surely you see that.'

'I do, and I am inclined towards your argument Matron. In fact, I believe I would be convinced if only I could see an end to my time here in Long Meadow. You will understand, I'm sure. Once free, I would have no reason to dwell on such matters. My memory would cloud like breath on glass. It would become a past I had no wish to resurrect but until such time, until some person, a man of standing, of medical authority, deems me fit, sane...'

'Let me stop you there, Mrs Gastrell, for I believe I know where your thoughts lead. My brother, Dr Eames, is just such a man, with such authority, and should you so wish, and should I request it, I have no doubt he can be prevailed upon to visit and would find you more than fit for release, cured in fact.'

'Cured? Of what I wonder, when I have nothing to be cured of?'

'Fit for release then.'

'And you can arrange for him to come and see me, and Phoebe too?'

'Phoebe Baines? I fear that might be a deal harder.'

'Nevertheless, if I am to restrain my better nature and keep our secrets…'

'He is away in Switzerland just now, with his wife, taking the air, but he is due back in a matter of weeks. I will speak with him as soon as he arrives home.'

'Thank you, Matron. I trust it won't be too long. And now I think I will join the women in the Courts and enjoy the roses before summer is gone, for God willing I will not be here to see them bloom a second time.'

They come with their gifts, before the morning bell, a ragged procession bearing tokens of farewell and goodwill. Alice is leaving. She is to be taken to the asylum in Yarmouth. Today. They bring what they have, no matter how small. They gather around her bed where she stands, already up and dressed for the journey. It is what they do, to send a woman on her way. To signal they will not be forgotten and nor will she. They place their gifts on her bed; a blown robin's egg, a sliver of sea glass, a postcard from Lyme Regis, two boiled sweets, a knot of dried moss, a pressed forget me not, a scrap of needle lace fashioned as a leaf, a watercolour painted by Phoebe. There are prayer cards and postage stamps, locks of hair, a brooch with the stones missing, a pocket almanac and from Simone, a gold guinea.

Alice gathers the offerings up into her meagre bundle of possessions. She hands her notebook to Simone, and says, in a voice with a raven's croak, 'Take it. I beg you, for safe keeping, so we are known, that we become visible. When you are away from here, I pray you will show them. Tell them. You will be witness for us all. Now be gone,' she says, 'all of you. No sentiment. I am happy to be away from here.'

The women trickle away. The bell sounds and Houndsworth and Matron appear.

'I see you are ready for the journey, Miss Semple, do you have your belongings with you. Have they been checked, Matron?' asks Houndsworth.

'I do,' says Alice.

Matron nods.

'Very well then, I shall discharge you into the custody of the driver and attendant who are waiting now at the entrance. But I believe I must cuff you first.' He draws a set of handcuffs from his coat pocket.

'Surely that won't be necessary,' says Matron. 'She is a woman well past jumping from a carriage. Let us not humble her. Let her at least arrive at her destination with dignity.'

Houndsworth hesitates but puts the cuffs back in his pocket. 'As you wish, Matron. Come with me please, Miss Semple.'

Simone skips breakfast, collects several books from her room and tucks them under her arm, careful to ensure Alice Semple's notebook is among them. She slips through the door from the vestibule out into the Airing Courts. The sun is already high, the sky blue and clear but there is a new bite in the air about her. A keenness overlays the last of the summer's perfumes, the slow decomposition of vegetable

286

matter, flowers are brown-edged and past their best, ferns rust and leaves yellow. Autumn beckons, another season stretches before her and still she is not free.

She hurries through the parterre, catching a stem of rosemary from the herb bed and rubbing it through her fingers. She makes her way down through the roses and lavender to the fruit trees and the bench tucked into the corner of the yew. Her hidden place. She settles into the bench and opens Alice's book. She reads without stopping.

Phoebe comes looking for her but does not disturb. She is content to sit beside Simone with her sketchbook in which she begins on a pencil drawing of a teasel head. Only when they hear the dinner bell and the call, 'All ladies in, all ladies in,' do they look up from their work.

As they close their books and begin the walk up through the garden, Simone considers how much she has learned from Alice's notebook. How much better she knows Long Meadow now. Phoebe's and Alice's lives, the lives of the women in Dormitory Twelve, all are catalogued and laid bare before her. The secrets of the Asylum have opened like a festering wound. The powder in the ale had been the greatest shock. Matron and Alice. What had Matron wanted? What did she know of the herbs Alice used? Perhaps less deadly than Matron thought or desired? It surprises and shocks Simone that they should act together and yet she sees how long they have known each other, how entwined their lives have become. How Matron held more against Farrell than she could ever have known or guessed. Enough to want him poisoned? Questions and uncertainties abound but Simone is sure she has gained another lever in her quest to be released from Long Meadow.

Before dinner, she goes to her room and for want of a

better hiding place tucks Alice's notebook under the mattress on her bed. She prays they will not come looking.

Word floods the washroom like a burst pipe, woman to woman, as they stand in their chemises readying themselves for bed. She did not make it to Yarmouth. She barely made it past Keeper's Wood when she jumped from the carriage and ran through a field of barley, disturbing the pheasants at their feed. Alice Semple has escaped. Disappeared. There is a search party out now and the attendant will be a dead man as far as Stafford is concerned. By all accounts he was asleep on the job and by the time he was woken by the driver it was too late.

'Took to her broomstick. It were the deadly nightshade, I would wager,' says Gladys Carter, and the women laugh and she snatches up an old mop and runs around the washroom with it between her legs, shouting, 'I'm a witch with a goose foot and free. Can't catch me.' And the others follow like a chorus. Even the *silent women*. Mrs Corey comes and tells them to hush and quieten down but there is no dampening their spirits and they go to bed rejoicing that one of their kind has escaped. Alice Semple is free, out in the world, sleeping under the stars, who knows where.

The rejoicing lasts but a day, when by order of Cornelius Stafford, the women are confined to their dormitories and rooms, allowed out for only meal times and one hour in the Airing Courts. The attendants call it lockdown. Stafford says that they must think on the escape and its consequences. They must have time to dwell on the gravity and foolishness of such actions. For, he insists, she will be captured, sooner or later.

At dinner, Houndsworth is overheard telling Mrs Corey that his Lordship was beside himself with rage. Demanded to know how, how such a breach had happened, every last detail being poured over. Swore he would be the laughing stock of the Senior Common Room again. Swore he would have his revenge.

'Nothing worse than an escape,' says Houndsworth. 'You watch, we'll have the Masters back, crawling all over us if we're not careful. By all accounts the Committee are raising hell, public safety and all of that though Matron's suspension, after all she was the one who decided to leave the cuffs off, has gone some way to appeasing them. If Semple had only been cuffed, as was required, none of it would have happened,' he muses, then adds, 'It's not my fault, you know. Anyway, the old witch is harmless enough. Not likely to take an axe to anyone's head. '

'I wouldn't be so sure,' pipes up Eveline Webb.

'Shush and mind your business,' says Mrs Corey.

They go back to their meat stew, heads down but ears up for any morsel of news, for they live, even more in these days, by the scraps gleaned from such conversations. They are sorry that Matron is blamed and wonder how she fares. Of late they have found an ally in her, one formerly an enemy. Poor woman, they say. It is always the women who take the blame.

No one seems to know exactly what suspension means. It is not the end, surely? Will she be allowed back? They'd like to see his Lordship run the place without her. And where is this new hoity-toity Deputy they keep talking about? Rumour has it he's having second thoughts.

For Simone's part, and for the furtherance of her plan, she can only pray with all her heart that the suspension is short-lived. The summer is at an end and Dr. Eames must surely be returning from Switzerland any day, yet Matron is no longer to be seen in Long Meadow's corridors and who knows how long she will be absent or if she will ever return.

Once again fate has taken her for a fool. A fool for allowing hope to sneak in, for daring to dream of freedom. In the long hours of confinement, she had begun to anticipate hers and Phoebe's release. She had made plans and there was money enough in the bundle left by Maria to carry them out. She had determined that once released, they would make their way to London. Granted, it would not be easy, having no knowledge of the city and its streets, though she had heard the tales of miasma, disease, typhus, smallpox, of pickpockets, street robbers, and the rookeries where no respectable person may venture. They would secure respectable lodgings, approaching a gentlewoman for a recommendation. It would not be the first time she had had to rely on the comfort or help of strangers. From here, armed with Clara's address, they would purchase their tickets aboard a liner bound for India.

Such plans she had made. Now she must put them away.

She must push thoughts of life beyond Long Meadow back into the far reaches of her mind. She will lock them down as they themselves are locked down, their days punctuated only by the bells and the single hour when they are allowed their brief respite outside.

Now the Airing Courts are mostly empty, and no one is present to witness the burnishing of leaves and the ripening of berries. From her window, Simone watches the wind blowing through the trees in Keeper's Wood, carrying the first falling leaf to ground. The pumps echo the dolent beat of her heart.

September

The regime is unrelenting. The dormitories stay locked. Time is a new dimension, slippery and unreliable, draped in fog, and measured in the muffled throb of the pumps. No destination in sight. There is only bell-time, time lived through but not lived. The devil they must sit with. Simone takes solace in her books where she inhabits another world, a world of nature, botany, a world of learning. And there is much still to learn. She thinks of Miss Nightingale and Miss Benson. How they wore their books like clothes, distinguishing self. How she wears these few books left her, like a cloak staving off loss, holding her steady until better times. She is a drowning woman clutching at the life raft of words. Do we become our books, she wonders? Who was Alice without her notebook? Without her story? Simone prays Alice fares well without the book of her own writing. She checks that the notebook is safe, still hidden beneath her mattress.

They are at breakfast, eating in silence, when Houndsworth bustles through the doors and approaches Mrs Corey. A whisper in her ear and she turns as white as a cuckoo flower. If it weren't for Houndsworth catching her, she would have fallen to the floor. The attendants gather around. They bring a chair. She sits down and bends double, her head between her knees.

It is the shock, they say. A body, a body has been found, pulled from the river and by her own son, Michael Corey, who had gone that morning to check his hives for eels.

'What body?' she says.

The room is hushed, the women all ears.

'It is not known,' says Houndsworth.

The name Amos Farrell is on everyone's lips.

Simone wonders how much Mrs Corey knows of what was in the jug of ale they fed him that night.

Later in the Airing Courts, beneath a sun as warm as any summer's day, the gossip mongers are abroad and the women hungry for the news.

'The body,' says Anne Bickerdale, 'twas a sight to behold, so they say. Reckon Michael Corey spilled his guts there and then. Alive with maggots it were, and green, with blisters the size of walnuts, fungus sprouting from the mouth, eyes scavenged by eels, else they'd popped out. No teeth, no nails. Taken to the dead house, though they reckon tis not a fit place to keep a dead dog let alone a human. The Coroner is on his way. Mrs Corey's got the day off, so Cook says, to go and see to her Michael.'

Death of a Patient

70. On the death of a patient, notice shall be given by the clerk to the Parish Officers, and to one of the nearest relations of the deceased (if her address be known) and they shall be delivered to them, if requested: if the body be not removed on the fourth day after death, it shall be buried under the direction of the Medical Officer and Superintendent.

Rules for the Government of the Pauper Lunatic Asylum situate at Long Meadow – prepared and submitted by the Committee of Visitors thereof, by virtue of the 53rd section of the 16th and 17th VIC. CHAP 97- state

The Superintendent's Cottage

'Take a seat, Chaplain, if you will.' The Chaplain sits opposite Stafford, on the other side of the unlit fire. 'Drink?' Stafford holds up a decanter of wine, but the Chaplain raises his hands, palms out, to decline. 'Very well, to business. You know what must be done. I don't need to remind you of the rules of Governance. Or your duties in all of this. A sad business indeed. It goes without saying I can rely on you to do what is necessary. But, it's not that I wish to talk about. What concerns me is people's perception. I'm sure you'll agree with me, Chaplain, too much scandal cannot be good for Long Meadow. Not good at all. And we've had our share. We are in the local papers again, for all the wrong reasons, and on the lips of the Parish, not to mention the Senior Common Room.' He sighs. 'We will be fortunate to avoid another investigation. The Committee is yapping at my heels, so to speak. There is talk of transfers at the highest level. I don't need to tell you what that means or to remind you better the devil and all of that. We are all of us at risk. There are plenty waiting in the wings who think they could do a better job. What I want from you, Chaplain, is your help in silencing our critics and restoring confidence and good order at Long Meadow. I still await my new Deputy and so I find I must rely on my existing Officers. Oh, Houndsworth does a good enough job but, between us, he is loose-lipped and prone to be swayed this way and that. I need staff I can rely on to carry my word and thoughts to the patients, especially to the women. Are you with me?' He swigs from his glass.

The Chaplain nods his assent, reserving his judgement, for you never know what Stafford is really about.

'I am relying on you to spread the message that all is well here at Long Meadow, despite recent events. We have just been the unfortunate recipients of bad luck. As from tomorrow, the dormitories will be opened and the women returned to their normal regime so they may take solace in work and in each other's company. To be honest, Chaplain, I find I now regret somewhat the cancellation of the fete. Perhaps we can consider another such social event? I'll leave that with you, and you will be ably assisted, you will be pleased to hear, by Miss Nightingale who, like Matron, is to be re-instated forthwith. Can you spread the word among the patients, as well as informing them of the death, dispel the gossip, especially Dormitory Twelve? I know you'll be very busy with official matters but I'd like you to find the time. I need to know I can rely on you for this. Good man. Now, shall we seal it with a drink?'

'Not for me, thank you,' says the Chaplain, 'but I will inform as you request, and willingly spread the word.'

The Chaplain closes the door to Stafford's cottage behind him and permits himself a smile. A verse comes to mind, *The beauty of Israel is slain upon thy high places: how are the mighty fallen*. He hurries off across the grass to the entrance, then along the corridors to Dormitory Twelve and beyond to Simone Gastrell's room.

The door is open, still he knocks lightly to announce himself. 'Mrs Gastrell,' he says, stepping into the room, 'and

Miss Baines. How busy you both seem at your books and your paints. I am sorry to disturb you.'

'Please, come in, Chaplain. Please sit,' says Simone getting up from her chair.

'No. I'm perfectly fine standing, thank you, this won't take long. I'm afraid I have some rather distressing news about the body, the body recently pulled from the river. I'm sure you've heard about it.'

'I have. Please, go on.' What news now? Is there ever news in Long Meadow that is not distressing? Simone takes a deep breath and stands tall, preparing herself for what is to come.

'The body has been identified, with some difficulty I might add, but it appears it is the body of our dear sister, Alice Semple.

Phoebe cries out and reaches for Simone's hand.

'No, surely not,' says Simone. 'It cannot be. I was led to believe the body was in a state of decay, how could they determine...'

'The sixth toe on the left foot, of all things. It seems she had a goose-foot. A distinguishing mark. The bones are still intact. Moreover, I am assured it is the body of a woman.'

'So, it is not the Chief as some had feared?'

'No, indeed apparently he was seen only yesterday by Mr. Houndsworth who came across him in the Dog and Gun public house, somewhat the worse for wear, I gather.'

'So, it is Alice then,' says Simone, sinking back into her chair.

'Gone to meet her love,' says Phoebe

'Shall we say a prayer?' says Daniel Hawkins.

Phoebe

knock the hives
silence the pumps
stop the bells
the queen is lost
alice is gone gone from us
drape ribbons
swat away september wasps
bothersome honey thieves
tremble dance on the boards
cluster
as do we in winter
more than one of us
our hive
she knew all each everyone
native from other region
nesting in cavities
peered in and knew our souls
alice is gone to the meadows
on high to the bright places
the gold
and clare is waiting

Summer lingers. But the morning grass is starry with dew and the evening moon yellow and fat. Swallows gather like regrets on the sills of the upper rooms. In the gardens, the fruit trees are russet and gold, their branches laden with apple and quince. The women of Dormitory Twelve have been out early in the Courts gathering what they may, for posies, for a Simpler's bouquet: rosemary for remembrance, rue for grace, lavender for peace, parsley for luck, yew for immortality, mint for joy in mourning. They tie them with scraps of cotton and wool got from the mending shops. They wear their caps. Simone wears the dress she wore to Long Meadow, its collar washed and pressed. Beneath her arm she carries Alice's notebook.

They have all come, the great and the good. The House Committee are here and Stafford himself, with Matron beside him. Mrs Corey and her son Michael, attendants, and patients all, congregate in knots, chattering among themselves outside the Chapel while they wait for the body to arrive from the Dead House.

Simone is intent on the notebook, holding it open at the piece she has chosen to read aloud at the service when a hand comes to rest on her shoulder. A gloved hand. She turns and sees that it belongs to Miss Nightingale.

'My dear Mrs Gastrell. How are you? I am sorry to be here on such a sad day and yet I am so very pleased to meet with you again.'

'And I too,' says Simone.

'You may know I am soon to take up my work for the House Committee here at Long Meadow again. We will resume our walks and I hope...'

299

At this point she stops for the crowd has hushed. The men take off their hats as the coffin approaches along the narrow path, between the graves, on the back of a horse drawn cart.

'But never mind that, quickly,' she whispers, 'I must give you this. The Chairman has tasked me with ensuring it reaches you. A letter. From India if I am not mistaken.' She offers the letter to Simone. Simone takes it and pushes it down into the pocket of her gown, but not before recognising her sister's hand. Her spirit soars like a meadow lark in song, a song of hope which she dares not trust and yet which rises up and will not be dampened. She turns to Phoebe who stands beside her and smiles. Together they follow the mourners into the Chapel.

In the dusty, speckled light of sun through coloured glass, while the congregation settles and the Chaplain begins, she retrieves the envelope from her pocket and opens it.

My Dearest, Darling Sister

I weep for the tragedies that have befallen you. Thus, I will not waste your time in pleasantries, for time is clearly of the essence. Through the offices of one Henrietta Gaule, who it seems has procured our address from the Foreign Office itself, I have come to know of your most dreadful misfortunes. She writes of the death of the child, Constance, her sister, and of your unwarranted incarceration at the Asylum, Long Meadow, at the hands of Gastrell.

Do not despair, my darling sister, for when you receive this, as I trust you will, then know I am already departed for England. I arrive in Tilbury on 13th of October and leave immediately for Cambridge.

Know I will not rest until you are free. I am...

Simone does not finish it, there is no need, and besides, Phoebe is standing hymn book in hand. Simone stands too, folding the paper, pushing the letter back into her pocket and begins to sing, to sing as never before, her heart in her voice, trembling with sorrow and unexpected joy, *Abide with me, fast falls the eventide...*

And when the singing is over, and the congregation seated, Simone comes to stand at the front. Stepping up to the lectern, and opening Alice Semple's Notebook, she reads: *So it was once with us. All of us. In our youth we were loved. Pale and green as fresh milk from the cow, untouched, untainted, sweethearts. Daughters of the May, our blossoming stolen, our mothers dead, our sisters dying. We are caged and yet we grow, as she does, as gives us hope, as fruit luscious and red. Our stems reach up far beyond these bars. We will wear new bones.*

Fatehpur Sikri – India – April 1876

I come when I can. It is a day's outing from the sprawling bungalow in the cantonment at Agra where we live now with Clara and Edward. Twelve miles to the west, Fatehpur Sikri, the Imperial Palace of the Emperor Akbar built in red sandstone, walls the colour of rust, azure ribbed roofs, chambers open to the sky and a silence filled with sound. In the Wind Catcher Tower, I hear lost voices keening on the wind, straining to be heard. I hear the soft swing of the elephant's trunk, a raised foot on the neck of a wayward princess, an execution, the cracking of bones. In a place beyond the net of words, a place of feeling and intuition, high on this rocky ridge, in palace and prison, I come to remember, for though I know nothing of palaces, I know much of prisons.

Phoebe comes to draw and paint with her sketchbook, paintbox and a canvas folding stool. Mahrukh, who tells me her name means *radiant like the moon*, and who is a housemaid and water-carrier at the bungalow, accompanies us. We wear straw hats, carry parasols and water, for summer has arrived and soon I am told we will be forced to repair to the hill station of Mussoorie to escape the fierce heat of the northern plains.

For now, we dwell in a luxury and peace formerly unknown, among well tended lawns and gardens filled with the rich, sweet scent of frangipani and jasmine. There are fruit trees, papaya, sour cherry, pomegranate, and flowers, roses, sweet peas, hibiscus and many plants whose names I have still to learn. By day the cicadas sing. By night on the terrace, the quickly folding dark, a vast covering of stars and new constellations, the call of the nightjar.

Most of all, there are the kind, healing words and deeds of Clara and Edward.

I have grown bold, fearing little, for what can be worse than the worst of Long Meadow. It took time to recover, time and Clara's patience. I had lost all ability to make choices for myself, even as to when I might take a cup of tea, or whether I might dare make it for myself. When to sleep, when to eat. In public, in London's crowded streets, I could not enter a shop and make a purchase, God forbid, though now I can do all these things without a second thought and I am teaching Phoebe.

Before we set sail, with the help of Clara, many new purchases were made for us both – new gowns and shoes, gloves, castile soap, bathing salts, handkerchiefs, bergamot and lemon oil. With the help of Edward, Alice's notebook was lodged in the hands of the Earl of Shaftesbury, Head of the Lunacy Commission, for what good it will do. I had taken the liberty of removing certain parts to avoid accusation for those who deserve better. Matron for one.

It is Phoebe's intention to draw every part of this great complex at Fatehpur Sikri and then to render it in paint, in pinks, oranges and reds, the tinctures of fire and sunsets, the coppery light that comes in the late afternoon. Today, she sits before the Diwan-i-Khar, also known as the Jewel House where the Emperor held his private audiences. Mahrukh holds the parasol while Phoebe works.

I sit on the palace wall. Below, in the west towards Agra, lies an oasis, an emerald ring in the desert guarded by a stationary white egret. I watch the bird as it picks its way through the shallows. I listen for the voices rising up from the plain. For strange though it may seem in this wild and foreign place, I hear them. I hear the women of Long Meadow and I tell them I have not forgotten, nor ever will. I tell Alice where her notebook resides and that I have a copy and have thoughts of publication in the future, if such a thing were ever possible. But for now I am content, a contentment far exceeding anything I had dared to imagine. I look up into a sapphire sky at the fretted wings of black kites, caught in the sunlight. They glide and circle on the thermals above me. I have found my freedom and I thank God for it.

Simone Gastrell

Author's Notes

Although it was not my intention when I set out to write *The Silent Women*, I find I have drawn heavily on my twenty-five years of working with women in prison. As I began to create the Victorian world of Long Meadow Asylum I found myself walking in a familiar space. Discovering the 1856, *Rules for the Government of the Pauper Lunatic Asylum for the County of Lancaster, situate at Rainhill, within the Hundred of West Derby*, in the online Welcome Collection, confirmed for me my innate understanding of the hierarchies that shape the life of a closed institution. This valuable document suggested certain structures and provided me with the unique opportunity to use authentic period text. It demonstrated, as did much of my subsequent research, the strong parallels between the asylum and the prison, between then and now, sadly, resonating as it does with the contemporary world of women's incarceration.

Other titles and archives that have proved invaluable in the writing and research of The Silent Women are: *Mad, Bad and Sad, A History of Women and the Mind Doctors from 1800 to the Present* by Lisa Appignanesi; *The Female Malady* by Elaine Showalter; *The Yellow Wallpaper* by Charlotte Perkins Gilmore; *Asylum* by Erving Goffman; *A Mind That Found Itself* by Clifford Beers; *John Clare by Himself* by John Clare; *Ten Years in a Lunatic Asylum* by Mabel Etchell; *Inside the Pauper Lunatic Asylum and Voices from the*

Asylum by Mark Davis; *Life in a Victorian Asylum* by Mark Stevens; *Behind the Wall – The Life and Times of Winterton Hospital* by Adam Lamb and Jack Turton; *Littlemore Hospital 1840 to 1960s, From Pauper Lunatics to Mental Health Patients* by John Stewart; *How to be a Victorian* by Ruth Goodman; *Gender and Modern Botany in Victorian England* by Ann B Shteir; *Lunatics, Imbeciles and Idiots – A History of Insanity in Nineteenth-Century Britain and Ireland* by Kathryn M. Burtinshaw and John R.F. Burt; *Culpeper's Complete Herbal* by Nicholas Culpeper; *The Useful Family Herbal* by John Hill; *Flora of Cambridgeshire* by Charles Cardale Babington; *The British Journal of Psychiatry*, including: *Electricity: A History of its Use in the Treatment of Mental Illness in Britain During the Second Half of the Nineteenth-Century* by Beveridge and Renvoize; *Proceedings of the Royal Society of Medicine, including: English Private Madhouses in the Eighteenth and Nineteenth Centuries* by W. L Parry-Jones; *Investigating the Body in the Victorian Asylum* by Jennifer Wallis, University of Strathclyde; *Bad or Mad? Infanticide and Morality in Nineteenth Century Britain* by Paige Mathieson, the *Midlands Historical Review;* *Some Notes on the History of Colney Hatch Asylum* by The Reverend Henry Hawkins, late Chaplain, Welcome Collection; *The Landscape of Public Lunatic Asylums 1808-1914* by Sarah Rutherford; the podcast series *Promoting Public Health Through the Lessons of History,* University of St. Andrews.

Acknowledgements

My thanks as always to my amazing editor Lynn Michell who gives me the confidence and support to continue writing, especially through the difficult times, and who has become a dear friend. I am full of admiration for everything she and Linen Press achieve, often against the odds.

Thanks to all the friends and supporters of my writing who help to make it worthwhile: my writing buddy and mentor, Wendy Robertson, without whom I would not have written a word; Chris and all at the Weardale Wordfest; my Writing Days newsletter readers; my dear friends Marney and Lynne and the women of South Terrace; Emma from Collected Books; my sister-in-law Jan; Anna; Mary-Jane and the writers at Casa Ana's November retreat – you were great and I had a ball! Special thanks go to Gillian for her eagle-eyed copy editing and to Ali for championing my work. Thanks to my daughter Kate and my-daughter-in-law Hanne, who in busy lives always make time to ask me about my writing.

Thank you to the men in my life: my partner John, first reader and copy editor; my brother Mark and my son David.

Last but not least my three beautiful granddaughters to whom this is dedicated and who are, without doubt, keeping me on my toes.

Milton Keynes UK
Ingram Content Group UK Ltd.
UKHW021819150923
428767UK00013B/523